Kneeling

Book 1
of
The Pastoral Noir Trilogy

JED OHLHUES

BOOK 1 THE PASTORAL NOIR TRILOGY
KNEELING

iUniverse books may be ordered through
booksellers or by contacting:

iUniverse
1663 Liberty Drive
Bloomington, IN 47403
www.iuniverse.com
844-349-9409

ISBN: 978-1-6632-2490-3 (sc)
ISBN: 978-1-6632-2491-0 (e)

Print information available on the last page.

iUniverse rev. date: 07/12/2021

For
Tonya H

AUTHOR'S CAUTION
TO SOME READERS

The following is a novel, yet sexual addiction is not a fiction.

This narrative includes scenes, themes, and descriptions which may likely be very suggestive and highly arousing. To those struggling with sex addiction – it is advisable for you to go at your own pace. If you get aroused and need to take a break – take one!

Do not risk a slip, relapse, or misstep by reading non-stop. Rather, set this book down as you need to, and return to it only after you feel it is safe for you to do so.

Your sobriety is to be encouraged.

Not tested.

"I form the light, and create darkness;
"I make peace, and create evil:
"I the Lord do all these things."

- Isaiah 45:7

The following fragments have been cut and assembled from a sobriety log, theology/prayer-journal, blog, tweets, and a year's worth of personal correspondence by the author to five different recipients.

✂- -

INTRO

Caught between two worlds.
>Black and white.
>Day and night.
>Saint and sinner.
>Purity and perversion.
>Can't have one without the other.
>Or, is it more like two sides of the same coin?
>I'd be a world renowned sex therapist already, if I
hadn't ended up as a priest instead.

✂- -

1

Easter Day

I. After Easter Celebration

At the end of service, as I exit the pulpit and walk down the center aisle behind the choir, you can tell I've pissed off the usual parishioners.

I can count on upsetting them four weeks out of every five.

That's just by virtue of my being me.

I don't believe church services need to be somber, severe, and joyless.

Which is exactly how they think services need to be, and why those individuals get pissed off at how I do things.

Don't think me paranoid.

I learned to stop fretting.

The bunny ears on my head are their problem, not mine.

✄ -

To hear them tell it, you'd come away thinking I don't take worship seriously.

I take *what* I do very seriously.

But not the *way* I do it.

✄ -

It's Easter, the end of service, and everyone else is smiling, except for the "sourpuss" family.

In the back pew, my little fan is waving frantically from her mother's arms.

That made the surrounding smiles even wider.

Most people like to see and hear little kids in church. They're the sight of life.

Those who dislike natural childhood noise, well, they're murdering the Church.

✂ -

Flashback:

At Ash Wednesday, I'd challenged the Sunday School kids: "If any of you memorize all Ten Commandments by Palm Sunday, I'll wear a pair of bunny ears on Easter."

Surprised me that one of them did!

Since a promise is a promise, I put on the rabbit ears and started down the center aisle to start off the service (then removed them after the announcements so they wouldn't be a total distraction all through the choir cantata.)

Following the benediction, but before stepping out from behind the altar railing to trail after the choir, I put the ears back on.

As always, I inwardly cringe and hope that no one notices the downward cast of my eyes following every step taken by Holly (the prettiest choir member) who is usually last in line.

My eyes drawn low.

Lovely ankles.

And it's no help to me that the only shoes she owns are stripper heels.

✂ -

The term you're looking for is more Retifism (shoe fetishism), than Podophilia (foot fetish), although neither really apply.

I simply meant Holly has the poise to walk on stilts without her ankles wobbling inward before lifting with every step.

✂ -

Pausing at my little fan's pew, I tilt my head and bent forward so the fuzzy ear tips brushed her face. With her distracted and giggling, I applied a foam rabbit nose to myself so that when I straightened back up – it would seem to her – that I'd magically sprouted a new nose!

She squealed louder in delight and clapped her hands.

I smiled to her and her mother, then proceeded to my usual position by the double doors, below – and to the left of – the huge portrait of Saint Mary.

✂ -

Turning around, my back to the wall, my eyes sweep the sanctuary for a quick inspection. I see:
- the backs of people as they gather up their stuff to leave
- the backs of those who pause to kneel for prayer before leaving
- the stained glass windows
- the things you don't see in many churches any more, such as

the raised pulpit (three steps to get up into it)

the large wooden rood screen (like a flower bed beneath the stained glass windows over the altar, except that it's function is decorative and not to hold anything)

- and the rafters and beams of the arched ceiling high overhead.

Always gotta check the roof isn't gonna collapse on me.

✂ -

Standing at the back doors, I was shaking hands with people as they exit the sanctuary.

There's one in every congregation

that parishioner who, every week, says they enjoyed the sermon.

On cue: "Reverend, good sermon."

Thing is, it's Easter.

I didn't preach.

Instead of my sermon, the choir sang a cantata.

Showing his habit, rather than sincerity.

BUSTED!!!!

✂ -

Standing at the back doors, I was shaking hands with people as they exit the sanctuary.

Happy smiles:

"Father, we love the way you engage the kids in service."

"Father, that was a wonderful service!"

"Didn't the choir do a marvelous job?"

"Really hit it out of the park today, Father."

✂ -

Standing at the back doors, I was shaking hands with people as they exit the sanctuary.

Another Easter service was over, and I wouldn't be seeing – nor hearing from – our "see-a-knee" guests for nine months.

"C & Es" (Christmas & Easter).

A smile and a handshake twice a year, that's about it from them.

✂ -

But isn't it always the way?

A line of folks behind, anxiously waiting to leave and a bi-annual visitor has to pause and ask, "Father, could you stop by and visit my mother?"

A smile, handshake, and I gesture her towards the side table beneath the portrait.

"Of course. If you'd take one of our prayer cards and write down directions and an address for me?" I asked.

"Oh! It's real simple. At the light make a left. Go down a ways, and it's right across the street from Cecelia Holmes' house. Cecelia used to be a parishioner here, and brought mom with her."

Things I'm thinking but don't dare say aloud:

1) "That's supposed to mean something to me?"

2) "Lady, I never met whoever, and I have no idea where they lived. And since you're using past tense regarding her membership here, I doubt she's still alive!"

3) "If my visiting is important enough for you to hold up the line to ask me to do it, then why can't you be bothered to take a moment and write down the directions for me?"

4) "Never tell a priest something on a Sunday morning because we won't remember what you said, along with everything else everybody else is telling us. When we ask you to write something down, it's for a reason!"

Just to get her moving out of the way, I said, "I'll get over to see her" (and pray I remember to).

✂ -

Standing at the back doors, I was shaking hands with people as they exit the sanctuary.

According to the church's insurance carrier, clergy should no longer be initiating physical contact.

No shaking hands.

No hugging.

("Because if a person doesn't want to shake your hand, they still will, even though they don't want to, because you are the priest, and they always have to be polite to the priest."

(It was called "Boundary Awareness Training."

(I call it "Six hours of my life I'll never get back!")

And yes, they mean we cannot hold the hand of someone lying on their deathbed.

Heaven forbid we offer a comforting presence there at their end.

Some simple human contact.

I guess those insurance idiots never realized that not every physical gesture in this world is sexual.

I guess they just see perverts everywhere.

✂ -

It all boiled down to their one and only point:

"Keep it in your pants."

✂ -

"If someone looks you in the eye, cast your eyes to the floor; because making eye contact will intrude on their retinal boundaries."

Where will the litigiousness end?

Malpractice insurance for clergy in case we preach an offensive sermon?

✂ -

There's a dry sarcasm here.

Hope you're reading with that in mind.

✂ -

And yes, there's Holly.

That choir member in her "do-me" heels.

Yes.

I checked.

She's in the choir, but not a member of the congregation.

She never joined.

There is no paperwork.

Like most people, she figured that attending regularly is what made her a member.

(Not according to the diocesan paper-pushers, though.)

✂ -

Maybe you're right.

Maybe I shouldn't be ogling Holly so much.

Especially since I've asked a pretty young woman to marry me.

✂ -

Standing at the back doors, I was shaking hands with people as they exit the sanctuary.

Usually the last to exit, Mr and Mrs Church (not their real names) were leaving early to make it to an afternoon Easter party with family.

Every church has folks like them
those who are in charge of everything.

Mr and Mrs Church; the "Sourpuss Family" as I call them.

Neo-Puritans, I swear!

So, you can guess which parishioners were first to take offense at my way of doing things with joy and humor.

I smiled into their disapproving scowls over my rabbit ears and foam nose.

Of course, she was still pissed at me about our conversation from before worship began.

✂ -

Flashback
Prior to 11 am Easter Morning service

I'd been talking with parishioner # 21 when Mrs Church barged up and interrupted us by thrusting her clipboard at me.

"Father! I want you to sign my petition!"

I had to excuse myself from parishioner # 21 and immediately give Mrs Church my undivided attention.

(It's an unforgiveable sin to make her wait.)

Yet I couldn't help pausing before taking the clipboard from her.

She sighed her displeasure, "I want to put this out for everyone to sign after worship. It's Easter, so we'll have a lot of extra people here who can sign this."

"What's it for?" asked parishioner # 21, editor of the parish newsletter.

"As you know, I am on the committee which reviews the applications for business licenses here in the village. He said he wanted to sell T-shirts and clothing, not dirty movies!"

Awkwardly, I smiled, said, "You know, we really should look into this first. Get all the facts."

"What facts??!! He wants to sell dirty movies here in the village!"

("Dirty movies? Does that mean porn? Or rated-R?")

I replied, "State zoning laws may prevent that."

"Why are you trying to stop me??!! Father! One would think you want them to open such a store!"

Yes.

God would do this to me.

I think God likes to see me squirm.

After all

a porn shop

open across the village square from the church??!!

I told Mrs Church, "I'm simply advising patience. A petition to stop a store from opening will only draw more attention to the store. Why give them extra publicity?"

"Father does have a point," parishioner # 21 said. "A book gets protested, and people buy it just to see what all the fuss is about. I know, because I've done that, and usually, the book itself was nothing without the scandal."

Thwarted in her latest crusade and moral outrage, Mrs Church had stalked off.

Fumed throughout the cantata.

Burned with further insult at my ears and nose.

Surprised me she came through the line to exchange pleasantries with me. Usually she'll exit by the altar to avoid having to exchange pleasantries with me (she just wants to make sure I don't miss how upset I made her on Easter).

Thankfully she had that family party to rush off to.

Otherwise I'm sure she would've held up the line to give me her opinion.

(As though hers is the only one that matters.)

I smiled, "Have a good party this afternoon."

It wasn't my whiskers that were singed.

✂ -

Standing at the back doors, I was shaking hands with people as they exit the sanctuary.

Disapproving frown.

That's Christian love for you.

Parishioner # 48, Church matriarch.

Old school.

Still attends church wearing a hat and gloves.

The voice that will accept no change to anything while she's alive!

So many elderly church-goers just want to keep things exactly the same as they've always been.

As if there's never been any changes to the church, or in the church.

Hello??!!

Um ... the Church of 1919 is not at all like it is in 2019!

And, by the way

there is a technological vacuum in this parish.

✂ -

The idea was raised my first week at Saint Mary's, whether or not to get a wide screen for projecting images like hymn lyrics, or video clips during a sermon. It was brought up because my first official duty (before my first Sunday in the pulpit) was to do a funeral. The family had asked for a wide screen to show a video the decedent had made (he'd been a twenty-something musician who'd recorded a song he wrote and sang before his drug overdose).

Sadly, there'd been no tech to show it on.

The old battle axe shaking my hand had brought that conversation to a dead halt by dismissing the "Jumbotron" (as someone else called it) and leading the vote to

"Not change.

"Never change!"

And parishioner # 48's sentiment had been echoed around the room with offense

"Jesus didn't have a big screen TV when he preached the sermon on the mount!"

"We don't need that!"

"It's unnecessary!"

"Never had it, never will!"

✂ -

And church-goers wonder why there aren't more young folks in the pews.

✂ -

I know, I know.

I really am trying to tone that down, but it's my knee-jerk reaction.

In my defense though, the photocopier in the office (with its hourly paper jams and ink smudges on every page) is the same one they've "always had" so it can't be swapped for a newer one.

And don't get me started on the story about the big upheaval that went on back in the 1980s when they scrapped the ditto machine to lease the photocopier they still have!

Way I hear it, the church roof almost came crashing down!

✂ -

Standing at the back doors, I was shaking hands with people as they exit the sanctuary.

My mind in a flurry of memories and stories triggered by each face.

Parishioner # 39, the farmer who lives up on the hill is next in line: "Father, I'm sorry, but we need to postpone tonight's dinner. Would you still be able to make it the night after tomorrow?"

(Their family tradition: Hasenpfeffer on Easter. His Grandfather had started the tradition after catching the rabbit which had been raiding their first garden on the new family farm 82 years ago.)

"Wouldn't miss it, thanks."

His three daughters are your quintessential cowgirls.

Pointed-toe boots, Stetson hats, skin-tight jeans, perfect skin, and slender figures without an ounce of flab. His son wasn't so lucky as he'd inherited nothing but fat, acne, and social awkwardness. All five kids did have bright white teeth which his wife says is a benefit of growing up on a dairy farm.

"We'll call you with the details."

I added, "Thanks again for the invite."

Released his hand to shake his wife's, and then their kids – in line – youngest to oldest.

His oldest daughter (still at home) had her nose bandaged up, and her eyes shadowed like a raccoon from the bruising after her nose job.

The only one of their five kids missing from church was their first-born. For her, they often request prayers of wisdom (to learn how to break the allure of addiction) and healing (to get and stay sober).

✂ -

Standing at the back doors, I was greeting people as they exit the sanctuary for the village square being dribbled on with rain.

The odd drop here and there didn't really qualify as a "sprinkle."

Next in line: an elderly man, took my hand and said, "REVEREND, I CAN'T HEAR YOU!"

Screaming at the top of his voice; still can't hear himself.

He sits in the third pew from the front.

At the top of my voice, "THE SPEAKERS ARE RIGHT BACK HERE!" and I stepped aside, Vanna Whiting the big black boom box in the corner.

Apparently what I offered him wasn't an answer.

(Not one he chose to hear, even if he could.)

He replied, "DON'T WANT TO LOSE MY SEAT! BEEN THERE FOR FIFTY-ODD YEARS!"

As I helped him down the church steps, one slow and wobbly step at a time, he repeated, "I DON'T KNOW WHAT TO DO! I DON'T KNOW WHAT TO DO!"

After helping him to his car, I returned to the top of the church steps.

How does he still have a driver's license?

✂ -

Is it just me?

Let's see – he could keep sitting up front, and not hear a thing.

Or, move to the back by the speaker, and hear more.

His vision's fine, no issues there.

Of course, if he'd get himself a hearing aid, that would help!

Trouble there is, he doesn't want people seeing he needs one.

But that's just more tics.

✂- -

Tics.
    T-I-C-S
            Things
            I
            Can't
            Say

✂- -

The worst of the occupational hazards priests have to deal with is not being able to say what we think. For my own peace of mind I came up with that mnemonic.

Without an outlet
                we've got to suppress it
                        bottle everything up inside.

That's why so many clergy have nervous breakdowns or turn into overly-excessive drinkers.

Me? I'll think it, but never let myself verbalize it.

Saying what I was thinking would be harmful to "The Collar".

By keeping my private thoughts unspoken I wasn't at risk of damaging God's reputation (since clergy are supposed to be God's representatives on earth).

So, thank-you, for listening to me.

It means more than you know!

Who ministers to the minister?

You do, by allowing me to let my hair down and bitch about work. Ideally the bishop is meant to be a priest's priest, but he's way too busy for pastoral work.

✂- -

You've seen me at work
- I make eye contact
- I smile (even if forced)
- I'm always cheerful (even if not feeling it)
- I listen to folks as they talk to me
- I demonstrate – and act out – the proper priestly image, and
- I don't dare betray any of what I'm actually thinking.

Since you wanted a glimpse "behind the curtain" I figured I could part the veil of my public "image" for you.

Here are my experiences as a priest, so you know what being a priest is really like.

No fluffy feel-good tripe.

No ignorance of the world = innocence.

Start by scrapping all the crap about how I shouldn't
       think this
            feel that
                  believe whatever
                       and so on, and so on, ad
nauseum.

✂ -

Unhooking the double doors, I pause to glance across the village square.

Our heavy doors open out onto a cement platform which offers a panoramic view of the shop buildings surrounding the grassy area in the middle.

In-between the two trees is a gazebo whose white paint is chipped and pealing.

Three-quarters of the storefronts in the square are vacant. Some windows are boarded up, papered over, others lay wide open showing the empty, dust-coated rooms within. The nearest shopping mall is twenty-two miles up the road going north. The nearest hospital is eight miles to the East. The closest Thruway on-ramp is thirteen miles west. The square has one traffic light on the far side of the MBT bank next door (the tallest building in town – three floors; not counting the attic under its pitched roof and squared-off facade). The most obvious blight upon the quaint village square is the other church at the opposite corner. It burnt down and its charred timber frame and scorched remains are still there after decades. Why they (village/town council) don't get rid of the ruins and build something new I don't know.

The biggest draw for the city folk to come to town is horse-riding in the summer

the town carnival

the ski slopes on the surrounding hills in the winter

the children are bussed to a neighboring town to attend school

there's one weekly newspaper (recent front page stories: "Burger Joint Worker Assembles Whopping Big Burger in 12 Seconds!" – "Dairy Princess Wins Scholarship for Raising Rabbits" – "Car Wreck On Main Street Takes Down Telephone Line!").

There are more cows than people.

You don't have to strain your imagination to know this is a village you'd miss if you blinked.

You wouldn't notice it while on your way to somewhere more interesting.

The youth are chomping at the bit to get out of here.

The elderly who still have teeth gnash them at the young couples moving in.

As those first-time home owner couples don't have kids yet, the churches aren't competing with each other to woo and welcome them to town. And after getting settled in the young couples don't take part in the local community events, which were probably selling points used by their realtors to entice them to buy the "quaint" homes.

Those couples keep to themselves and only moved into the area for its rustic, rural appeal, and because the houses can be bought for cheap.

The sound of horses in the nearest stable two blocks uphill can be heard during quiet moments like Sunday mornings after church.

It helps me feel lost.

I like the idea of doing "frontier" ministry.

Being out here in the vast, virgin, territory, with no one to rely on but myself (read: no bishop looming over my shoulder watching every move I make).

It's like I can momentarily imagine myself as a preacher venturing out as a pioneer.

I like it.

It's peaceful.

It's quiet.

It works for my self-imposed exile.

✂ -

They'd just hung the banner.

The dates for Copthorne's 79th annual summer carnival.

It's stretched in-between the two poles which support the square's solitary traffic light. One pole is at the corner of the bank, and the other is in front of the liquor store's picture window, which makes the wire cross High Street at an angle. Fortunately for me, I'm able to see the banner and read its lettering from the front steps of Saint Mary's because of the angle its at.

✂ -

Used to be you could count on Spring always getting warmer as the year advances towards summer, but not for the last many years or so.

It had been warming, then a freak drop in temp, and snow covered the ground again. I stood outside the double doors, waiting for the last parishioner to drive off. In-between folks, I'd glanced around the square.

Looking from the burnt out Baptist church at one end of the opposite side, to the corner bar at the other, I notice that same 10 speed pedal bike parked outside the bar door again.

Snowing. Cold. Guy still rides his bike to the bar because the wind-chill ride into town takes less time than walking. He has a long beard the same white as the thick hair on his head. I'm tempted to tell you he's the town Santa Claus impersonator, but you wouldn't believe me if I did.

✂ -

Closing the double doors I take a deep inhale and say under my breath that prayer I say every Sunday morning when I lock the doors of Saint Mary's Episcopal Church:
    "People are strange – God love'em."

✂ -

My Seminary education was great for deconstructing my faith, turning me into an atheist, and then rebuilding my faith back up.

And through that I came to see how the church has its own trade language meant to make everything sound loftier and grander than it really is. Like how I can't just want to change locations by transferring to another (higher paying) branch of the franchise.

Nope
        in church I'll have to claim I am "called" to that larger, better paying parish.

As if God has blessed me with the opportunity to get a raise.

(TICS: "Funny how no one ever gets 'called' by God to go to a small church that can't pay as well as the bigger churches.")

How I avoided getting a pay-cut by moving from the city to the country is beyond me; but I do count that as a blessing.

✂ -

Like my cousin said, "If you love everything about your job, then it wouldn't be 'work.'"

You bitch about your job, so I can bitch about mine.

You just think I'm not allowed to have anything to bitch about because I'm not allowed to be human. That I have to love all my neighbors ("turn the other cheek" does not translate into "Let yourself be victimized").

Truth is, you love your Uncle, but you're always bitching about him.

You sleep with your boss, but you're always bitching about her.

So cut me some slack and be a friend who lets me vent and rant about my job, too.

✂ -

I'm gonna tell you something now, even though you'll forget I said it:

I love the ideal of what the Church could be; I'm just not enamored with the reality of how it actually is. Reason I keep my job is I love parish work, I'm just not keen on anything higher up the diocesan (read: corporate) ladder – that's where the Church loses its soul, and Heaven forbid any bishop or any minor church politician ever hear me say that!

I'd be out on my ass, is why!

The "Godfather" (read: bishop) and his toadies won't want to believe any clergy actually think what I just said, even though more clergy do than they'd ever want to believe. Rule number one in all church doings: "Don't be heard, so don't voice it!" which is why self-preservation has left me mute. The minority in power live for that political shite, and they expect everyone else to as well, so we pretend, and adopt the guise of pride in profession, since members are supposed to care about the club they belong to.

Right?

Me – I care about God, and faith. I'm a pastoral minister first and foremost.

My calling is to help people grow closer to God (however they understand God).

Not preach blind obedience to human organizations.

I'm trusting you'll keep my secret.

✂ -

II. Eastertide

The "Flower Duet" from Delibes' Lakmé accompanied me into the cemetery.

Funerals are a problem for me!

It's not because of Necrophobia, nor that Necrophilia is in the Bible. Rather, it's the
young women today
sex kittens in seductive little black dresses, what can I say?

It's good to know they know the tradition of wearing all black, but must they really come to funerals wearing cocktail dresses, patterned stockings, and skirts with slits up their thighs?

✂ -

Pulling into the cemetery, I looked around and recognized the family.

They had a visitor with them, someone who hadn't been at the funeral back in January!

That petite and cute little blonde all in black was the first new woman to catch my eye in a while. Sure, I've noticed Holly ("Yum")
the town librarian ("Hot Mama!" "Ssssh!")
the farmer's daughter (not really my type, but still very sexy) and
the village's popular barber-barmaid (I'm not dead).

Even though it was Spring on the calendar, and the morning's snowfall had melted by afternoon, I'm used to that, but not used to seeing many young women wearing wide-brimmed Grandma hats anymore, and that gave the leggy blonde a quality of apple-cheeked innocence, combined with the cartoonish giraffe tattooed on the outside of her left leg, and the butterfly on her left bicep.

She was a source of cute'n sexy fun within the bleak funeral setting.

Youth combined with antiquity.

Why did she look familiar?

Her dress was a black sleeveless number with a stripe of glossy vinyl running straight down the front's middle, accented with a wide red belt and low-heel shoes.

Walking up to the family at the cemetery, I'd looked over her profile before she turned my way and offered a radiant gap-toothed smile that lit up her face and crinkled the bridge of her nose. It was that same kind of friendly smile many wear when they see The Collar, but don't see me.

Her fair hair under that hat almost concealed her pearl earrings.

Pale face, grey lipstick, wonderful green eyes!

Why she had to spoil her charms with a brass nose ring is beyond me.

I offered my condolences to all present, then looked back into the eyes of the goth hottie who was all legs in that dress. Sexy figure, twinkling eyes, and banana knees. She hadn't been able to attend the January funeral service but was able to join the family for the burial.

✂ -

The cemetery was calm.

Quiet.

Established on a hillside.

Stepping away from the family, I went over to greet the funeral director, not too far from the square hole of a grave.

Being still early in the year, the trees had yet to grow leaves, and the grass was still that sickly lightishy color. By mid-summer the entire landscape would be alive with vibrant foliage. So much so, that it would seem like town was the only settlement in an untamed forest.

Cut off from the rest of the world.

You won't even see any gaps where lines of trees were cut down for roadways.

Like a solid, unblemished, frontier wilderness.

I love it!

✂ -

Except for that black and rusted industrial blight on the next hill!

✂ -

You have to go out of your way to get to town.

Getting off the Thruway at the nearest exit still requires a drive along winding, twisting, tree-lined, forest-like roads to get here, and once here, you discover **THERE'S NOTHING HERE!!**

Except for those abandoned buildings and chimney stacks on the next hill which stick out like old, rusty blocks.

The factory.

For almost seventy-five years it had been the biggest employer in the area.

Now closed.

Discarded.

Corroded.

Abandoned.

✂ -

The funeral director reeked of too much cologne, like always.

His black suit and tie immaculate and ironed with creases sharp enough to cut paper.

I think of him as "Cyranose" because he'd bought the Bergerac Funeral Home, and kept the name (keeping an established name was better for business than switching to an unknown name). My name-calling might sound horrible, but when I think that name in my head, it's said affectionately.

(In college theatre I got to play the title character in Rostand's *Cyrano DeBergerac* due entirely to my using the opening monologue from *Richard III* for my audition.)

Cyranose sends a lot of extra work my way.

✂ -

Started the committal service, my eyes homing back in on "Legs," and her knees with their slightly backwards bend. From her, I forced myself to look over at the other folks on either side of her, each in turn.

After finishing the prayers and concluding the committal service, I stepped back

the funeral director stepped forward

knelt down on a pad of fake grass to place the urn inside the square hole.

"Oh! You know, can you open that up?"

Cyranose, elbow deep in sod, looked up, "I'm sorry?"

"Grams wanted her ashes to be scattered on the wind!"

There was enough breeze to ruffle the director's wig and he had mud streaks on his black coat sleeves after removing the urn from the grave.

It wasn't the type of urn which was made to be reopened.

It was the type which needed a flathead screwdriver to be used as a wedge to pry it open. Once popped free, Cyranose removed the lid and the clear plastic bag inside which contained all that remained of Gram's earthly remains.

The Granddaughter tore open the bag like it was a bag of chips, and reached in.

Removed a handful of ashes.

Threw the ashes up into the air.

The wind was slow in picking up.

The ashes weren't carried away.
The funeral director's black suit was greyed.
I repressed a smirk.
Some of us were wise enough to step back.

✂ -

Bag of ashes back in the urn.
Lid back on the urn.
That square mouth in the ground swallowed the urn anew.

The family had drifted off to the far side of the cemetery by the wooden fence. The barely sprouting cornfield on the other side descended across a gentle hill.

Cyranose was getting back up on his feet as a voice carried: "GROSS! I got some of Gram under my fingernails!"

✂ -

Once "Legs" started to move towards her car, half of me was happy she'd be leaving, so I wouldn't be able to keep looking at her, and half of me was saddened that she'd be leaving, so I couldn't keep looking at her.

Only, Legs moved to get into the passenger's side of her car to retrieve a bottle of water.

She looked familiar but I couldn't place where I'd seen her before!

Drives me crazy when I can't place a familiar face! You know I pride myself on being able to recognize someone, especially since I'm terrible with names.

I remember stories and backgrounds before names.

I'll talk personal history and private details with people before I know what to call them.

✂ -

"Grams" (Saint Mary's Christian Education Director – Parishioner # 16) had died just before Christmas.

25

She'd tumbled off a step stool while hanging Christmas decorations up at home the day after Thanksgiving. Following a stay in the hospital, during which she never awoke, the family did not call me in when they decided to pull the plug.

(Then they blamed me for not being there when the time came.)

Then her burial had to wait for her family to come back to town at Easter break.

(They couldn't be billed for the grave digging, but they could be billed for snow removal, so they'd decided to wait.

(TICS: "Nothing says familial love like cutting corners for a lower bill!)

None of her family had continued going to church after they all grew up, and yet – and this is neither surprising nor uncommon – they still wanted a religious send off for her. Just

not in church.

So, by not calling me in they could then feel justified in thinking that since I wasn't there for them

the Church is not there for them

therefore they don't need to hold any loyalty to the Church.

People don't need to look hard for a reason to avoid church.

That's just the way it is.

Keeping the faith can be an uphill struggle, and it should be. The issue for me is whether or not a person's faith is in God, or in the institutional Church.

The funeral director knows I'll do funerals for families who don't go to church. My view is, if someone wants the comforts of God (church-goer or not) then it is not my job to block them from God on the basis of church attendance.

Rather, my job is to extend such comforts to all as I am able.

(The minister at the church down the street won't do any funeral services unless the dead were faithful – and regular – attendees at his church.

26

(I really should thank him for that, since his refusal brings more part-time work my way.)

✂ -

Watched Legs pour the expensive bottle of water (it's adverts claimed the water was melted off an arctic iceberg – frozen back before pollution started – so it's the purest drinking water available) over the granddaughter's ash-covered hand.

I waited beside Cyranose for the family to leave the cemetery.

Then he gestured for the vault guy to lower the casket into the ground for burial.

"Well Father, it's been nice working with you," the funeral director said as the last car started up.

"Heading back down to Florida for a few months?"

"And not coming back."

"Retirement?"

Cyranose had to add a final shot: "Try not to run into any more horses after I'm gone, ok?"

The man in the ash-covered suit wasn't as funny as he liked to think he was, and I could only hope he'd put in a good word for me with his replacement.

✂ -

You remember back when I first moved into town?

Flashback:

I was following behind my moving van (read: tailgating) when the sort of tragedy that people constantly talk about – happened!

My arrival to town soured my reputation before I stepped into the pulpit.

That had been the same day a multi-ribbon winning white stallion got lose and went for a run around the parish. It's gallop ended when it ran out in front of the moving truck filled with all my stuff

27

the day <u>before</u> it was scheduled to fulfill some million dollar stud contract.

Funny how the facts get distorted when stories get retold from gossip
> to gossip
> to gossip.

People now think – incorrectly – that I was driving the vehicle which splattered the horse. Which is why the funeral director has always worked my "hitting a horse" into every conversation he and I have had, beating his dead horse joke to death.

✂ -

I could only hope that when his niece takes over Bergerac that she'll have a better sense of humor.

"I told her all about you," Cyranose promised.

(TICS: "Great.")

I wished him well, and offered to pray for safe travel with him.

I was reminded (as I peeked mid-prayer) of all the bitterness surrounding that whole derelict factory complex on the next hill.

✂ -

Most small towns still hold their traditional festivals with locally-related themes.

I've heard of

Winefest	Winterfest
Burger-Fest	Oktoberfest
Maplefest	Fall Fest
Dairy Festival	Corn Festival
Apple-Umpkin Festival	Garlic Festival
Honey Festival	Latex Festival

✂ -

I say "bitterness" because the owner of that industrial eyesore had once been given a chance to keep the factory alive and going, but he'd refused to expand the factory's range of products. When pressured to allow the change in product lines, he cited his Baptist conscience and how that prohibited his selling the property to any company that would make black latex fetish suits.

His morals killed the local economy.

And set the village/town of Copthorne on a path towards a slow and lingering demise.

✂ -

Then

he moved to Arizona.

So, what's he care about the people, or town, left behind?

His property has yet to be sold, and since its closing twenty plus years ago, local teens have taken to using the old factory buildings as a place to park for backseat sex and keg parties, scattering used condoms on the grounds of the factory which had made condoms during WWII.

✂ -

According to the town's history book, historical society, and sign plaques posted about, I can share that Charles Goodyear created a pliable, waterproof, moldable rubber, and patented his "vulcanization" process (remove the sulfur then heat it) in 1844 (patent # 3,633). The first rubber condom was made in 1855. Then in 1920, Latex was invented, and latex condoms were thinner, and lasted longer, so they were a popular selling item by 1929.

(Charles Mackintosh's rubber raincoat in 1823 was the start of rubber fetishism in clothing, though it didn't really reach mass popularity until much later.)

The factory was opened in 1925, and then shifted to producing condoms by 1940 to supply the Allied troops (because the only European supplier was German, and they were the enemy, so who would trust their condoms?). The military gave them out to every soldier. I'd imagine a big governmental contract helped finance the factory through its change in product line from shoes and tires – to condoms – and back again after the war ended.

The idiot owner (the one in Arizona) took over the factory from his father back in 1960, and after fifty years of making rubber gloves, ran it into the ground.

Instead of seeing his home town gainfully employed, he chose a cock-blocking attitude regarding rubber fetish gear, designer condoms, and "kinky sex suits."

Since he wouldn't sell
        the buyer went elsewhere.

The factory owner is still on permanent vacation.

This town is still out of work.

Who wins when people deny human sexuality?

✂ -

Local history has it that some moral watchdog group had tried to incite the factory workers to strike rather than make contraceptives.

Back when the US entered the war, and the men went off to fight the Nazi regime, the women took over the factory work. They wouldn't strike because they needed money to feed their children, and nothing would get in their way of that, even it it meant actively doing something to stop the spread of STDs (which were touted then as being a divine punishment for sexual misbehavior!

(Some irrational arguments – like "sex education encourages sex" – just never die...)

If you're wondering how this small, rural village/town, in the middle of nowhere is able to hobble on rather than become more of a ghost-town

about eight miles up the road is a 700-plus acre landfill facility. Of that, only about 125 acres are actually used for trash storage, as the remaining area has clay pits, wetland, leachate pumping and a methane power station. Apparently, what is under the ground is just as important a factor on where a county dump can go as is what's above.

According to some, that owner figured the dump would be in operation for about another thirty years (more like 10 now), and with the dump paying property taxes for local residents, he probably figured no one needed to keep working.

Not only was he a prude
       also sounds like an ignorant ass to boot!

✄ -

My car started up to "You Don't Know" by Kobra and the Lotus sending an overloud crescendo echoing around the headstones (always forget my car's mute deactivates whenever the car is shut off). Starting out of the cemetery I ignored the touch screen's warning about not taking my eyes off the road.

I wouldn't have to look away if they still sold cars with CD players!!!

Touch screens are supposed to be easier?

Fuck no!

There's no texture to work by touch, so you're forced to effing look!

Flustered, I pulled my "Symphonic Metal" USB stick out of the car's dashboard, resentful of how the car radio industry screws you over if you don't have an effing smartassphone! Probably could've left it in, but I'd had that stick plugged in for the past week and was due for a change. Rather than search, or go back to the classical radio station, I turned off the radio to get a little quiet time for reflection.

Ended up contemplating our Puritan heritage instead.

I figured that's largely why we're all so effed up about sex.

The Puritans arrived in America, denying their sexuality, and then the slaughter of native people began as more and more white folks moved in and took over.

End result: sex is bad, violence is good.

Why isn't our culture as shocked and scandalized about violence, as it is about sex?

We – as a country – don't talk about sex, which is why there are so many sexual problems; not the least of which is sexual addiction.

✂ -

The very first thing you need to understand about addiction is that it is not universal.

We want to think it is, but it isn't.

Some people can drink without becoming alcoholics.

Some can eat food without over-eating.

Some can look at a sexy person and not stare.

Some people can use/view porn then turn off the TV.

It's not the behavior; it's the person. The mystery why some folks become addicts and others don't has yet to be solved conclusively, but that does not mean addiction is fake. I think addiction is caused by the trinity of: environment, genetics, and drug-of-choice. Without the combo platter of all there (and yes, there is a biological overlap in there, too), addictions don't develop.

(Some scholars believe there were recreational drugs in the Biblical era, and that the Apostle Paul likely took something which influenced his writings [Wine, Opium, Nutmeg, Harmal, Pomegranate, Agarwood, Saffron, Blue Lotus, and even Frankincense, and Myrrh]).

So I'd encourage you, not to be so closed-minded.

✂ -

Because we simply do not talk about sex, I usually have to lay a foundation for open acceptance and communication free of judgement or blame.

To do so, here are the things I tell all my addiction clients before we get started:

1) There is no such thing as being sexually "normal".

2) There is no "sexual sin" God will not forgive.

3) While we may start by talking about a sex addiction, be prepared to find the issue really isn't about sex after all. In most cases, the sexual component is just a symptom of a larger/deeper issue, and sex is rarely the issue itself.

Some find these statements disorienting (especially # 2, with my wearing The Collar).
We have this notion in our heads –
    based on stereotypes,
       church tradition,
          faulty theology,
             biased Bible translation work,
               and the societal expectation
                 – that personal sexuality must always be kept secret. I say: be open to an awareness of where our ideas came from
    because these are the very *things* we must struggle against
    and redefine for future generations
    if we're ever going to provide those generations with a sex-positive Gospel ethic rather than cursing them to the same sex-negative afflicition we've all suffered from.

✂ -

The fallout from centuries of bad attitudes about sex has prompted a dual approach to my work.

I do clinical work.

I do pastoral work.

And honestly, there's a lot less pressure in my secular office.

Yet my church setting is probably where the harder work needs to be done.

And my aim is specific:
                the buck has to stop somewhere.

✂ -

Sometimes people are reassured.

Sometimes they're scandalized.

But when parishioner # 55 came to talk with me about her husband's porn habit, well – that's always trickier than counseling a non-churched person because – the pressure is on!

Say the wrong thing in the wrong way, and the parishioner might leave the church.

But then, it's often the case that after a parishioner has an open discussion about their problems, they sometimes leave the church anyway (because now the priest is aware of their dirty laundry) and the internalized notion of "JUDGEMENT" kicks in.

They can no longer face anyone who knows their deep dark secrets, whatever those may be.

The self-conscious invariably see judgement in my eyes.

For myself, I can say it will not ever be there.

But they'd be seeing it in the eyes of anyone who ... *knows.*

So it's not my eyes, personally.

To her weeping, I offered, "I know you feel hurt, and that this could be a painful conversation, but if you'd like to talk through this, maybe I can help."

"Get him to stop watching, you mean?" she asked through her sniffles.

"Help you."

"Me? How? I'm not the one with the problem!"

"Well, for example, can you say why you have a negative opnion about pornography?"

"It's porn! It's dirty movies! My husband's sick!"

(TICS: "How do you know they are 'dirty'? When did you learn porn = sickness?"

(TICS: "The reality is, you can find porn all throughout history, and even as far back as pre-history when you look at some of the cave paintings. Porn will always be around.")

✂ -

"You want your husband to stop watching porn. I get that. But I also want to help you. To do that, there're a few common misconceptions we should talk about.

"Like, are you still in love with your husband?"

"What's that got to do with anything?"

(That riled. Need to return to it.)

I offered what I always hope is a comforting smile and appeased, "You are.

"So, what if I told you he's still in love with you?"

"What's he said about me? Did he talk to you about this already?"

"One common misperception is that a man does not love his partner if he watches porn."

"How could he love me, and watch that stuff?!"

(TICS: "Meaning, you alone should be the only woman he ever looks at? A common enough greeting card fantasy, but totally unrealistic.")

"Men can love their wives, and still find other women attractive. Haven't you ever found other men attractive?"

"I might look, but I'd never touch!"

(TICS: "'Look, but don't act on it. Don't touch the attractive woman. Don't touch yourself while watching an attractive woman'"

(Add a fear of sex into the mix and common sense gets all short-circuited.)

Tried something different, "Tell me, are you worried the porn will replace you?"

"It's a movie! How could it replace me?"

"Let me ask you this. Given the choice, of one or the other, would you rather know he watches, or that he lies to you about not watching, but then watches in secret anyway?"

"I'd rather he not watch it at all!"

(TICS: "Good luck with that!")

"Would it help you to hear that your husband's not sick just because he watches pornography?"

"Why are you defending him, Father?! It would help me if you'd tell me what to say to him to get him to stop!"

"Two questions for you:

"How often does he watch?

"And, does he neglect doing the things he has to do, so he can spend time watching movies instead?"

"Dirty movies!"

"'Dirty' is a value judgement."

"Father!"

Forced myself to smile.

Hope it's reassuring.

"I'm just trying to help you be aware that if you want to have a conversation with your husband about his porn watching, and how badly that makes you feel, then you need to know what words not to use. 'Filthy' is one, 'naughty' is another, because these words will throw up a wall and he won't hear you."

"What are you saying? That I can't call his dirty movies 'dirty'?"

"'Dirty' is another one."

(TICS: "Don't voice'em. Same way I'm not calling what he does 'porn use' instead of porn watching."

(To be blunt, there are shrinks who claim there's no such thing as "sex addiction" and they cannot conceive of porn as a drug-of-choice. But porn use can become compulsive, and then addictive. That being said, I do not tend to villify porn because my view of porn is that it is simply another genre of entertainment. Name the categories of movies you like: "Westerns. Comedy. Rom Coms. Mystery. Suspense. Classics. Musicals. Porn." See? Even video rental shops used to have special sections in the stores for porn, like with action and horror or sci-fi.

People react to porn like people used to react to Rock-n-Roll with Elvis and the Beatles.

(And to the people who disbelieve in sex addiction, I'd remind them that AA has been around for 100 years yet still people doubt the validity of alcoholism as a disease. There will always be believers and non-believers. Goes with the territory.)

I summarized, "Think it. Just don't say it."

And I returned to my query about how often her husband watches porn.

"Too much!"

(Again,) "Is he ignoring other things to go off and watch more?"

"Probably! I don't know! I'm not always at home!"

Like pulling teeth.

The pain of shame, and hurt feelings of embarrassment that her husband's eyes roam elsewhere. Not easy to talk about with that in the mix.

Can't establish if he's a porn addict, or just a casual user from what she's giving me. There's this entrenched notion in her mind about how things are supposed to be in life, and porn is not a part of it.

The unwritten/unspoken monogamy understanding that men are not told about.

How many couples define monogamy for each other?

Why is it that folks get so bent out of shape by people having sex, but then turn a blind eye to mass shootings, crime, starvation, homelessness, the slaughter of endangered species, ecological terrorism, pollution of the oceans, melting of the ice caps?

But, people having sex.

No greater crime, no bigger sin, no worse thing people can do!

And then ... to film it?!

✂ -

I have this problem.

I don't stomach the status quo easily.

I don't conform just because it's easier to be a clone.

I don't swear blind obedience to a club just to be a member in good standing.

Trouble is, I'm a priest who does not believe
    that sexual activity is sinful.

Yet everyone else in the club says YES, absolutely!
    Positively!
        Of course!
            Sex is a sin!

I don't buy that.

And not because I want to be contrary.

Not because I want to be different.

I'm not trying to upset the apple cart.

The Church has held this view for centuries
        and yet, here I stand.

I'm just looking for what God actually says about sexuality.

Not just absorb those words the Church put in God's mouth.

Not swallow human doctrine without question.

I have serious doubts that the Church accurately reflects God's truth.

They say we preach what we most need to hear ourselves.

✂ -

Saint Mary's has a paid staff of three:
    Priest
    Organist
    Sexton (read: janitor/repairman)
    And a volunteer staff of:
        Secretary
        Treasurer/Signer
        Precentor (read: hymn leader)

Staff meetings include all six of us (I hate meetings, so my mind usually wanders), The secretary gets pretty steamed if she's ever not included in any kind of discussion about parish business. She's constantly quoting, "If I don't know about it, I can't put it in the newsletter!"

Which usually causes conflict with parishioner # 21, editor of the newsletter.

Parishioner # 32, not only leads the congregation in song vocally, but also by accompanying the organist with his playing of harmonica, guitar, and ukulele (though not all at the same time, and he's too shy about bringing in his digeridoo for worship though that's the instrument he enjoys playing most of all). What I appreciate about him isn't just that he's funny, but also that if I need someone to cover for me, he's the perfect guy to lead worship in my absence.

✂ -

Across the street, next door to the single-yard cemetery entrance, lives
   the world's most annoying neighbor!
   Headlights on a riding lawn mower, 11pm!
   No muffler, revving his motorcycle, 6am!
   Beat-up pick-up truck, name of his self-employed contracting business on the side in-between rust spots, also needs a muffler, boisterously announcing whenever he comes and goes!
   When does the guy sleep?!
   Rumor is, he's the town drug dealer.
   Rumor is, he has a fiancée in Rochester.
   Tell me when he's ever visiting his fiancée given how often he's across the street in his dilapidated, run down, should be condemned by the town, house with crumbling basement walls.
   For a contemplative priest who enjoys silence, I hit the jackpot moving into the rectory!

✂ -

Cranky from the guy across the street making so much racket (before the sun had even risen)
   that I couldn't roll over and go back to sleep
   I dragged myself through my morning and got to the bar on time.
   Our monthly ecumenical lunch (typically always falls on the day after my monthly Saint Mary's staff meeting.)
      set up in the back room like usual.
   Whenever a bunch of clergy get together
         it's not to "shoot the shit" like you'd expect.
         (TICS: "They'll never be that honest.")
   Rather, we gather for "holy conversation."

Forget letting your hair down around your peers; everyone knows everybody else is only there to get the latest dirt on whoever
     screwed up since our last meeting.

It's not a celebration of gossip.

Rather, once somebody fucks up royally, all the others call dibs on who gets to go poaching parishioners.

Case in point: the Roman Catholic priest got up into his pulpit on Easter morning, confessed to a porn addiction and to having two on-going extra marital affairs with a couple of parishioners. He then walked out on the parish, abandoning it on Easter Sunday without anyone to lead worship in his absence.

(TICS: "He made it sound like he was diddling married women while being a film buff afficianado, but really, I know what actually happened with Client # 3.")

I'd already extended worship invitations to our RC neighbors, but they're more elitist than the Baptists.

✂- -

"Denominational envy"?
     Good one!
    "Theological exclusions"?
     Not so much.

✂- -

The Pentecostal suggested that the RC priest left in such a hurry because he got caught doing something with children and the police had been on their way.

That he needed to run while he still could.

The Amish minister (who rarely joins us) was of the opinion that not allowing priests to marry was why the RCs always had that kind of trouble; and thank God for the media, running all those sex scandals in the news.

Rather than risk client confidentiality, I kept my mouth shut.

✂- -

III. Cooked Bunny for Easter Dinner

You ever see it in a movie, where a character reacts to a person or situation in a homicidal rage? And then after the blood is done spraying like a gushing fountain, the scene reverts back to that moment right before the killing started?

I don't have impulses to respond with physical violence.

But there are snippy, snarky, self-amusing, sarcastic comments I'd love to actually voice out loud, but have to bite my tongue on instead.

That's what the TICS are for me.

(In the movies, it's called a "Voice-Over" where you hear the narrator while you see they are not talking.)

For example, Parishioner # 18.

Sitting in her pew, leaning close to the person seated beside her.

Talking all through my sermon this past Sunday.

Then, turning around to tell the pair of little giggling sisters in the next pew, "Ssssh! the priest is talking."

I want to call out from the pulpit, "Good advice!"

And then, having interrupted my own sermon, and in the hush of a church as silent as a tomb, follow that with, "In fact, while we're at it, why don't you shut up, too?"

My fantasy impulses: the TICS.

✂ -

No, I don't verbally call my parishioners by number.

In person I'll greet them by name.

But as I write to you, I'll categorize them either by number or name.

The ones you'll hear me talk about more often will have names, while that faceless crowd of anonymous folks in the pews will get numbers.

To guard client confidentiality, I won't tell you their names, but give them numbers, too.

The higher the number, the more recently I met them (same with the parishioners).

I'll try to include a detail or two on everyone, but why should you be keeping track of dozens of names to people you'll only hear me mention once, or maybe twice, at most?

✂ -

I drove the three miles to the farm for that delayed Easter dinner of oven-roasted bunny.

Expected that when I got there, I'd be hearing the latest in the saga of poor decision-making and bad life choices made by the farmer's (eldest) daughter.

I was ready to hear
        she'd quit her job
        been dropped by her live-in boyfriend
        checked herself out of rehab early
        had returned to her nasty habits.
I considered what to say to that.
        How to word my prayers with the family.

✂ -

Rather, as dinner was ending, Kelly – voice distorted by the bruising and healing of her nose job – asked, "Father?"

All eyes turned to her at the end of the table, seated beside her boyfriend.

She must've been nervous and unsure how to proceed once everyone's attention was on her.

Kelly had blonde curls, a black concert T-shirt, button fly stone-washed jeans bedazzled from hips to cuffs, and purple army boots.

Small breasted, trim waistline, rounded hips.

Dark rings penciled in around her eyes, with short lines angled outward beneath her temples.

I could appreciate her charms, even though she wasn't to my taste.

✂ -

Just because the expression, "Not my 'type'" is more common, I still think it's misleading; whereas "Not to my taste" is more accurate.

And absolutely! Kelly could be "seasoned" to my taste
once the nose work is finished
and she used some goth make-up for a stark white face, red lipstick, kohl eyes, and dyed-black curls tumbling all the way down to her waistline.

That's a look that could really bring out the color of her blue eyes and excite my old Morticia Addams crush!

She said, "We were hoping you'd be able to marry us?"

(TICS: "Scratch that!")

Cue up: scratching-a-needle-across-a-record sound!!
Delete all memories of Kelly!
Stop having sexy fantasies of her!
Inner brain hiccup.
Sorted.

I replied, "It would be my pleasure."

Her nerves weren't on edge about asking me to officiate the ceremony, but because she had to follow that query with the revelation that the wedding invitations had already been printed with a date.

✂ -

Back when in my active addiction, the world was alive with color! Now that I'm sober it's reduced to a black and white environment.

Yet the only full color I see any more
are those women I'm attracted to.

And they aren't just in color, but are full-body **4K Ultra Hi Def TECHNICOLOR** from head to foot.

They're the only vibrant colors inside a black, white, and grey landscape.

Yet by asking me to officiate her wedding, Kelly was drained of all color in my eyes.

From full-color beauty to being as black, white and grey as the rest of everything else.

She ceased to hold my attraction because she'd be getting married!

✂ -

A winter wedding?

Cuz they met in winter?

Not a bad idea, and certainly the wedding photo sample album she showed me looked wonderful.

Brides in white gowns with roses on a field of unblemished white snow.

Brides wearing furry hats and furry boots along with their lengthy gowns.

I didn't want to be discouraging, but when you plan for an event which depends all on the weather, too much can go wrong.

Betting the farm on one day's weather.

Hit or miss.

No guarantees.

End up with

       a bride crying all day because it isn't snowing

       a bride crying all day because it hasn't snowed enough to cover the ground

       a bride crying all day because there's too much snow, the roads aren't plowed, and her family can't get to church

       a bride crying all day because of freak rainfall melting the snow and turning the day grey, wet, and muddy.

It'd be so much easier to just plan their engagement photo session for a day with snow. Three people (the couple and photographer)

       one phone call

         quick drive

           get your pictures that way.

But, they'd already had those pix taken.

Instead, they were looking at having to deal with one hundred people unable to park their cars in the village square (due to high snow banks, same as last winter); not to mention those friends and family who might not get plowed out in time to make it.

So, I didn't say anything about anything.

I find the most tiresome part of my work is always having to put a positive spin on everything and always pointing out the silver lining to folks.

For a cynic like me, it's effing exhausting!

Sometimes, there just isn't any good to be found, and life just plain SUCKS!

Closing the album and leaving it on the table before me, I eased back in the stiff wooden chair, "They'll make wonderful pictures. I especially like the one of the couple in front of the Christmas tree."

"With all the colored lights! Right? That's my favorite!"

I smiled.

(TICS: "Good luck with that.")

(TICS: "According to the guy in the White House, Global warming is not a thing. And yet, used to be, back when I was a kid, it snowed before Christmas every year. These days, I'm usually not in a Christmassy Spirit since there isn't any snow in December.")

✂- -

As dessert was served, I ceased my imaginings of a Christmas wedding with Kelly in a festive gown instead of the traditional white.

"So, that won't be a problem?" Her fiancée asked about the date, shoveling pie into his piehole.

(TICS: "When you're giving me more than six months advance notice?")

I smiled, "No problem at all."

Guess they felt compelled to explain: "His family's Roman Catholic, and they'd like their priest to take part in the service. That won't be a problem, will it?"

Her fiancée offered, "My priest was going to do the service, that's why we did the invitations already, but then, he couldn't."

Farmer Dad (parishioner # 39) interjected, "He wouldn't!"

I was wondering: was their priest on the "Naughty" list?

(Named in the news for being under investigation for sex abuse charges?

(Was he already one of my clients?)

Kelly added, "I kinda need to be baptized."

Ah. There it is.

"His priest was asking if I was, but since I wasn't, and ..."

I could protest.

Rattle my sabre.

Being their second choice and all.

Make a fuss.

Hem and haw.

Make a mountain of a molehill.

Serve my own bruised ego.

In the end, I replied, "Tell you what, why don't we schedule that for two Sundays from now? That young mother who's been bringing her baby to church? We're baptizing her daughter then, and it would be a nice service to have an infant baptism, and then an adult baptism."

That's the kind of priest I am.

(My love and passion are for parish ministry, and nothing higher. Church politics do not call to me. I have no interests beyond being a parish priest. You might say I lack ambition in that regard, but that's not a point worthy of discussion.)

Yet since it had come up, I turned to Kelly's parents, "You know, would you like any of the other kids baptized?"

House of seven.

Of course they would!

Oh. Shit!

Be writing a very short sermon that week.

(TICS: "The shorter ones are always harder to write!")

One infant baptism followed by five adults. Three daughters, one son, and Farmer Dad himself. All but

Kelly's mother (who was baptized as a baby) and their eldest daughter (who was up in the city, and won't be there).

The family nick-name for their first born was "Elder," by the way.

✂ -

After dessert Kelly, her fiancée, and I retreated into the TV room for a brief introductory session, and for me to spell out for them how our eight pre-marital classes would go, and what we'd do at each (have to call them "sessions" as her fiancée bristled at the school-like reminder).

My back was to the wall of family pictures so I could face the couple.

All business, I started my speech, "I want this to be a fun learning experience for you. So don't worry about there being right or wrong answers. I promise you right now, we'll have your wedding, but we're doing this so I can get to know about you, and you two may learn more about each other than you know now."

Then, I prepared them for my questioning style.

Give them an example of what to expect.

So, I asked her fiancée, "What's Kelly's favorite candy bar?"

Should've been an easy question.

Surely he'd bought her chocolates and flowers?

Er ... he had, hadn't he?

I began to wonder, by his silence and hesitation, if I'd put my foot in my mouth.

(TICS: "Showing my age, huh? The young don't do flowers and chocolates anymore? How sad!!!!")

Was his exam phobia so strong that he'd just retreated into a shell within his mind? Panicking, rather than feeling at ease?

(Fight
(Flight
(Freeze!)

Aren't guys so forgetful that we forget birthdays (my "Favorite" woman's was on 12/12/**), anniversaries (I met her 11/27/**), and various holidays and Valentine's Day?

His mental paralysis threw me off so bad that I forgot to go through my usual opening exercises, like asking each to define monogamy (you'd be surprised how many people NEVER discuss that until a porn habit is discovered. So, is porn a violation of monogamy? Strippers? Phone sex? What do you include as part of your monogamy expectations?)

✂ -

Wondered if I should cut the guy some slack.

Kelly answered instantly.

His was a plain Hershey's bar.

I figured it was best to set a date for our first "session" at church, and then left.

✂ -

2

Pentecost (i)

I. Exorcisizes in Exorcism

Parishioner # 29 phoned to ask if I could do a blessing of the new fire engine.

"I'd be honored to!"

Made plans for him to pick me up on his way to the fire hall for their monthly meeting (but I didn't have to stay for the meeting if I didn't want to.

Figured ducking out early would be too dismissive, so I'd stay for their meeting.

That's the kind of priest I am.

Hanging up, I was reminded – I don't have a good history with this sort of thing.

✂ -

Flashback:

There was a parishioner at the city church I was at, had a car that kept breaking down.

Asked me to bless it after worship one Sunday.

I did.

Sprinkled blessed water on it.

Did the whole 9 yards with all the frills.

Then she got caught in the middle of a three-car accident on the way home.

I figured the blessing didn't work.

She figured it had, since her insurance got her a new car on a silver platter.

✂ -

Flashback:
Then there was Pizza Shanty.

Came from the office, so I had the collar on.

Was earlier than the people I was meeting.

As I waited, the manager, and assistant manager, came up.

"Do you mind if we sit down for a minute?"

They proceeded to tell me the restaurant was haunted. Oven turning itself on at night. Food turning bad in the freezer. Restaurant built on an Indian burial ground. A couple other details from movies I did recognize – which they probably figured I'd never seen.

Would I do an exorcism of their restaurant?

Of course.

Don't know what they wanted, but I went back that night just as they were closing up.

Had them fill a bowl of water for me.

Said a prayer asking God to bless the water.

Went room by room, burning sage in hand, making the sign of the cross in grey smoke. Sprinkled water with my free hand.

Told them not to empty the bowl but leave it on the floor so that as the water evaporated, the blessing was carried into the air of the place.

Was given a "free pizza for a year" gift card.

✂ -

Whole place burnt down the next week when someone tripped on that half-filled bowl of water.

The second pizza shanty revoked my gift card.

(read: customer dissatisfaction.)

✂ -

Given my history, I approached the fire hall cautiously.

6 bays.

4 vehicles.

Attached garage for their snowmobiles and pick-up truck (support vehicles).

They rolled the new fire truck out of the main bay.

Shiny finish, new paint, not a smudge on the chrome.

Volunteers lined up around me.

Said a prayer asking God to bless the water.

Said a prayer asking God to bless the "apparatus" as they called it.

Sign of the cross on the front hood in blessed water.

(It was a reach, given how high up it is off the ground.)

I added a prayer, "Dear God, deliver all who ride in this vehicle safely to where they need to be. Strengthen them to use this apparatus safely as they deal with all incidents this vehicle is called to. Protect these men and women as they continue to be of service to this community."

✄ -

I hope it works.

Hate to think they'll have to ask the Baptists or Charismaniacs to do the blessing all over again because the Episcopalian one didn't take.

✄ -

Reception afterwards.

Got lost looking for the rest room.

Ended up in a supply closet.

✄ -

Parishioner # 9's grandson was hit by a car.

She hadn't requested I visit him in the hospital.

Had even tried to dissuade me from going when I'd offered to.

But I went anyway – knew it would comfort her if I did.

The nurse was in his room, fluffing his pillows, and asked me to wait in the hallway for a moment.

He already had a visitor, already waiting in the hallway who acknowledged me when I came back out of the room, "You must be Reverend Pervert."

Said the way so many do – as though it were an euonym.

I smiled, "It's pronounced *Purr-veer*."

(Though I've heard it mispronounced as *Per-vey* by some

> *Per-voe*
> *Pur-veh*
> and *Per-vaire*, by the cleverest telemarketers.)

✂ -

If I ever seem a little touchy about a simple mispronunciation, here's why –

imagine a little boy in kindergarten on the first day of school.

The teacher taking attendance; calling out surnames, gets to: "Pervert?"

The surrounding kids snicker.

And repeat that every year throughout grade school.

And every year, I'd offer, "My family says it's *Purr-veer*."

"That's not even spelled right!" the other kids would call out.

That, and "Who're you foolin, pre-vert?"

(Try using my parents' examples on kindergartners and first graders!

They don't get it when you tell them Merlot, bidet, or Escargot, don't use the "T" sound,

> or that knife doesn't use the "K" sound.

Such explanations weren't accurate enough to satisfy my classmates. Only a "T" example in a proper name would, and sadly, it never occurred to me to point out the girl in the corner (who ate her own toenails) and mention how her name "Margot" is spelled with a "T" that isn't spoken.)

I was only mocked more loudly by their calling me "Pervy" with a haughty accent.

Kids can be cruel.

Especially the kids in church Sunday School classes.

(And teachers stayed out of it; even turned blind eyes to such bullying.)

I mention this because, well – Labeling Theory says that if you call someone by a name often enough (like "pervert"), that person starts to believe that's what they are.

So I grew into a "pervert" identity.

Which evolved into my wanting to be a sex therapist.

Now imagine how that went over every time I was asked, "What do you want to be when you grow up?"

(Fortunately, when it came time for my Junior Prom, my date's father was a Psychologist, so he didn't respond with immediate offense. He asked if I'd read any of Freud, and I'd countered by saying I preferred Jung, which got me instant brownie points with him.

(Yet killed my chances with his daughter.

(Nothing kills backseat Lust quicker than when your date's parents approve of you.)

(So much for giving up my virginity before Senior year!)

✂ -

I'll go slow.

I'll be gentle.

It's typically easier to talk about sexual activity when we're talking about someone else doing *It*, so I'll do that. But first, let me bring you up to speed with a little psychoeducation 101. It'll sound like a classroom lecture, so please forgive me.

But before you'll be able to fully appreciate what I tell you about my clients, you need to know the underlying basics:

One of the things which often happens with female sex addiction clients is, they don't jump right in, not the way guys do.

(Women with vanity who've been insulted by a partner's infidelity [real or imagined] are another matter.)

Their 1st session reluctance is down to the sexual double standard.

Men, allowed to sow their wild oats, will tend to brag.

Women, told to be chaste till marriage, tend to keep secrets rather than brag.

✂- -

I maintain a second office at a rehab center.

Went in for an appointment.

Pastoral Counseling specific for people addicted to sex.

Since we all know, sex and the Church are such good bedfellows and always have been ...

✂- -

It's important to identify the exact nature of a client's addiction before any sort of treatment program begins.

I use Narrative therapy, which externalizes the presenting problem.

As I use it, the addiction ("Addi" as one client refers to it) is talked about like it's a presence apart from the person. Rather than saying the person is worthless because of their addiction, the client is helped to think of their addiction as

    something separate from them

    something against which they feel helpless

    something that tells them they are worthless human beings

But they aren't!

That's just the voice of their inner addiction, doing whatever it can to make sure it survives, at the expense of the addict.

I have one client who compares their addiction to a parasite.

"It's not a symbiotic relationship like the addiction tells me it is, rather, its slowly sucking my life away, bit by bit by bit!"

With help, clients can defeat the "devil" within (a lot of religious clients go to that as their default language).

Just to be clear though:

I'm not a spokesman for the school that trained me.

I don't speak for it.

Sure, I know how to use the 30 Task Model with clients, but I don't always immediately make clients start that program (which is great for helping clients to stay busy, rather than giving them time to get bored and seek another fix).

Just keep in mind that not every therapist/counselor I trained with uses Narrative therapy, so don't generalize that all sex addiction counselors do things the way I do.

They don't.

And they shouldn't be expected to.

✂ -

Puritanical prudery and The Church.

These are what really effed up our cultural notions about healthy sexual activity.

In my opinion, our modern Church doesn't care about correcting itself.

Rather, it would go on with the status-quo, teaching people to feel guilty about normal human pleasure.

Teaching that denial – not moderation – is key to salvation.

I'm all for fasting as a prayer discipline, don't get me wrong.

But I'm not convinced that prolonged/enforced fasting from all sexual activity is healthy in any way whatsoever if it goes longer than 90 days.

✂ -

It might be easy to think of church as Dr Jekyll, and sex as Mr Hyde, but while that focuses on the two different personalities, I tend to focus on the single body they both inhabit.

"Sexual sin" is a misnomer, hence renouncing, condemning, and vilifying sexual activity is not something I do. It's a common (read: popular) stereotype to say that because I am a priest I have to preach sex is wrong, immoral, and evil. It's ignorance which says that

    as a pastoral counselor
    and as a sex addiction counselor

        that I will tell folks they can't have sex. Reality, for me, is that sex is simply a pleasing biological function that should not be infused with moral and ethical ramifications.

My mission: to help others find a "healthy" sexuality for themselves.

My quest: to assist them in integrating a sex positive attitude into their religious lifestyles and spiritual practices/beliefs; if they are desirous of doing so.

My goal: to see people enjoy sex without all the guilt, shame, self-loathing, and religiously–based baggage that comes along with it (pun intended).

Anyway, **Jekyll and Hyde** me all you want, if that helps you reconcile how I can go from talking about church to talking about sex.

Within an open-minded conversation, I'm very matter-o-fact.

My hope is that you won't be disrupted for long – by my going back and forth from church to sex and back again – but that you'll get used to it.

By getting used to it, and integrating these two conversations, you'll find yourself moving further into a world filled with an awareness of God's love and acceptance

        rather than God's wrath and punishment.

✂ -

As a priest who counsels sex addicts, I tend to mostly see the following types of clients

- wives who never learned to let themselves enjoy sex
- parents who want me to treat their gay son because the only way they'll get grandkids is if he gets married to a nice Christian girl
- men who claim to be sex addicts while mistakenly thinking it's a great excuse to use when caught with their pants down (with someone who isn't their wife or partner)
- couples who are sexually incompatible
- priests coming to me in tears because they've had sex with a parishioner.

Don't get hung up on the 5 categories above. The genders mentioned are not absolute, and can apply either way. Such as -

- husbands who never learned to let themselves enjoy sex
- women who claim to be sex addicts while mistakenly thinking it's a great excuse to use when caught naked with someone who isn't their husband or partner.

Still think sex addiction is not a thing?

✄ -

Just don't make the mistake of thinking sex addicts are only unattractive losers, or creepy men with a penchant for wearing raincoats in movie theaters, because anyone can be a sex addict. It's just, we only want to hear about the beautiful and sexy people from Hollywood having oodles and oodles of raunchy sex. But I'm not peddling that porn myth.

I won't ignore the issue like Ms Grundy would've.
I'll tell it to you like it truly is
And the reality is, anyone could be a sex addict, e.g.
your next door neighbor
the guy down the street
your local librarian

> your kid's schoolteacher
> your church's choir director.
> Your anyone, really.

Marrieds, bachelors, spinsters, divorced, polygamous, cohabitates.

Anyone.

Attractive and unattractive.

Overeaters and anorexics.

Elderly, and even some kids who haven't reached puberty.

Sex addiction can afflict anyone!

Addicts may act-out with partners or while alone.

Some sex addicts never physically act out with a partner at all, and their entire addiction may be confined to within their own private thoughts coupled with excessive masturbation.

The reverse is also true – everything I just said about sex addicts also applies to sex avoidants. They can be anyone, not just church-prudes.

✂ -

Not every sex addict I counsel is also a religion addict, but as a minister, I tend to find them running as concurrent addictions.

In my own way, I'm trying to correct centuries of sex-negative theology, one sex addict at a time.

✂ -

Every so often I'll encounter such a disagreeable Christian that my very Calling comes into question.

It's not God I doubt.

But some of Christ's followers!

(TICS: "Don't you get it? Did you even read the Gospels?"

(TICS: "Am I even doing the right thing with my life?")

✂ -

A detour on my way to the clinic and I get asked to wait out in the hospital hallway before I can visit with Parishioner # 9's grandson!

(TICS: "Come on, the clock's ticking, I only have so long!")

First thing his visitor says, "Let me ask you: Do you think the Jews are going to heaven?"

(TICS: "This question? Again? WTF??!!")

What I voiced was, "Yes."

"How can you say that?! They turned their back on Jesus! Don't you know that's why the Holocaust happened?! Jesus is the only way! The only truth! The only light! Believe in Him and you will never die!"

Clearly she wasn't looking for anything other than for the guy in the dog collar to validate whatever exclusivist bullshit theology she was gobbling down at whichever fascist fundamentalist church she went to.

(Probably the one up on the hill that plays with snakes.)

✂ -

Religious loons like her have minds like cement.
        All mixed up
                and permanently set.

✂ -

Reminded me of the bumper sticker:
    "Too bad closed minds don't come with closed mouths."

✂ -

I didn't bother mentioning John x. 16, about the sheep and how the sheep that aren't part of the flock are still welcomed anyway.

✂ -

Glad I didn't share how my father was Jewish (from New Zealand).

It was an argument I didn't feel like having with that harridan.

In-between Mum (she was an Irish Proddie) and Dad, I came to believe quite strongly in "Universal Salvation" as the thing – which, is a big no-no in Church by the way; so sadly, you won't hear me preaching it from the pulpit, even though it's my own personal belief.

Theologically liberal? Yes.

Gnostic? Hardly.

Rather, I

gotta tow the party line.

gotta obey all club house rules.

✂ -

It's ironic, I know.

I have no tolerance for the intolerant.

As I meditate on that, I pray: "Nice irony, God.

"Like teasing me with that porn shop going in next door. Good one!"

✂ -

The nurse let us back into the room.

Never a good approach to ask a patient, "How are you feeling?"

Rather, I voice, "What's going on?"

(If you think about it, a priest who doesn't talk about God is like a doctor who doesn't talk about your illness. Even so, in the spirit of having love for others, I won't thrust my beliefs on people, nor entitle myself to shove religion down someone's throat. Rather, I first ask if they mind if I share with them.)

I had the sense that this religious intolerant wasn't inclined to leave me alone with Parishioner # 9's Grandson.

Maybe that's why he asked her to go to the cafeteria and bring him back a cup of coffee and slice of pizza, to soothe his hunger pangs.

She protested with
> didn't he have to wait for a hospital meal?
> > was he allowed to eat something different?
> > > did he absolutely have to have it right then and there?
> > > > couldn't he wait a while?

Probably feared I'd corrupt him by preaching the Christian ideal of love and acceptance of others the way Christ intended it.

And clearly she couldn't let that happen!

(Not that I was doing any better at feeling more tolerance for her than she felt for me.)

I was just glad she went away.

✂ -

The story of his accident went like this:

he'd been hit by a car while walking across the parking lot of a grocery store after shopping.

"There was this blonde, and she had her car's back door open. It was parked facing away. She was standing there bent over, top half reaching across the back seat. Bottom half jiggling and wiggling, so I was distracted. I admit that.

"When I looked away from her for a moment, a car was coming my way. I figured the car was gonna turn into a parking spot. So I went back to looking at her. Then, when I glanced away from her again, make sure I wasn't gonna miss my car, I saw that other car coming right at me! Right before he hit me, I saw that driver was watching the blonde too!"

Clearly he was dying to tell that rubber-necking story to someone because he couldn't share it while his other visitor was around.

I think he just wanted someone who could hear the story without lecturing condemnation with a side of harsh judgement.

Being a priest, I couldn't exactly chat about the beauty of his bent-over vision.

Butt I could listen.

Just, not envision or imagine.

✂ -

Truth be told, I constantly ask myself the question: "Where does being a guy end, and being a sex addict begin?"

And I've yet to find the answer since

       1) not all guys are sex addicts, and

       2) what is "normal" anyway?

✂ -

Actually, I prefer "common" instead of "normal" since the latter is only illusion.

Whenever I'm asked, "What's normal?"

    "There is simply that which is common."

✂ -

Parishioner # 9's Grandson told me that his other visitor was the woman he rented an apartment from.

As she returned with coffee and pizza for him, she must've figured she needed to play nice because she gave my church a back-handed compliment: "I'm always so glad to see your church when I get into town. I love that it doesn't have a steeple!"

(Saint Mary's has a square bell tower without a spire.)

People often think a church's highest point is its "steeple" but in church architecture, steeples are made up of tower and spire. Sometimes, but not always, built atop the four-sided tower is a belfry (where the bells are), a lantern above that (for lights at night), with the spire (long, conical structure capped with a cross) on top.

The Saint Mary's spire collapsed around 1902, and while it was scheduled to be replaced, dropping attendance since WWI diverted the steeple funds to other more pressing, operating expenses.

From her comment, she then launched off on the pagan origins of steeples being how they replaced the obelisks which drew people's attention skyward, towards the sun god Ra.

(TICS: "And which crap documentaries have you been watching lately?")

Here's the thing; she probably watches a documentary on TV and buys into it like it's the Gospel truth and nothing is missing.

Probably fails to understand that the film-makers have a bias and an agenda.

That they want viewers to think the way they think.

She was on a roll.

A one-hour B-S documentary, and suddenly she's a master scholar on ancient Egypt?!

Church steeples have always been tall but that is so people would always be able to scan the distant horizon, spot the tallest structure and know that is where they could go to worship God.

Used to be, faith was much more important to people than it is today. Nowadays so many folks have no time for anything that lacks an immediately visible reward.

I left her to spout off on how people worshipped false gods

and how any god other than the one she believes in, is false.

I stayed quiet, let her

> rant
> rage
> protest
> preach.

I just

> rolled my eyes
> ignored her
> visited who I'd come to see.

Soon as etiquette allowed, I was out of there!

Her "Blah blah blah..." echoing down the hallway after me.

✂ -

It's just semantics, really.

As though the name her church uses for God is the only name anyone can ever use for God.

And yes, I've encountered priests who take great insult to the name "Higher Power" because they think that only by using the name "God" is one connected to that supreme, all-knowing, all-seeing, all-powerful, ever-present, ever-living, deity who created the earth, heavens, and humanity.

If they believe all that about God, then how can they be so narrow in their conceptualization?

To hear them say it, God is a Christian.

And yet Jesus, who was a Jewish rabbi, spoke about the very same God these yahoos are now claiming exclusive ownership of.

Think it through.

Think it through logically.

If God is omnipotent, omniscient, and omnipresent (the Alpha and Omega, the beginning and the end of all things, etc etc), then why do human beings ignore all that?

Whenever any one tribe claims ownership of God, they are – in essence – limiting all of who God is allowed to be, because they're insisting God conform to their tribal notion of who God is.

Humanity limiting God.

Think it through – what do you say you believe about God? Does that line up with what you expect from God?

If God is as great, awesome, and mighty (as Christians teach their young) then why are they threatened by every contrasting view of the divine (such as Brahma, the Hindu concept of God which is comprised of a lot of little/lesser gods)?

If God is all that Christians teach God is, then why do they not also teach that there is room enough for God to fulfill multiple different human understandings for what God could be?

A name, by any other name ...

it's all just semantics, really.

Nothing more than tribal arrogance and selling a package deal.

They claim a belief that God is all loving and all forgiving.

Yet they then insist God doesn't love everyone, and God doesn't forgive everyone.

They send the message that God plays favorites, so no, I don't really wonder why church attendance is going down given such exclusivist bullshit.

I don't know about the God they know, but I know a God of love and acceptance of me for who I am, faults, warts, and all.

Those Christians give the rest of us a bad name while also assassinating God's reputation.

Religious abuse.

Spiritual abusers.

Face it, if God is not the way they want God to be – well, they'll just find a different God, right? Thing is though, they don't because they need the centuries of church tradition to validate their authority as being "called" to put words into God's mouth.

They just use God like a dancing monkey or performing seal since they alone can say who God will love and hate.

(The part they ignore is how it's not for them to tell God who God is allowed to love.)

✂ -

Some find this very threatening, but here's the thing with me:

I'm looking for God's truth.

Not human truth.

✂ -

II. Pastoral Counseling

Sex Addiction is a thing.

As a certified counselor it's not my job to tell people they are wrong, bad, sinful, and going to burn in hell.

For me the equation is simple

God created humanity in God's image.

Therefore because human beings are sexual, God is also sexual, since we share the Creator's image. Sex cannot be considered evil and sinful because it is a biological function, and God did declare all things in creation were good (Gen i. 31).

I may be a priest, but I will not rebuke someone for having pre-marital sex.

Nor, for any form of sexual behavior with self, or another consenting adult.

The Church's sex-negative view has done us more harm than it ever did us any good.

That's the problem with Origen.

One of the earliest Church fathers.

The guy takes Jesus' comment (Mt v. 29-30; Mt xviii. 8-9; Mk ix. 43, 45, 47), "If thy eye offends thee, pluck it out," and "if your foot makes you stumble cut if off" in a very literal way, and hacks off his own "offensive" bits.

(TICS: "Did Christ – a guy who taught in parables and metaphors – seriously intend for self-mutilation to be a literal answer?"

(See: Deuteronomy xxiii. 1, also Lev xxi. 16-20.)

(See: The Sentences of Sextus, mid-3rd century; there were a lotta guys who followed the self castration trend.)

My point: neither castration (whether anatomically or chemically), nor penile amputation, will exorcize all sexual urges!

Also, phallic substitutes are not in short supply.

✂- -

Sometimes, to break the ice with a new client, I'll ask them to name any movie title that sums up their sex life. I stipulate, "Not the whole movie, just the title."

Here are some of the answers

Lady and the Tramp	*Moby Dick*
Lethal Weapon	*World's Greatest Lover*
Rear Window	*Midway*
Punisher	*Whore*
Spare Parts	*Teeth*

If I don't start with that exercise I'm liable to start with some sex trivia (but usually follow the movie title with trivia) since most people don't find it easy to talk about sex.

For example, the Reverend Sylvester Graham (Graham Crackers) was convinced that men lost their "vital fluids" whenever they ejaculated, and John Harvey Kellogg (Cornflakes) believed that plain food kept sexual desires from arising.

The big thing is to set a non-judgmental tone to the session, so the client feels accepted

for all that they are

for what turns them on.

Another thing I try to do in any first session is to help clients realize what turns them on. There are a lot of people who know when they're turned on, but couldn't tell you what turns them on. So we look at that.

For client # 18 (and it was my third session with him) it's redheads.

He knew he'd always gravitate towards a red head first, but never gave much thought as to why that is.

He was even able to ramble off a list of actresses for me who always got him hot and bothered. His Arousal Template definitely ran in one clear direction, which was helpful.

I offered the trivia that the Sistine Chapel paintings by Michelangelo show Eve as a red head and not as a blonde.

Granted, the pool of acting out partners for him is limited by hair color, the problem he's facing is how he tends to get a bit aggressive in his pursuit of those women. You might use the terms "stalker" and "peeping tom" but those are not labels I can use in session.

Stepping away from the look of the women who get his attention, the next aspect of his Arousal Template is what he likes to do while acting out.

What-all this information gives me, as his counselor, is an understanding of why he'd spent over $100 a week on visiting one particular girl at a hot oil massage parlor.

The complication is that the girl in question retired.

He'd first seen her in a strip club (bought her home-made sex tape), and followed her when she changed jobs. He'd been going to see her for over two and a half years at the hot oil massage parlor (you do the math$) where/when she'd shared a fair amount of personal information about herself. Enough information that he was able to send flowers to her at her home.

To write cards.

To park across the street (as he says, "Just to see her, and know that she's doing alright for herself").

She'd filed a restraining order, which is what brought him in to see me.

"I would've married her!" he cried and wept at the loss of the dream he had for a future with her. But he desired a future with her sex worker persona rather than who she was as a person.

We agreed on a plan to navigate through who she was as a person, and who she was as a working girl. And how he related to her (in her persona) when her boundaries dropped and she shared personal information.

Clearly she had been using her personal info like the carrot, dangled in front of him to keep him coming back to see her.

And there would also need to be some grief counseling mixed in with this.

✂ -

Sex addiction is a thing!

A consultation appointment.

"I'm not gay."

"Alright."

"Just want to make sure you know that."

"I'll take your word for it, but tell me, why do you feel that should be the first thing you tell me?"

"Your ad! It says you're LGBTQ-friendly. I'm not gay."

"So, what brings you in?"

"Last counselor I saw was all about guilt. A friend said if you're open to homosexuals that you probably aren't all about guilt and shame."

"I'm not all about guilt and shame, you don't have to worry," I assured the potential client. "And I don't make judgements, either."

"Good!"

"So how can I help you?"

We live in a media-driven age. Technology is commonplace. Ever since silent movies, some people have had trouble keeping the fantasy of their favorite movies separate from their notions about real life.

Another guy who mistook porn for the way real sex should be.

Has a girlfriend who claims he's using her.

If he doesn't get help, she will leave him.

I start by asking for his perspective on the relationship. Will it last? Does he want to marry her?

"You're the third counselor I've tried, so I guess so."

"Tell me about your relationship to porn."

"What do you mean? Like, what kinds do I watch?"

"No. How does it make you feel?"

"Feel?"

"After the movie is over, what are you feeling? Better or worse? Guilt? Shame? Regret? Self-loathing? Calm? Satisfied? Happy? Uplifted?"

"Oh. Well, I don't feel worse, I guess. But it doesn't put a spring in my step, either."

"Indifferent, would you say?"

"Yeah. I guess."

"Alright, so why do you watch it then, if it doesn't put a spring in your step?"

"Something to do."

"Boredom, then?"

People don't know how to talk about sex because our society has done everything it can to make sure people do not talk about it. So if it seems to you like this was a belabored coversation, it really wasn't. My suggestions weren't given to lead him, but to help him learn how to talk about sex.

The emotional baggage of "don't ever talk about sex" will be dropped, he just needs some help letting go of it, and learning a permissable vocabulary to use.

Most clients do.

He answered, "Yeah, or I get home, and just feel horny."

"How many of your sexual fantasies are based on porn?"

"You mean, do I dream of being a porn stud?"

I asked, "Do you?"

"It'd be neat, wouldn't it? Having sex with all those beautiful women."

"When you and your girlfriend start getting intimate. How much of what you ask her to do with you, comes from porn?"

"We aren't talking by then."

"Do you talk it over beforehand?" I asked, already guessing the answer.

Here's another point of interest for you: many times people presume porn is the problem when it really isn't. But if the problem is sexual or relational, then porn becomes the all purpose scapegoat. And that's down to all the fear and blame society has heaped upon it.

"How well would you say you and your girlfriend communicate?"

"About sex? Not at all."

"So, rather than asking if she wants to try something, you just nudge her into a position?"

"Well ... er. Is that wrong? It's what they do in porn!"

(Porn is not a documentary! It's not a how-to video!)

"Now, you do know porn is a movie, right? That the director and performers talked about what they'd do before the cameras started rolling?"

"They do?"

Psychoeducation 102 (i.e. clue him into some trade secrets): I explained to him how that's the part of porn you don't see. The communication behind the camera that happens first. By not showing the verbal consent in-between sex partners, porn presents a skewed notion of sexual activity. Like mainstream Hollywood sending the message that there is no love without sex (since sexual activity is just a visual depiction of emotional expression).

And other aspects of behind-the-scenes (porn-set-business) are pausing for a photographer to shoot some stills, the start/stop element in the sexual activity for the repositioning of cameras, lights, and the awkward staging of the performers to gain the best camera angles. The continual make-up touches, and application of lotions and lubricants.

(TICS: "And then there's the barf bucket hidden from the camera but kept within the actress's reach because an overlong phallus might trigger her gag reflexes."

(TICS: "And there's the lighting. The heat that builds up ends up baking the sweat and bodily fluids throughout filming. The longer a scene takes to shoot, the greater the stink.")

So, it's not quite start the camera, go at it, finish up, and yell "cut!"

There is a lot more involved that is never shown
nor heard of

and very rarely talked about in interviews.

I assured him, "But they do have those talks about what'll happen."

"Guess I never ..."

"Which is why I mention it."

From a Pastorsal Counseling approach I shift into a sex addiction assessment approach because, if he wants to stop a behavior but cannot, that would strongly suggest compulsion and/or addiction. If the presumption is that since porn is involved he must be an addict, that is not always the case.

"So you watch porn when you're bored."

"Yeah."

"Do you want to stop watching?"

"No."

"Has your girlfriend told you that you have to stop?"

"No."

"If I recommend you can't watch porn for the next 30 days, how would you respond?"

"I'd wanna know why I can't."

"I'm not seeing that you have a problem with porn addiction. If you're here for a sex addiction issue, then what is that, would you say?"

"She's says I'm sick because ..."

Turns out, he needs to bring her in for couples' counseling, rather than his seeing me for sex addiction counseling. The issue, as described, is his uncommon fetish, which because of how uncommon it is, his girlfriend has jumped to a conclusion that he is a sick deviant since he watches "such kinky bizarro porn sex" (her words).

Rather, he's just a guy into Intercrural sex (rubbing his penis inbetween his girlfriend's closed thighs).

I give him points for talking about his preferences with her – most people go their whole lives without ever revealing to their partner what turns them on.

(Sexual incompatability because people don't share – usually because everyone's so afraid of being judged and being called "filthy". Thing is, reactions like that just make a person feel rejected rather than loved and accepted. The next response is to clam up and not share what your fetishes and fantasies are. Which may then lead to orgasm incompatability, by which time a couple is on such a sexually frustrated downslope that they're in need of major couples' therapy!

(All because they won't talk about sexual activity with the person they're having sex with!)

We set a follow-up appointment, and he'd bring his girlfriend in with him.

I'd help them debunk the greeting card myths about romance.

✂ -

Client # 5, after Prostate surgery, can't get as many erections as he used to.

I do more grief counseling with him for his libido than anything.

Don't laugh.

Mourning the loss of a hard-on.

Adapting to life with a hard-off.

Have some compassion.

✂ -

Most common concerns men visit sex therapists for are:
1) premature ejaculation (# 1 complaint)
2) diminished erectile firmless (erections just get softer with age)
3) loss of erection during sexual activity (when ignored they disappear).

But since our culture does not talk about sex, guys tend to think they're the only ones suffering from these – just because they're never told – common truths!

✂ -

Client # 11, young guy.

Found himself (as many porn addicts do) watching

porn that he wasn't interested in. He was watching the sort of things that he never used to watch. An indication of porn escalation where "normal" sex ceases to be arousing, so even though something (insert whatever your dirtiest imagination can imagine) never did it for him before, he finds himself watching that now, just because it's new and he's overly-familiar with what he used to like watching.

And, from porn the situation also occurs elsewhere.

As he told me in session: "I was in line at the grocery store, and I noticed the cashier was a bit heftier than I like. But as the guy in line ahead of me grabbed up his bags and left, and I moved up in line, I saw the cashier use both hands to pull up the front of her black yoga pants. And you know, that got my motor going. I never would've given her a second glance, but something about her pulling up her pants like she did, seeing the shape of her in them, just did it for me."

I hear quite a few stories like this: about how things that never would've been arousing before, have become so.

If the client wants to understand why something new is suddenly arousing, we spend some time on that, like reviewing their arousal template, and what else within the situation might have led to their "surprise" arousal at the unfamiliar.

Sex addiction is a thing!

✂ -

This latest media-darling court case really pisses me off!

You know the one: guy in Alabama, driving around looking for hookers?

Kept driving past the same black girls and never picked them up.

Now he's on trial in a discrimination case!

Because he only hires white prostys, he's being told by the court that he now has to pick up – what was it? – how many black girls every year?

Just to maintain some employment percentage!

Like a john looking for cheap sex is some kind of employer!

Yet because of the pay-her-to-do-a-job aspect, they're treating it like the unfair hiring practices of a fortune 500 company!

It's just one guy, looking for a good time!

Now he's being faulted for knowing who he finds attractive!

And today the latest – his home computer.

He browses online porn and there's a gazillion clips on his hard drive.

Nothing but white girls.

Not a single black, hispanic, or asian girl, anywhere in all that.

Culturally we've now gotten to a point where having a specific ethnic preference for our sexual partners is discriminatory and illegal!

What's the world coming to when a guy is told he has to download porn he doesn't like just to maintain some kind of racial equality?

What's the world coming to when a guy is told he has to be an equal opportunity letch?

If this doesn't scare you, it should.

Scares the shit out of me!

Like passing a law requiring all priests must be neutered.

(We're not all kiddie fiddlers abusing our authority you know.)

✂ -

III. Patches

My work as a sex addiction counselor began with perfect inspiration!

Flashback:

Five years ago; my second year at Saint Mary's.

Writer's Block.

Sermon trouble.

Doesn't happen often, but sometimes I have a dry spell.

It was Black Friday, so I'd left the rectory office for a stroll through the church, and then crossed the village square to go into the coffee shop for a tea.

I took notice of the brunette in line ahead of me.

The indented outline of her tweed coat, tight at the waist (with dark brown paneling and elbow patches), and wide at the shoulders and hem.

Knit hat capping a long cascade of straight elbow-length hair.

Her legs, coated in flesh-toned nylons, were visible from knees to ankle boots.

Called to the counter, she returned the ceramic mug she'd been holding and asked for another, "to go".

While I appreciated the hourglass shape of her, I inwardly dreaded that I was gawking too long.

I needed her to turn around so I could see her face and add identity to her wonderful backside!

Getting her cardboard cup with plastic lid, she turned, and I noticed her horn-rimmed pink framed glasses as she paused, looking at me.

"Sorry! I'm in your way" and I stepped to the side as she replied

"Never."

"Always."

Then, I added, "Depending on who you talk to."

I'd turned so my words would follow her

but she was gone.

Stepping to the counter I ordered my usual Earl Grey tea with two flavor shots of Cassis.

Waiting for my drink, "Lust" dubbed the previous customer with the name "Patches".

Soon as I'm able, I always check for a wedding ring, and I'd noticed she didn't have one.

Yes, that is one of my boundaries.

I will not fantasize about married women.

I had smiled.

She'd walked out without returning a smile.
Sometimes, the collar gets that response.

✂ -

Having gotten my tea I was moving towards the glass exit
when I saw, through it, that Patches was stepping inside
an alcove doorway two storefronts down.

Drizzly afternoon, solitary antique shopping with her
antique glasses?

Might she be looking to get picked up?

Had she stood outside the antique shop until seeing
I was on my way out of the coffee house? Then gone in,
hoping I'd follow her inside?

Dare I hope she wanted to take me inside?

Lust suggested the possibility, and my imagination
was instantly alight with lascivious scenarios.

Was Patches a day tourist looking for a quickie
hookup?

Her idea of mixing the pleasures of shopping with
schtupping?

Lust was weaving me a fantasy with that.

Lust compelled me.

Teased me.

Suggested rationalizations and justifications like Lust
always did.

Always sounding reasonable and rational, and leading
onwards to the next step

Instead of going straight across the village square
back to church, my body was drawn to turn left!

I had to know if Patches wanted me.

I had to know if I could have her.

Lust's voice in the back of my mind enticed *Don't
forget, you have been hoping to find a pair of heavily
weighted book-ends.* That cover story was all I needed
to enter the same antique shop I'd seen Patches go
in to.

Tiny Christmas bells tinkled as I'd opened the door,
and the string of lights (stretched along the wall over

the cashier's counter) blinked the typical pre-Christmas dance.

"You'll be able to get in another good gawk of her while you shop for bookends; so that's a plus, yeah?"

Damn Lust!

✂ -

Coffee in her right hand, left kept in her coat pocket, I kept a covert watch on Patches as she moved slowly through the various alcoves and clusters of items displayed on the creaky hardwood floors of the ancient building.

(Holding my tea in one hand, I also kept my other in a coat pocket. That's the best way to resist the temptation to reach out and touch something.

(Something she and I had in common?

(Do we think alike?

(I'm always encouraged when I see an attractive woman who shares one or more of my mannerisms, idiosyncrasies, or habits.

(Anything we have in common to bond over, that's what Lust watches for!)

Pretending to shop while secretly staring, I removed the plastic tab from my collar and undid the top button.

How to strike up a conversation?

Lust was always impatient, wanting only to get right too the casual sex!

I imagined Patches and I shopping while holding hands, so that neither of us could touch and break something.

I imagined neither she, nor I, had felt the touch of another person in a very long time.

Was Patches looking for an alternative to the toys she had at home?

Could I get her into a back room to lift her skirt and drop my pants so that together, we could satisfy our mutual need for basic human contact?

The creaking floorboards of the upstairs level may not be the best place to take her. They'd only announce

every delightful thrust as I start slow on her, then build
up to a frantic creaky speed at my release, followed by
sudden
silence.

✂ -

Dare I hope Patches is an online porn-watching addict
looking to act out in person?

I'd be happy to help Patches mimic whatever porn
clip she had stored on her cell phone. She could use me
for whatever she needed to in her desire to copy whatever
sexual antics she wanted to impersonate.

And I'd thank her for using me to do so!

✂ -

I wondered if, maybe, she wasn't wearing anything other
than lingerie under her coat.

Stockings, lace garter belt, and matching bra, because
she was looking for a man to use?

(The way I looked for women back in my active
addiction, when the world was still in full color
everywhere I looked.)

She looked my way and I offered her another smile; she
shyly looked away without any hint of acknowledgement
(or invitation).

Just two people who noticed each other in one shop.

And then in another.

Accidentally (on purpose) running into each other.

I hoped she'd be thinking that.

To me, a smile = invitation.

I'd give one more smile, then give up.

Maybe she'd never smile.

Maybe she was figuring me to be some kind of creepy
stalker?

Maybe I misread the details again, and wasn't really
to her taste, the way she was to mine?

Wouldn't be the first time I was attracted to someone who didn't find me attractive in return.

Maybe she wants a man to be forceful and take charge of her.

Push her around, just so she can tell herself she didn't initiate it.

Shook away the voice of Lust.

I don't swing that way.

My kink: a woman has to be willing.

My fetish: a woman has to be with me voluntarily.

My hang-up: I need to be – physically and personally – desired.

✂ -

Having decided I would not pursue any further, I felt a need to attempt to hide what I'd really been up to, and left the room Patches was in, for a back corner room.

A coffee table in the room's center. Floor-to-ceiling bookshelves filled with old encyclopedias; books that have been out of print for fifty years, and over-sized coffee table picture books.

Lust indicated: *There is a walk-in closet right there! Could be private ...*

Probably wouldn't happen the way Lust was spinning my imagination.

Yet it seemed plausible.

Lust can be that convincing.

Because I wanted the world to be the way Lust said it would be.

I chased the fantasy
                          to get the hit.

The entry door and closet door were both along the same wall, so while in the closet, one would be hidden from anyone passing along the hallway and glancing into the corner room.

Why was I still thinking like that?

Like I needed to find some privacy for us?

Hope springs eternal, Lust whispered to me.

Told myself I needed to leave.

Didn't want to scare someone.

Why was I stalling?

My awareness of that closet was dismissed quickly as I began looking across the shelves

then the clip of high heeled footsteps on the aged floor came closer.

"Why do you keep smiling at me?"

I turned.

Patches, standing there in the doorway, slipping into the room while reaching up to draw her hair into a ponytail.

Suggestive lift of her long and thin eyebrows.

I answered her first with a shrug, then, "Was hoping you'd smile back."

"Why should I?"

"Because I'd like to see it."

"My smile?"

"Yes," I answered, smiling some more.

(TICS: "Will the third smile be the charm?")

She shrugged

stepped past me

moved towards the corner closet.

Said, "Fine" and with a hand on one book shelf, she proceeded to bend over while drawing the hang of her long coat over one side, revealing a black skirt which she then lifted to show the black silk of a thong.

"Beautiful smile" didn't need to be articulated.

I didn't hesitate.

Stepping closer, kneeling behind her, kissing her bared bottom.

She didn't protest or move away.

You might think what I did was presumptuous and/ or sexual harassment.

But I took her not moving away as an invitation.

✄ -

After doing my thing, and dizzied by disbelief, she straightened up, and circled around to back me into the closet. Like I had, she must've figured we'd go unnoticed by anyone passing down the hallway and peeking inside the room of over-sized books without entering.

Kneeling.

There, on that hardwood floor, she reached for my belt.

I didn't stop her.

Wouldn't.

Couldn't.

Partially naked with her.

✂ -

Cob webs were everywhere, and the stink of decaying paper mustiness and something not alive filled my nose.

The owner's aged dog wandered free in the shop and left puddles.

✂ -

We'd started with a condom

discarded it mid-way through.

✂ -

Yes. I do pray after sex.

My prayer: "Thank you, God!"

✂ -

Refitting our askew clothing.

"Do you always take that long? It's like you were *lingering* back there."

I gave an awkward shrug.

Couldn't help but take that as a criticism, so it elated me when she offered, "Here's my number."

Her smile crinkled the corners of her downturned eyes.

"This could be the beginning of a beautiful friendship," I mimicked badly.

Her eyes. Straight at mine. Voice cool. "Don't fall in love."

I glanced at the slip of paper she gave me.

A ten digit number.

"No name?"

"Figure it out before you call," was all she said as she walked out on me.

✂ -

A week later, I'd tried, "Is Patches there?"

"Who?"

"Er... Patches?"

"Say again?"

"Patches."

"This is she."

"This is the antique guy."

"Oh, right. My coat has patches on the sleeves. Clever. You want to get together again?"

We didn't bother with a condom then, nor ever again.

And when we finished that second time, she just repeated, "Don't fall in love."

✂ -

"Don't fall in love," said every time.

✂ -

Of course, I did exactly that.

Couldn't help myself.

Brunette. Glasses. Tall. Slim. Exactly my type and taste!

(Always has been!)

More than that though.

My dirty fantasy.

She was my porn dream made flesh!

We kept getting together for the next nine months, and I wrestled with the nature of what we had.

Our "relationship" was strictly physical at first.

There was the risk and thrill of anonymous sex in public.

A rush!

(Only thing that stopped my post-addiction regret/remorse was that fact that she was one of the more beautiful women I'd ever been with, and I would not have to struggle for a defense of my lustful actions because ... well, "Look at her! She's lovely! Like an angel!")

But the thing is, a sex addict chases variety.

Always going after whatever is different from whoever they're with.

Yet Patches and I kept getting together, at least once a week (sometimes twice).

Deliberately.

I'd drive an hour to the city to see her.

No chit-chat.

Got right to it.

Mutual satisfaction.

Slowly, chit-chat started to evolve.

Instead of just making a "booty call" we began to hang out, not needing to always rush out of our clothes.

Became "Friends with Benefits".

(Although being old-school, I preferred to think of Patches as my "Mistress".)

Then I'd drive an hour back to the rectory and never once question the wasted drive time (two hours round trip), nor the physical nature of our relationship.

How does the saying go?

"Men are liked hardwood floors. If you lay them right you can walk all over them for life."

Yes.

I was hooked on the Pretty Patches.

(Replacing one addiction with another is not uncommon.)

Antique shopper Patches became my drug
    a replacement for all the vintage porn.

✂ -

Who needs nun porn when there's a girl willing to let you be her number one fan?

Locked all my porn away in a storage shed (a foot locker was too small to hold it all).

Dubbed her my "Favorite Woman"!

And knowing I'd be seeing her again soon helped me to cease drooling at every sexy woman to pass me by.

It was a new experience.

To recognize beauty, yet not feel a need to respond to it.

✂ -

I only had eyes for Patches
    because I was a "Love-and-Sex Addict"
        with some OCD mixed in
            so once Patches and I were going at it, I couldn't stop myself.

Whatever she wanted.

Whenever she wanted it.

"Don't fall in love."

I was enslaved.

The sex was a way to gain her love.

When I couldn't see her I went out of my mind!

"Don't fall in love."

But it wasn't just about the sex for me.

The sex became incidental.

An excuse to just spend time with her.

"Don't fall in love."

She had me over to her place, made dinner, would take me out in her car so I wasn't always driving.

"Don't fall in love."

It was the best relationship (9 months) I ever had with a beautiful woman.

What do you do when you're addicted to another person?

Call it "love" and ask them to marry you.

That's what I did.

I don't know why, where, or how, but the inspiration struck one night while we were sitting on a park bench beneath a full moon, eating take-out.

We'd been there often enough, and on that night we hadn't yet done anything physical, so it wasn't a post-coital afterglow which inspired me to offer myself to her in marriage.

And then, she was gone.

> All of a sudden.
>> No word.
>>> No messages.
>>>> No farewell.

From all that wonderful togetherness to zilch.

That night was the last time I saw my "Favorite Woman".

Something put her off.

Or maybe it had nothing to do with me, and Patches had just grown bored and moved on to a new playpal.

In many ways though, I'm still not over her. It's almost been 4 years!

Cue up: the Cowsills, "The Rain, The Park, & Other Things".

She's still in my mind.

In my heart (or, for whatever passes as a love-and-sex addict's heart).

Thoughts of her distract me.

Fantasies of her keep me up nights.

Echo of her voice, "Don't fall in love" in my ears.

(I know you think **she found someone else and moved on** but honestly, I don't want to believe that. And I also know, soon as I hear from her again, I'll drop everything and be out the door to see her!)

Is it love?

Is it codependence?

Is it obsession?

I don't know, but it's an unhappiness which brings happiness with it.

("Limerence" if you want the clinical term.)

That was my addiction.

Told myself it was a bona-fide relationship, not a just-sex thing.

I legitimately cared for her.

We could've hung out and not had sex, and I would've been better than OK with that.

You see, used to be the more I got to know a woman I started dating, the less I liked her. But with Patches, the more I got to know about her, the more I wanted to know.

I wanted to know all about her past, her dreams, her fears, her feelings.

✗ -

I'm too introspective for my own good at times.

Occupational hazard – when you make your living with your head rather than your hands sometimes you get too cerebral and get lost in your own thoughts.

My time with Patches had been enjoyable, and yes, I was aware of some less than happy times with her (along with a time or two when I swore to myself I wouldn't ever go out and see her any more).

Only I kept on seeing her.

Until she no longer wanted to see me.

In her absence, I found my way to a certification as a sex addiction counselor. From there into a PhD program.

These days I don't have much in the way of vices.

Not like I used to.

Now that my dissertation is finished, I'll be struggling.

Gonna have a whole lot more free time on my hands than I've had for the past four years.

✗ -

3

Pentecost (ii)

I.

9 am

Standing at the double doors, I was shaking hands with people as they exit the sanctuary.

Parishioner # 9 (I'll just tell you, her name's Dottie), back from her annual trip to family in Texas, came through the line, "Thank you for going to see my Grandson, Father."

"You're welcome."

(I knew it'd mean a lot to her.)

"His land lady's a right nutbar, isn't she?!"

"Yes, she's confused."

Dottie laughed, enjoying the euphemism.

"She runs that church she goes to, I hear."

"Oh? Is she their pastor?"

"No, more like president or something. Crazy woman," and with her joyous cackle, Dottie proceeded down the three steps in the darkened bell tower to the doors below. I'd shifted the angle I stood at, as I do whenever she passes by.

I've learned to keep my posterior as far from her as possible.

Not because I minded, but to prevent her from insulting Mrs Grundy (by displaying more comfort and familiarity with me than the Churches clearly thought anyone should have). I'd figured Dottie was just being cute

and had probably been quite a flirt back in her day
> still
parishioners shouldn't pinch the priest's ass!

✂ -

Standing at the double doors, I was shaking hands with people as they exit the sanctuary. A snowbird just back from Florida.

I hadn't missed Parishioner # 92 at all!

Had taken me a while to figure it out, but every time she comes back from a diocesan ECW meeting, she's always like

"Father, do you know Father Wuzzhizname?"

Usually not.

And that's followed by something like

- "He does this.
- "She does that.
- "He jogs five miles a day!
- "Her sermons always tie the Gospel, the Psalm, and the Epistle readings together!"

And always the follow-up: "Why can't you do the same?!"

So, so, tiresome.

(TICS: "You want me to be like everyone else? Do everything the way they do it.")

At these Episcopal Church Women's' gatherings, the ladies clearly sit around bragging about the priests back at their home parishes.

Gotta one-up each other.

Which makes me wonder, with all that boasting (read: gossip) going around, how much is actually true?

Still, given how many clergy are workaholics who turn to alcoholism and/or have nervous breakdowns, maybe it is all true

> maybe I really am an underachiever.

✂ -

11 am

Mr and Mrs Church are a real pair!

He's the sort that, unless he's the one doing the handyman job, it's not being done right.

She's the sort that, if an idea isn't hers, then it's not a good one.

An unscheduled and overdue visit to my office brought the shitstorm: "Father! I want to talk about my petition! I gave it to you on Easter. You said you wanted to look into it."

"Yes. I'm sorry. I haven't had a chance to get to it, yet."

"The clock is ticking!"

"This week. I promise."

"I trust you shall," she actually sniffed disdainfully. "It's been a month! Your delay makes us question if you welcome such a store."

(TICS: "'Us?' Ah, yes, the infamous and always unidentified *'they'* in every church."

(By quoting the unknown and mysterious "They" an individual presumes the weight of public opinion, even though there is no real *They* who ever actually said any such thing, and you'll never ever find out who that non-existent "they" are who have supposedly been quoted.)

"And I promise you, that is not the case," I answered honestly.

(Yes. HONESTLY!)

Impressed myself that I could hold her gaze as she ranted, "Those kinds of movies are a curse! We must protect children from seeing such things!"

(TICS: "Then we better shut down the internet while we're at it!")

✂ -

Yes. Honest.

Think about it.

I wouldn't be able to go into that T-shirt selling porn shop!

Too close to church.

Parishioners might see me.

But what a rush it had been

in that antique store in Copthorne's village square!!!!

The risk of being spotted

identified

caught

and having the news spread all over town!

Risking my job

livelihood

God's reputation

just to let a hot woman get my rocks off in the back room of an antique store while she wore her antique glasses!!!

I can't let myself get so carried away I do something that stupid ever again!!!

So, a porn shop in the square by my church?

I'm not concerned about protecting something that would benefit me.

Rather, the presence of a porn shop in the village square was no use to me at all beyond its being an amusing sight gag to irritate the prudes, like the nasty, prudish parishioner #92, and Queen Victoria Church (not her real name).

Basically, I won't sign her petition for one simple reason:

I cannot support anything that encourages censorship in any way.

Now that the SJW censors have started, freedom of artistic expression is going to be eroded away to nothing until it's dead and gone!

Not even history is safe!

Not while history's being rewritten to ignore unsavory facts.

(Then again, it always has been, even in the Bible - armies went to war, and whoever won got to write the history and boast God was with them!)

No matter what we talk about, someone somewhere will take offense at everything.

Mrs Church continued, "I don't understand why you just won't sign it right now."

She's used to having people cave rather than delay.

"I do want to look into it first."

"You can't be saying you want such a store to open!"

"I'm not saying that," I answered. "But there are different aspects to consider. Not the least of which is, I don't believe such a store can actually open. Legally, I mean. I'm thinking that proximity to a church falls under the same guidelines as being too close to a school."

"How do you know that?"

"I don't know that. That's why I think we should ask about it."

Might be, the shop cannot open.

Why generate local interest and encourage the shop owner to rent a different storefront further on down the street just so he gets beyond the designated no-porn zone surrounding a school or church?

She wasn't happy, and I know Mrs Church won't let it go.

Her sacred mission; remake the world to her idealized notions!

✂ -

I do try to be encouraging rather than squash my parishioner's enthusiasm for doing what they think is right.

Often though, that means I have to bite my tongue since I see things differently.

I'm Theologically liberal.

Placed in the pulpit of a Theologically ultra-conservative parish.

Yeah.

There's friction.

(If my seeing sex as a biological-pleasure-that's-not-always-sinful, doesn't say it all, then I'm not sure what will.

(Survival technique: it's easier for a liberal to pretend to be a conservative than the other way around, and in church, most parishioners presume I'm as conservative as they are. Let them think whatever comforts them, and also be highly selective when picking my battles.)

You see, people have a fast food franchise mentality – they equate a denomination to being a franchise, and no matter which parish they stop at, they expect to find exactly the same thing as what's in every other parish.

Yet

>each parish has its own personality.

>each priest has their own personality.

These two do not always line up with each other!

When shopping for a church, people aren't just looking for denominations anymore. They're looking for convenient locations, and available programs. But what they should be considering first is the Priest's Theology, the congregation's Theology, and then find the church with the most similarities in-between the seeker, the priest, and the congregation.

Not all Christian denominations match, and it's a mistake to think they are all exactly the same.

✂ -

Parishioner # 25 is college freshman, eighteen.

He'd been baptized, Confirmed, and received a scholarship from the Church to go to college, and came home for summer vacation with a problem!

(Caught me for an impromptu appointment after worship.

("Father, I have a question. It's personal."

("Of course," and I drew him aside, in view of others, but far enough away his whispers would not be heard.)

He's got an addiction to online porn.

(As he said, his mother insisted he confess his viewing habits, and he expected I'd be shocked, scandalized, aghast, pointing a finger of blame and condemning him to hellfire and brimstone. He didn't expect a calm and rational reply.

We scheduled an appointment for the following day after mid-day prayers, and I had no doubts that he felt more encouraged and reassured than he'd felt when stepping inside Saint Mary's that morning.

That's what being a pastoral counselor is all about for me!

Helping people know God as a loving God

not as a vindictive, and wrathful one.

✂ -

Standing at the double doors again, I was shaking hands with people as they exit the sanctuary.

A couple of cackling ladies came through; reminded me
        tomorrow
                time for my bi-weekly trip for Communion supplies.

✂ -

"I got a guy."

A bunch of bakery gals, really.

Being a country church, St Mary's missed the invention of the Communion Wafer and has "always" used real bread for the sacrament. It's a matter of pride for some of the church ladies whenever their turn comes up in the rotation and it's their week to bake the bread.

Apparently it's a shared recipe which dates back to ... I dunno, 1701?

Sunday mornings – a ball of bread, a chalice of wine.

The bread is shaped that way so that every person can have a torn piece of bread with some crust on it (the crust is to make it easier to hold and pull apart as each bit is torn free). I pull it off the lump, place it in their flattened palms (or place it on those tongues some stick out at me).

When Parishioner # 16 had her accident back at Thanksgiving and could no longer bake the daily bread for mid-day prayers I had started going to the closest market every other day to pick-up a few Portuguese rolls, and use them instead.

Knew I'd remembered seeing "Legs" from somewhere!

(Very easy to spot the Easter burial Goth hottie inside the baggy bakery whites with heavy powder all over her face, just not so easy in a cemetery without the coating of white.)

✂ -

"I got a guy."

A winery guy.

Ten miles up the road, a local winery.

The owner had converted a disused dairy farm into a wine and beer brewing factory, with new silos and barrels added annually as they expand.

They give tours

samples

and have a bar which serves every weekend (and uses those old style beer barrels as a decorative motif).

Took almost two years, but my guy finally whipped me up a Cassis wine to use for Communion. Every two months I'll stop by and pick up a case. Three bottles for the rectory, five bottles for Church. He and I got to know each other during the trial and experimentation phase when he was working on getting the flavor just the way I like it.

Thing is, all the left-over wine after Communion needs to be "consumed" so if I'm going to be knocking back a full goblet six days a week (not Saturdays), I want to enjoy the taste of it!

✂ -

Flashback:

In line for the winery counter, I'd heard from behind me, "Father! I'm surprised to see you here!"

I turned.

Kelly, in line behind me, with her sisters.

Long fair hair, old nose, eyeshadow and kohl accents. Decked out in all her country-western finery. Plaid shirt unbuttoned to her cleavage, hat, bedazzled (skin tight) cut-off denim shorts, long legs, and pointy-toed snakeskin boots.

I greeted Kelly, then her sisters, by name.

"We haven't seen you in so long!"

That was two years ago, the day he got the black currant flavor just right, and the girls were the first parishioners to try it.

Apparently the three of them stop by every week, rather than stock up, and ration out their booze (the way I've learned to do with my stash - in my now-fully-stocked wine cellar).

I knew from past afternoon visits to their farm, that Kelly usually showered and changed clothes in-between morning and evening chores because her afternoons were spent away from the farm.

She always likes looking her best, and not smelling like she'd just come from milking cows.

✂ -

Call me "Rev. Wingit" if you like.

Every so often you have to just go with the flow and work with what's available. You make do with what you got.

I had to make a house call.

Do a funeral.

Backyard burial.

Crying child.

Dead cat.

Cardboard boot box.

First time a family pet died.

Holding the prayer book open in front of me, I closed my eyes, and just prayed out loud since there isn't a prayer for pet burials in "The Book." Made sure my prayer named the cat ("Baxter"), the crying child ("Natty"), and the "Rainbow Bridge."

Acknowledged that pets are family. Added descriptors like his being a grey striped cat with a really long tail and over-large paws. Emphasized the "let them be reunited someday" aspect.

I spoke briefly about how God intended for animals to be saved on the ark, and how Jesus could not fulfill prophecy without a donkey to ride into Jerusalem. Then, to make sure the whole to-do sounded official, I concluded with, "And let us keep in mind the instructions found in the Gospel of Mark which tell us 'Go into the whole world and proclaim the gospel to *every creature*.' Which reminds us, don't share the Good News only with people, but also share it with all the animals."

(You don't need to ask, it's Mark xvi. 15, and "every creature" is the exact KJV phrase – I don't have the Bible memorized, I just always look up my quotes before writing to you.)

✂ -

II.

An orgasm triggers a release of natural feel-good chemicals the body makes for itself. In my case, it was the Oxytocin and Vasopressin cocktail which hit me every time I was with Patches. My body's since stopped production of them and boosted its production of Serotonin, which is the body's natural "cold shower" chemical.

That loss ("withdrawal") of general arousal is why I'm irritable and cranky.

That's why whenever I have a dream about Patches, I wake from the dream with an erection and awash in those feel-good chemicals, and I want MORE!!!!

I want to go back to sleep and dream of her over and over, just to get that familiar rush.

Which is worse, do you think?

- The substance addict who can only get a hit with that external supply?

- The behavior addict, who can get a hit by just thinking about (and remembering) their drug of choice?

An experiment for you: when you see a pretty woman, try not to undress her with your eyes.

· Try not to fantasize about the positions you'll use.
Try not to even look!

✂ -

The 3 second rule.
    You can look.
    But don't stare.
    You can appreciate.
    But not for long.
    Do not fantasize.
    Do not memorize.
    Do not use memories for a thrill.
    Sex addiction is a thing!
    If it helps, think of the term "Sex Addiction" as an umbrella label. Under it are several sub categories, like
        Porn Addiction
        Masturbation addiction.
        Love and Sex Addiction
            and it's sister, Romance/Relationship Addiction.
    After waking from a 4 am dream of Patches, thoughts of her kept me up all night, chasing after memories to score another hit to help me relax and go back to sleep.
    Whenever I wake from a dream she's in, it's heaven on earth!

✂ -

I just wish I had more dreams of her.
    Sad, right?
    Best thrill I've had in months was subconscious.
    In the Middle Ages that would've been attributed to a succubus.

✂ -

Sat down with the scholarship student in my church office and went through some basics with him.

Help him understand the what and why of his concerns.

Porn addiction differs from sex addiction in that, without porn, he cannot get aroused.

Imagine: a real person does not excite you, but the movie gets a rise out of you.

He cannot get an erection without watching some videos.

And then, with the co-eds he's been with, he needs porn playing in the background (so he can watch it and maintain his interest in the live person there with him).

✂ -

P.I.E.D.

("Porn Induced Erectile Dysfunction")

It's becoming increasingly common.

Boys suffering from it are getting younger and younger.

And yes, the number of girls who watch online porn is on the rise!

Last study I read said that one in three women are watching online porn.

Some imagine that by watching they'd be clued into what boys like girls to do.

(Is it art imitating life, or life immitating art?)

(Is being on the beach at sunset romantic because it is, or is it only romantic because we see it in romantic movies?)

Other women watch it because they escape into the fantasy scenarios of the videos, chase the sexy romance. Which in its way is not too far removed from people obsessed with mainstream Hollywood movies for the escapism value.

Porn just adds graphic sex to that mix.

Most often though, it's depicting unrealistic sexual encounters.

Porn would not exist without people wanting to watch it.

If there isn't a video of what you want to see, tell a porn company, and your video will be available online within hours, if it's not already (and you just haven't found it – Rule 34).

It's all available.

There used to be specialty stores.

Now it's all out there on the internet.

It's all affordable.

Without materials (plastic and cardboard) there are no manufacturing costs.

Digital can be free on certain websites (though nothing is ever really free).

It's all accessible.

Easy to find, easy to watch, easy to start it playing.

✂ -

With the click of a button, the online realm can offer a video for any, and every, type of fantasy.

Doesn't matter what it is.

Click–Click.

Click.

Click.

Click.

Heterosexual.	Homosexual.
Toys and vegetables.	Zoophilia.
Urophilia.	Spankophilia.
Polymastia.	Haptosis.

Doesn't matter what we talk about.

You name it, it's out there!

"Something for everyone!" as they say.

You never know what someone's up to within their own mind.

Or, what people get into behind closed doors ...

✂ -

Name whatever it is that really disgusts you.
Go on ...

✂ -

Consider this fun fact:
Somewhere in the world, there is somebody who gets turned on by the very whatever you just named.
I'm not kidding.

✂ -

I advised my college student (new-client, # 19) to attempt moderation.

His addiction is a recent development, so I figure we could try starting him at phase 2 rather than phase 1 even though he's spending more than two hours a night searching online for porn (2 hours is the average minimum, BTW).

Going online is like looking into a bottomless pit.
It's a wellspring of porn that'll never go dry.
I suggest a kitchen timer.
Set it for two hours, go two weeks.
Set it for one hour, go two weeks.
Set it for half an hour, go two weeks.
Set it for fifteen minutes, go two weeks.
No more porn.
Go a day without thinking about porn.
Go a week without.
Go two weeks without thinking or remembering.

Ideally, he should go 30 days without thinking, recalling, or using, porn (but that always sounds like such an intimidating mountain to climb), so I suggest the goal to work towards is halving the time incrementally. Keep a journal as he goes. Many people find they use porn to alleviate boredom, and/or to satisfy curiosity, and once you realize that about yourself (if that's the case), then filling your time with other activities becomes key to abstaining.

The average time to a solid sex detox is to go three months without doing it
> thinking about it
> remembering it.

With behavioral addictions, thought control is vital, because just thinking about it can deliver a hit of your neurochemicals, and you want to break away from needing that hit, which means not thinking about certain things.

Easier said than done.

But it is do-able.

✂ -

In session, cell phones must be turned off.

But when treating someone in recovery – or struggling to gain sobriety – from online misuse, I strongly encourage them to downgrade from their hi-tech (mini-computer) phones (I've had to make that a condition for on-going sessions with one resistant client).

Seeing that a client has limited their phone's capacity and capability is a good indicator of that client's commitment to their recovery.

This isn't punishment, but an attempt at limiting accessibility.

Client # 19 wasn't thrilled at the notion.

Few clients ever are.

Yet if he wanted to be a client, that was a condition of therapy.

Hi-tech mobile phones (whatever name they're going by now) are simply a means to porn access 24/7
> with no days off
>> no time off
>>> and not much material that stays the same!

✂ -

I tend to waive my usual fees for parishioners only because my primary job is ministry.

I suppose I shouldn't, but when you think about it, I guess church membership should have some perks, right? Especially in these times when people don't come to church

so they really don't know what amenities they're missing.

✂ -

Typically I'll turn my attention towards the sermon for the following week each Monday. I generally spend a few days thinking about which passage to use (lectionary or go browsing for one), mulling that over, do the research, and compose it in my head.

Then, around Thursday I'll sit down to type out whatever message has been percolating in my mind for those days in-between.

On those occasions when I'm stuck awaiting inspiration for a sermon, I'll walk the square since my church doesn't have cloisters.

Of course, my dry spell/writer's blocks no longer discourage me since they now remind me of the joy of Patches and the afternoon she and I met.

Leaving through the church's front doors (they make quite a clatter and ruckus with the old metal hinges, heavy oak boards, and creaking wood frame), I cross the street.

Best way to describe it: There are two double-lane streets. One goes north-south (the major pass-through for traffic going both ways along the oldest side of town), and the east-west road (which brings most of the city visitors into town, and then takes them home again). Add in two one-way streets (both paved by brick cobblestone), that begin and end within the right angle of the main streets' intersection, and you have the formation of our village square, the central hub of local activity.

Bracketed by a deep stream on one side, and mostly unused railway tracks on the other, the square in-between has (in no particular order) a

> bank
> pharmacy
> bar/restaurant
> coffee house
> post office and town hall building (called the "Grange"), and also
> four antique stores
> one private, asymmetrically designed residence (turned into a public library), and
> two churches (Saint Mary's, and the burnt-down ruins of the other).

The rest of the buildings and store fronts are left in neglect.

One block outside the square is the Bergerac funeral home.

Five blocks away is the fire hall.

Two blocks over is the local Legion Post for veterans.

And behind my church is the rectory, which fronts a side road running parallel to the east-west-running street in the square.

The original cemetery had been relocated in 1861 (a two-year job) to clear up the center of the square for a village green when the anticipated railway was coming through. It had been moved to the other side of the rectory, so the priest's front window looks out on the gravestone-lined entrance going up the hill across a somewhat busy two lane road.

To put it all in perspective for you, when the store that sells everything for one dollar opened down by the fire hall, that was <u>BIG</u> news! The local pharmacy had protested, since that meant retail competition and while some in town still refuse to shop in the "chain" store, most others do.

Story is: there had once been an old warehouse building which was sold.

Demolished.

And the new "chain" store (with parking lot) was built on that site.

That made the local government nervous about other "chains" buying property to tear down and rebuild within what is known locally as "downtown". The square itself is not on the historical buildings registry, although two of the buildings within it are.

Yet for all that, there isn't a book store within thirty miles, and you'd think there would be a cell phone/computer shop here at the least, but there isn't.

One block outside of the square is a barber shop run by two young ladies who both dress up like old-style "pin-up" girls and they cater mostly to the older men in town who get a thrill by being reminded of their youth.

(I was told that gimmick caused quite a stir with the local housewives, the gossip being the barbers were selling themselves as well as haircuts. Of course that wasn't true, but small-town, small-minds.

(You've heard how it goes.

(The two women were dressed more "Rosie the Riveter" and "Julie the Janitor" than Bettie Page – which didn't appease any of their vocal opponents.)

I'm still not sure where the women go to get their hair and nails done (mall probably).

Welcome to life, as Norman Rockwell would've painted it (which, by the way, the bank's free calendars are always filled with his paintings).

I stroll the square, past the store front windows covered by sheets of newspaper. The one with a handwritten sign "Enter In Rear" taped to the inside of its door was rumored to have been where the "dirty" movie shop would've been.

I then pass

the antique shop on the corner (with its exciting back room)

and come to the coffee house directly across from Saint Mary's.

A familiar face from Sunday mornings was leaving.

We exchanged smiling nods in passing, and knowing they're friends with Holly, I look for her at a table inside.

Holly's not there.

Drank my tea alone.

I'll smile, nod, and call out pleasantries across the room, but for the most part, people don't come over to join me.

Unless of course, they want to talk shop.

Usually, I'll run into people who feel compelled to tell me all their excuses for why they don't come to church.

Yet every so often there'll be somebody who has to ask a question that requires more than 30 seconds to answer (provided they want a serious answer, rather than for me to just affirm whatever they already think).

✂ -

Took my tea to High Street, and listened to the stream running behind the oldest buildings in town.

It's hard to imagine – when you see how wide the banks are, and how shallow the running water is – that this stream was once deep enough to allow for the passage of ships importing and exporting goods.

The backsides of some of the High Street buildings (pharmacy, two antique shops) still have their rickety and crooked jetties and docks from back when the boats would tie up to load or unload goods and people.

The stream itself connects to one of the world's few north-running rivers, and after about one hundred years the railway came along, running parallel to the stream; so buildings went up on that side of town to accommodate the loading and unloading of goods and people by rail.

The square then formed naturally as the two sides reached out for each other to fill the empty space in-between with the influx of a resident work force population. The older side along the stream is flat-faced, unadorned colonial buildings, while the opposite side is more Victorian/Gothic-looking. Covered porches, pillars, and that single Queen Anne revival home (with rounded tower in place of a corner; on the historic buildings registry) which is almost identical to the Bergerac Funeral Home.

I still haven't figured out how Copthorne's biggest business – historically – had been cheese.

Seriously!

Cheese!

Using ice houses in the summer, loading it into orlop decks, storing it below waterlines when transporting all that cheese in natural refrigeration by boat, maybe?

I'd speculated that the earliest big business for the area had to've been grapes, so a town founded as a wine and cheese society had appealed to me before I took the pulpit.

Sadly, it had been the oldest living parishioner in my congregation who had told me that vineyards hadn't come to the area until recently (also confirmed by my wine guy).

✂ -

I stroll down along the curb by the pharmacy and liquor store, pass the single traffic light, and then I am out of the square and at the bridge which spans the stream. Turn right, over the bridge, and you've departed 1911 and are off and running to the twenty-first century.

(Or, go one more block, turn left and head up that side road to the front door of the rectory across from the hillside cemetery overlooking town with that bad neighbor next door to it.

A nice, soothing time, sipping my tea as I go.

Yet no inspiration.

What should I preach Sunday?

I felt stuck and creatively befuddled.

(I'm fortunate in that I don't often experience writer's block, but I was having a bout.)

✂ -

Into the sacristy (read: robing room).

Into the cassock, the surplice, the chasuble, the bells and whistles, accessorized with a stole and orphreys.

Stepped into the sanctuary to greet people on their way in.

The mid-day prayer service is held at quarter to one so that people have time for lunch first, and can then end their lunch hour with a quick church service before returning to work.

At fifteen minutes, it's hardly an intrusion on people's lives.

And yet the highest attendance count for that service can still be counted on one hand.

✂ -

Parishioner # 31 makes the daily service because she no longer attends Sunday worship.

She'd stopped attending church before I "hit the horse."

Flashback:

The first thing I'd asked my congregation to do for me when I arrived seven years ago was write up a list of people who used to attend church, but no longer did.

I took that list and made house-calls my second month.

The name of parishioner # 31 was on that list.

She had greeted me at her door and told me how she was in the middle of making lunch. I could return later or share her lunch.

Unaware of certain details about her, I accepted, and joined her for a lunch of

Tomato Soup (yuck!) and Grilled Cheese sandwiches.
She's a widow in her forties
     has fair-haired dreadlocks
          wears a camo overcoat with matching boots
             drives a beat up pick-up truck
               and goes around collecting roadkill.

The other church ladies won't eat her cooking, and that's why she no longer attends church on Sunday mornings; yet she faithfully attends the mid-day prayer services.

✂ -

I should say my **yuck!** means I'm not a soup person.

But, to be polite while visiting, I will eat whatever is put in front of me.

And no, contrary to local gossip, I don't believe # 31 cooks up the roadkill she gathers.

Rather, she views that as a community service, so I don't question her about D.O.T. removal.

And the "grill" she's suspected of having behind her barn, is a fire pit to cremate the animal remains

not barbeque them!

✂ -

Where do people come up with this stuff?

✂ -

My mid-day prayer services have an average attendance of three.

None of my predecessors had ever done that type of service, so it isn't really something many people come out for.

"Too catholicy," had been one complaint about my doing it.

(As if only the Roman Catholics have mid-day prayer services!)

Those who attend do so for various reasons.

One (# 25), because his mother is in the hospital and he feels she needs all the prayers she can get.

Another (# 21) because she was looking for a daily routine to help her keep busy (I'd suggested she become editor of the parish newsletter).

My concerns are not for what brings them through the church doors.

My concerns are seeing to their spiritual needs, whatever those may be.

(Matt xviii. 20: "'Where two or more are gathered in my name, there I am in the midst of them!'")

✂ -

III.

Cyranose had called, asking if I could do a funeral for a family who didn't attend church but still wanted a religious service for their family patriarch.

Got the name, dates, details.

The trend seems to be becoming a single day of visitation at the funeral home, followed by a brief in-home service immediately afterwards (with grave site burials usually scheduled for Saturdays, Mondays, or Fridays).

Then, off to the party (etiquette insists we still call it a "reception").

If there's a gravesite committal service, the family will do that while the partiers gather and start drinking.

(Weddings are worse!)

I arrived at the funeral home and Cyranose opened the door for me, as he did for all guests. Bergerac's inner foyer was white with paisley-print wainscoting, Georgian chairs, an ornate clock that chimes from a mantelpiece over their stopped-up chimney. A wall niche with a fake potted plant is on the left side of the five steps which lead up to the main floor at the far side of the room. As an entering visitor I took the sunken room to serve as a gate, halting people before they ventured too far inside. The foyer room itself was part of a recent addition (1980s), though for years I thought it was part of the original design, thinking those five stairs were mimicking a grand staircase (on a small budget).

Entering, my eye-sweep through the foyer ended up on the main floor where

shit.

Holy Shit!

HOLY FUCKING SHIT!!!!

I would've instantly recognized her in an antique shop, but almost didn't in the Bergerac funeral home!

But I have a good memory for faces.

And hers in particular!

My stomach sank before my excitement faded.

Suddenly I was standing there, petrified that I was about to be publicly outed, renounced, condemned, and vilified, as another priestly hypocrite caught with his pants down!

First response: heart beating faster.

I've missed her so much!

My second: "Oh, shit," because seeing her again hinted at a potential of seeing her some more – and I knew that addicts should never hang-out with people they used to act out with because, sooner or later, they'll end up acting out together again. It's the association, you see, the person revives the memory, the memory has its allure, allure leads to temptation. And temptation leads to relapse to getting another hit and fix, and with the person right there, it won't be hard to fall back into an old and familiar addictive pattern.

My "Favorite Woman" as I thought of her!

There, at the top of the stairs, elbow-length hair in a right-sided ponytail.

Waiting for the family slowly moving up the stairs to that main floor landing.

Antique dark Oak buffet – used to display pictures of the decedent – behind her.

(TICS: "Patches!")

    Here!

        In the foyer of Bergerac!

(Cue up: the refrain from "Mz Hyde" by Halestorm [her favorite band].)

You don't know how often I've stepped into city hospitals and area nursing homes, hoping I'd see her again!

And now

    here she is

        back in town!

What was she doing in Bergerac?

Other than looking so sexy in her black skirt, black crushed velvet jacket, and wedge heeled ankle boots.

How many times had I dreaded the moment when an ex-lover turned back up to ruin my life with a tell-all story?

Panic and paranoia!
>What if she had tracked me down?
>>What if I'd knocked her up?
>>>Was she here for revenge?
>>>>Was she here to extort money from me?

People would say I'd diddled around!

Just the ammunition the Churches and Cathedral Sisters would need to get the Bishop to pull me out of Saint Mary's and send me somewhere far, far, away!!

✂ -

My fear eased its stranglehold on my throat when Cyranose called out to her.

(TICS: "Has time frozen for everyone else, or just me?")

"That's my niece. This is her, here," he said, drawing my attention to the framed picture amid a few others on the wall by the mantle. It was of him with his arm around a 600-pound woman and an 8 year old girl in-between them (until meeting her, I'd though the large woman was his wife. Rather, Cyranose's wife had taken that picture of him with his sister and tiny niece). "She'll be taking over. I'll introduce you."

Never occurred to me, any of those times I'd gotten naked with her that she'd be related to Cyranose!

Could I say we'd met at a city bar, and one thing led to another?
>To another
>>and to another
>>>and to another
>>>>fifty plus times?

Wouldn't make a difference.

Details like that would quickly be lost in small-town gossip.

I'd be reduced to nothing more than just another priest caught screwing around!

A deadbeat dad since I wasn't married to the woman who had my child.

Did we have a kid somewhere?

(TICS: "Forget that I'd asked her to marry me, and haven't seen her since!")

I couldn't get my mind to shut off the possibilities running through it.

Did she recognize me?

Did she see me as a familiar friend?

Did she regard me as contemptable scum?

What was she thinking as she saw me in the dog collar standing there with her uncle?

Did she remember me from the coffee house before I followed her into the antique shop?

✄ -

I was adrift in rapids, being swept away!

There she was.

In the same room with me again

sharing the same air

smelling the same burning candle

hearing the same siren as the ambulance drove past outside.

Joy of joys, I'd have the pleasure of getting to know her all over again, as though we were meeting for the first time.

(Every time I saw her, she'd insisted on acting as though we were just meeting, since first time sex is more exciting and it was her way of attempting to continually reclaim that excitement.)

Even though there'd been all that pretending going on back then, what always excited me most was knowing I'd already been inside her in every way, and that she had intimate knowledge of what I like, and how to get a rise from me with just a breath from her mouth into my ear.

Nothing had been taboo between us, and I felt close to her because of that.

It elated me.

It terrified me.

I was excited.

I was scared shitless.

I'd been standing at the Bergerac threshold, silent and staring, for how long?

I recovered; looked throughout the foyer at the mourning faces, prompting myself to move forward to the stairs with Cyranose as she began to descend them (though I saw her do so in slow motion).

A tiger-striped silk scarf was the only color she wore.

Just seeing her again, I could feel the calming waves of oxytocin and vasopressin flooding me. I was back in a place of peace and tranquility, thanks to the sight of her.

Whenever I'd see her in my dreams, I'd wake with the same feeling.

A feeling I chased.

A feeling I wanted.

A feeling that was flooding me anew!

Bringing back those familiar sensations!

She could lead me to my ruin and I'd happily let her.

Well, she must've known I was a local.

Cyranose introduced me to his niece, Paget. As the three of us stepped up to each other in the center of the room, that memory of Lizzy Hale's vocals of nightmares in her head creating a monster in the bed, subsided in my mind.

(TICS: "Patches.")

And then he told her about my love for driving into horses.

(TICS: "Asshole!")

Paget smiled politely.

Didn't laugh.

If I hadn't already been smitten, and hadn't almost done the whole Kama Sutra with her, I would've taken an instant liking to Paget when she didn't laugh at the bad joke.

My mind was awhirl with memories of all the sex I'd had with her.

How there wasn't much she didn't do.

How there was less she wouldn't do.

Out of habit I almost reached forward to hug her

take her face in my hands to start kissing her the way I used to

back when I'd only known her by the name "Patches."

Who knew we'd be hand-in-hand again, after all my wasted trips up to the city which ended with continual disappointment over my not finding Patches in any of our old haunts...

Where had Patches gone after my proposal?

What had happened?

You may not believe it, but after she disappeared, that's when I began my struggle to gain my sexual sobriety. From that, to sex addiction counselor, and then to a PhD in Sexology.

And now, to have Patches-Paget here, in this parish!

Seeing her again

touching her, bare skin to bare skin.

Welcoming Paget into my real world.

My day job.

While Patches had belonged to my double life.

That "night life" I'd escaped to with her all those times.

The family's heart-shaped face she'd inherited was almost a distraction away from her figure.

Almost.

But not really.

Tall, thin.

Rounded hips, wider than her shoulders.

Firm thighs.

Nice legs.

Glasses (not the horn-rims she'd worn when we met).

I had to be careful.

Didn't want Paget, or Cyranose, to notice my ogling.

Were people starting to notice me?

My hesitation?

My awe?

Same wide, toothy smile she's always had, lower lip dropping further down than the right side, revealing a few of her lower teeth (when photographing her I'd had to shoot her from her left side to de-accent her uneven smile). No earlobes, wide bridge of her nose, smooth cheeks, creased smile lines under the outer corners of her downturned dark chocolate eyes.

I was glad to see she hadn't tried changing herself with surgery.

I couldn't stay mute. Finally, I managed some pleasantries.

After a few moments of Cyranose's yammering (time spent forcing myself to hold eye contact with him rather than keep looking her up and down), I was able to interject a word of congratulations to Paget on her engagement.

I noticed the odd look which passed between her and her uncle (she was wearing an antique diamond ring). Thought no more of it beyond how, if Paget's engaged then there's no chance of our going back to what we did non-stop for nine delicious months!

Damnit!

Tearing myself away from past delights, I struggled to focus on the here-and-now.

She was all set to take over the family business as soon as Cyranose and his wife left for their retired bliss next week (they'd already been delayed twice from leaving).

Called away (to take care of the grieving family's needs), Patches-Paget excused herself from us. Cyranose and I moved back to the door which he held open for people coming in and going out.

In-between people passing through, he told me Paget's story, unaware that she'd kept this whole part of her life secret while sharing all her bedroom secrets with me.

I mused: addicts do tend to keep a secret life (their addiction life), apart from their daily lives. And we may have had sex fifty times, but not once did she ever tell me she'd been interning/apprenticing at a city funeral home.

That she'd graduated mortuary school (two year program).

Had taken the two licensure tests and the one for state laws.

Was licensed as an Embalmer and Funeral Director in NYS.

Was a member of both the state and county Funeral Directors Associations. With the former she stayed current on the legal changes to the profession. Took her continuing education (twelve credits every two years) from the latter.

I hadn't asked for her CV but figured he thought I'd want to make sure she was fully qualified as if I might possibly decide not to work with Bergerac any more. "You'll still be the owner though, right?" I queried (feigning concern).

He launched off on that answer and really, my mind was only on how she'd never told me anything about her job. But I knew it now, and with her replacing him as manager of Bergerac, maybe Cyranose's bad joke about my equestrian roadkill would finally die the death it deserves!

✄ -

I wanted to get my hands on her some more!

Massage her. Reacquaint myself with her body.

Smell her again.

Taste her again.

Feel her again.

I missed her body, her soft voice, nice lips, her touch, her presence, our companionable silence.

You don't have sex with someone fifty times, in multiple ways, and not develop some sort of affectionate feelings.

All five of my senses had been suffocating without her!

Seeing her again, alive and well, was the deep gasp of air I'd desperately needed!

And if we did have a kid together somewhere, that idea didn't fill me with dread like it had with every other woman I'd ever been with. Rather, it excited me: that we would have a life-long connection to one another. That there would be another person bonding her to me, and me to her.

Distracted myself by asking Cyranose to introduce me to the next of kin

> as they came out of the main room
>> and down the stairs on their way outside.

I offered to say a prayer with the family, which was hesitantly accepted.

(Clearly they felt a need to be polite and accept my offer of prayer, rather than fess up that they weren't really interested in what I had to say.)

Decline my offer if you're not interested.

I'm OK with that.

I'd rather people own their reality than pretend the social niceties.

(TICS: "If church doesn't mean anything to you, don't pretend it does for my sake. I don't give a rat's ass, and telling lies to a priest doesn't pull the wool over God's eyes. Just so you know.")

My ability to focus on the family rather than day-dream of Paget didn't really surprise me.

I do have some sense of detachment, professionalism, and (now) self-control.

Once the family came back inside (from their brief trip to a car out in the lot), we all moved back into the "Slumber Room" (don't you hate those euphemisms?) where I called out and asked everyone present to gather in a circle as best they could.

Two immediate family members placing a hand on each end of the casket to include the decedent from head to toe.

Cyranose called it the "Reposing Room" which was split from the next room by an accordian wall. Wakes in one room, collapse the wall, roll the casket into the next, close up the partion wall again, and have a religious service (move the casket along, from one room to the next, kinda like an assembly line for back-to-back funerals).

That next room, the "Chapel", was a plain room with an open area for the casket before a thin altar-like side table and podium. The square room was filled with an uneven arrangement of twelve church pews (bought from a RC city church which had been closed down).

The family wouldn't be moving into the next room until morning, but a prayer in the Reposing/Slumber/Viewing room was not out of line.

(Funny how we change names for things depending on how quickly our context for them changes.

(Like, Patches – Paget.)

I didn't realize Cyranose had called her into the room until I felt her warm hand take mine just as I began to lead the circle in prayer.

Loved her short-cut fingernails.

Wanted to feel those fingers raking my back some more.

(Dermagraphism – as evidence that my fantasy is my reality.)

Having her hand in mine focused my whole being on Paget, giving me a jolt of neurochemistry.

It was all that O/V flooding my system again.

The "attachment" chemicals.

Been a lonnnnnnng time, my old friends!

Glad to have you back!

✂ -

After the prayer I told the family I would be around in the building if they needed me for anything during the calling hours.

Then I followed after Paget as she left the room, my eyes sweeping up and down her delectable backside.

I knew I shouldn't be doing that.

I shouldn't be chasing after a quick fix, but with my ex-lover turning up unexpectedly, my motor's over-revving.

"You had my leg hair standing up while you were praying in there," Paget confessed as we paused at the edge of the landing. She then went down the stairs to the foyer to do her job and I returned to the room with the casket to do mine.

✂ -

She and I had been together fifty times (I don't keep saying that to brag of my virility. I say that because for me, returning to the same person is significant, and cannot be understated.

(Throughout my life I'd never been with anyone else as often as I'd been with Patches.)

✂ -

I sat in my usual place, on a couch with flowers carved into the wood. Densely padded cushions covered in velvet.

Placed in the far corner of the room by the wall with the accordian door, facing the casket.

Unless needed, I pretty much stay in that spot unless some parishioners turn up to pay their respects (in small towns, there is always a parishioner near-by; except in antique stores). I'll get up and go over to greet them in the condolence line, and then return to my seat, knowing that (after speaking to the grieving family) those parishioners will join me at the couch and sit beside me, or in the wingback chairs on either side of it.

There are things only a gawking ogler would notice.

For example, as I watched Paget cross the room to talk with the widow (in a chair set beside the casket and bier), I noticed a white line running up the back of her right leg.

A soft, caucasian tan on either side of that line.

Not softly tanned legs.

But a run in her stockings.

The detail raised my interest from curiosity to Lust.

Why would she have cut the feet off her nylons? I know she had because as she stood on one leg for a while, she slipped a bare foot in and out of her ankle boot while talking with the widow. The bunched up material had created a tan ring above her ankle from that darker color of fabric whenever sheer nylon gets bunched up and folded over itself.

Considered a strategy to prevent myself from objectifying her.

Took my own advice
    asked myself, "What is unique to Paget?"
        She had no tattoos that I could see
          no facial piercings
            no crazy hair coloring
              was unblemished.

Being "undecorated" was probably her way of not putting off any potential – and traditionally conservative – clients.

She probably hadn't gotten any tatts since I last saw her, but I can't tell for sure until I see her naked again.

But I can tell you she still prefers silver jewelry to gold.

✂- -

Funeral services run about twenty minutes, and may go longer, depending on how many people have memories to share of the decedent when I invite them to share.

This crowd stayed mute.

On my way out, Paget and Cyranose were at the double doors, greeting people as they exited. I gave serious thought to lingering until the last family member had gone; but since I'd only be doing that to feast my eyes on Paget some more, I figured the wiser thing to do was leave, rather than stay and stare.

I went for the door, thanked Cyranose for the call, promised to pray for his safe travel south, then moved to the threshold.

Offering her hand, Paget said, "Thanks for coming."

"Thanks for having me," I said.

Cyranose simply smiled, blissfully unaware.

She remembered me!

(After fifty times, I'd be crushed if she didn't!)

Walking back to church I just hoped Cyranose would stay permanently unaware.

✂- -

IV.

Getting back to the rectory I quickly dove back into the past (read: before Political Correctness reared its ugly-ass head).

Noir – not the sort of thing my parishioners would expect to find me reading, but hey. It's my way of giving my mind a rest from all the doctrine, dogma, and ecclesiastical militancy that fills more of my days than I'd like.

Nunsploitation – not the sort of movies my parishioners would expect to find me watching.

But hey, we all need a little escapism from work, and what better way to blow off some steam than work-related quasi-pseudo soft core smutt?

Hopefully the fast-paced book plots and movie costumes would keep me from dwelling on Patches-Paget in Bergerac!

A lost cause.

She was back!!!!

And when I nodded off in my seat I dreamed of Paget in a habit.

✂- -

My dream.

(No; not a sex dream.)

You know I'm a big fan of noir, right?

Can't get enough. Of the corruption, the greed, apathy, femme fatales, the stark contrast of blacks, whites, and greys, the bleakness, the pessimism, the cynicism, the lack of trust in authority. It's shadowy and foreboding; and expresses what already lurks within me: Jaded. Bitter. Frustrated. Kicked about. Lied to, taken advantage of. Heart broken, cheated on, stolen from, screwed over, ripped off, had the heart torn out of me, been rejected, been insulted, been down, and still kicked in the ...

Noir is an attitude.

A lens used to view the world.

It could be in any genre (although, yes; it's typically crime).

I'd love to find an investor to fund my dream project.

I want to make a movie that tells the story of Christ in the genre of noir. Bogart as Jesus. Really make an impact with the audience who is unlikely to ever imagine the Christ story the way I do – until they can see it projected up on the silver screen in full Hollywood glory.

A statement to say that today's church leaders are no different than those Jewish authorities (Pharisees, Sadducees, Sanhedrin) who incited that mob to call for the crucifixion, or the Roman stooges who carried out that execution (which they wouldn't have bothered doing if it weren't for those religionist complainers).

And since the main characters in noir are always flawed (yes, it's typically addiction), get this:

our main character's tragic flaw?

In a selfish world, Jesus actually cared about other people.

✂ -

Like they say,

of one hundred parishioners, 20 will try anything their priest asks them to.

20 will complain and criticize without trying it.

60 will wait to see how it turns out, and then - compliment or criticize, depending.

Obviously, I bitch about that group of 20 critics more than anyone else. I know, I should celebrate the 80 who go along with me

yet why is it - the negative always makes a stronger impact?

You bitch about the people you work with, and yet you don't quit because you like what you do.

Same with me.

It's just too bad our jobs force us to deal in customer service.

✂ -

Tell you what

once I start calling my parish "Saint (Typhoid) Mary's" then you'll know I'm ready to pack it in. The best indication that I can't take any more, and need to be assigned to a new parish is when you hear me use any variation of "Saint Mary's of the Typhoid."

Got that?

But until I start making such references, please believe that even with all the bitching and complaining and griping I do – that I truly love what I do, and I do indeed enjoy the people I minister to (even with all their attendant B-S).

Why Your Priest Hates You as a title for my ministry memoirs? Naw!

It's really not that bad for me, you know.

The Passion of Rev Pervert is too obvious.

Though I like your "Rev Pervert's Naughty Christmas" title suggestion best!

✂ -

If I start calling Mrs Church my "Nemesis" then it won't be because of hostility and resentment, but more from irritation.

The same way you get irritated by the folks you work with who don't see eye-to-eye with you.

Example:

Vestry meeting.

Agenda item 1: Organ Replacement.

The Organist was growing increasingly upset with the instrument not playing, and bulbs burning out, and the only place to get replacement bulbs is in Germany.

"Could we replace the Organ with a newer one?"

To disguise that the issue was more about not spending money than anything else, the rebuttal went around the table about how long the current Organ's been there.

That we couldn't trash it without offending the family who donated it.

Etc. etc. etc...

It was settled; we'd start an "Organ Restoration Fund" and initiate it the following Sunday.

Agenda item 2: We typically have two worship services on Sunday mornings. One at 9, and one at 11. Every Spring the question gets raised, to merge the two into one service at 10 am and bring both congregations together for the summer months as attendance drops at both services.

As always, "We've never done it that way before!"

"We can't start now!"

(TICS: "Heaven forbid!")

Agenda item 3: A replacement for parishioner # 16, our deceased Christian Education Director.

She'd been retired, had donated all her time. Paid for the materials out of her own pocket as part of her tithe to the church.

She'd had her accident at Thanksgiving, died the week after Christmas, and her ashes got under her Granddaughter's fingernails on Easter.

Our Director's temporary replacement (parishioner # 70) is a single mother with two daughters who works as an dental hygienist, and was being swamped by the volunteer workload held by her predecessor.

Either parishioner # 70 gets help, or she'll resign as Christian Education Director.

What to do, what to do, what to do ...?

It was settled, Saint Mary's would offer to pay her a stipend to complete the year.

I already knew that wouldn't work (she wanted help, not money), but Mrs Church (since my idea wasn't hers) prodded the Vestry to ignore what I had to say. Rather than find a permanent solution and start advertising for it as a paid staff position, Mrs Church just wanted to bandage the issue in the typical Church approach to financial expenditures:

"Penny wise, dollar foolish."

✂ -

Sex Addiction is a thing!

There are no obviously outward signs to indicate who is, and who isn't afflicted by obsessive porn viewing (anyone can look exhausted and sleep deprived, it doesn't mean anything).

The unspoken instruction given from the Church to its clergy

"Don't get caught."

Forget the percentages of clergy marriages impacted by porn infidelity.

Forget that one in every two clergy watch porn.

We – as an institution - still don't talk about this.

Why address something that's better left ignored

right?

Don't bring it up

so parishioners don't think about it and wonder.

✂ -

Sex addiction is a thing!

"I don't want to hear you telling me I gotta give up my movies!"

"I won't."

My movies (read: porn).

"That's what my ... er, you won't?"

"No."

"You are a Sex Addiction Counselor, right?"

"I am." I gave Client # 21, in his denim overalls and rubber boots, a moment to cool. "And you've seen at least two different counselors, and you didn't like what they had to say."

(TICS: "Since they were not specialized in this field, that was probably wise.")

"I just know who I am! I get cranky, and pissed off when I can't watch my movies."

"What brings you in, then?"

"My boss says I have to."

(Probably watching porn at work, on his cell phone. Cannot stop, probably resents he's being told he has to stop even though he doesn't want to.)

Had to bite my tongue, his being a career dairy farmer's helper, and all.

(TICS: "I'm sure the cows don't mind."

(TICS: "Question is, are only cow teets being stuck in the milking machine?")

Phase One: I suggest "Watch all the porn you want."

"Really? How's that – ?"

"Two conditions. First, you can only watch when you are at home."

He didn't like that.

"Second, whatever you watch, it has to be a certain type, and only that one type. OK?"

This usually gets their attention.

Weary, "What, *type*?"

"Watch any movie you want, whatever that is, as often as you want, provided –"

I pause, make sure he's listening. "You pick one particular performer."

"OK."

Again, "You can watch any type of movie you want, so long as that performer's in it."

(Have to phrase it that way just in case he's into men instead of women.)

"OK."

"If you use the movie for a release, then you can only use those scenes that your chosen performer is in."

(Whether mainstream, or porn, or both.)

"OK."

"Do you know who that will be?"

"I have a good idea."

A woman.

He described for me what he liked watching her do.

Knowing that will make our conversations a little easier for which pronouns I should use

(although, her credits and talents don't add to our conversation).

Then, I stipulate: "No lesbian scenes. No threesomes. No group scenes. Just straight one-on-one, or solo, scenes."

"Er ... ok."

(The first client I suggested this approach to went crazy with orgy scenes – as a loophole – because his named actress was in it, but so were several other women he could also watch. Same with lesbian scenes, that's two women, and he could focus on either one.)

"There's a reason for this," I began. "We want to exchange variety for individualism. If you only watch one performer over and over, you'll start to notice details and you'll get familiar with them in particular."

"And get bored," he grumbled.

I continued, "But you'll start noticing details, peculiar to them. They'll stop being an object of lust, and you'll start to see her as a person."

"Father, you ever hear 'familiarity breeds contempt?'"

"Of course I have. The question for you is, do you want to stop endangering your job?"

"I have to!"

"Here's the approach we'll start with, to make sure you keep your job."

"What if my girlfriend and I make a sex tape? Can I watch that?"

Typical addict: immediately searching for loopholes to keep the addiction thriving.

"You can pick your girlfriend as your performer, but you can <u>only</u> watch movies she is in. With you, alone, or with another man."

"We only made the one. That'll get real old, real fast."

"See what I mean about variety? That's the allure of porn, how it offers you so much choice. You stop seeing people and start looking only for what's different. We want to bring you to a place where you are creating a connection to an individual."

I'd dubbed this the "Patches Approach" because she was the reason I stopped constantly looking around and began to have a sense for being a one-woman kind of guy.

There are risks with this as a "long term" therapy, as it can become a problem all on its own. But, as an initial and temporary approach, it serves its purpose. Once he starts to realize what I'm saying about his chasing "variety" rather than a particular person, he'll have an epiphany.

Which will, hopefully, switch his thoughts into other avenues.

(On a side note: here's how screwed up our thinking is as a culture:

(We're so hung up on how many partners a person has, right?

(Yet we don't give two seconds worth of thought to whether or not those fewer partnerships people have are good ones or not.

(Seriously, shouldn't we be more concerned about people having quality relationships rather than butting into the quantity of their relationships?)

Phase Two of the process – as I recommend it to my clients – involves doubling down over a period of time.

The porn addict goes from an unlimited and unrestrained habit

to having certain criteria to establish limits and boundaries and

within those limits, frequency is incrementally decreased.

I go into Psychoeducation mode, and lecture: "This may sound self-defeating, but we want to be practical. You will slip a time or two. That's usual. When you do slip, document it. What you watched, who was in it, why you were drawn to that one instead of your chosen actress, what was going on during the day you slipped, and what were your feelings before slipping. And also after.

"I want you to think about this.

"We need to identify your pattern.

"We want progress, not perfection.

"One slip doesn't equal failure so don't just give up. Think more like falling off a bike. You pick it up, and keep on going. In this situation, you want to learn about yourself. Things you may not realize. For example, do you turn to your movies only when you're bored or when you've had an argument with your girlfriend?

"We want to get you to a place where you're not thinking you need to watch, or that you have to.

"But until then, when you do, why do you?

"That's the missing piece of the puzzle, and once we know that, we'll be able to build on it."

Phase Three: "Keep meeting with me to discuss progress and set-backs."

He'll likely try it for a couple sessions, tell himself I'm a quack, go on a binge, get in trouble at the barn, reconsider what I told him, and start again. Within a week to ten days, he may call and cancel his second appointment.

Some do, some don't.

Some call back to cancel their cancellation, and reschedule.

Depends on how badly they want to stop.

And how desperate they are to keep their addiction going.

The clinic encourages counselors to offer a discount rate for those who pay for multiple sessions in advance.

Porn is everywhere – on farms and in city skyscrapers.

From town, to country, wherever there's good cell phone reception, and Wi-Fi for laptops and PCs, there're sex videos being watched (and used).

Still think Sex Addiction isn't a problem?

✂ -

4

Pentecost (iii)

I.

Standing at the back doors, I was shaking hands with people as they exit the sanctuary.

You wouldn't expect to find a man in a dress in small-town America, but my congregation has one of those.

At first I thought it was just a very unattractive woman with a deep voice.

Then, someone told me the truth.

Thankfully!

(People often presume – incorrectly – like I know everything about everyone, because God whispers it to me or something!)

S/he'd be a pre-op if their insurance would cover it.

It won't.

Started coming in for worship shortly after joining the twelve-step program that meets in the Saint Mary's building.

(Sometimes I'm surprised that the congregation opened up to, and welcomed, a guy dressing like a woman. Being so conservative in so many other ways [under the leadership of Mr and Mrs Church, and the Cathederal Sisters], I'd thought alternative gender identity would not be something they'd be open to.

(But people can surprise you sometimes.)

Since Christ never said, "Love your neighbors ... but ONLY if they're as normal as you are," my approach is always to show love through acceptance.

Meet people where they are at, and start from there.

(Or, in my case, hide my inner reaction, present an outward appearance of absolute acceptance, and do not mention Deut xxii. 5; nor xxiii. 1.)

If s/he wanted to be called by a certain name
     be a man treated like a woman

     I didn't need to know what was under that hideous thrift-store skirt, and I certainly didn't want to be within reach of those tentacle leg hairs poking out through cheap nylons.

A smile and a warm handshake
sure.

But I draw the line at hugging a tranny.

Don't wanna be worrying about what's under my robe rubbing against what's under his skirt.

✂ -

No.
     I don't want to have a "swordfight"!
     Smartass.

✂ -

A cross-dresser is a man who likes wearing women's clothes. Born a man, identifies as a man, and stays a man without any surgical alterations.

     A transvestite is same as a cross dresser except they get off by wearing woman's clothes.

     And a Transgender is any person who feels trapped in the wrong body, no matter where they're at physically. Some go surgery with implants or removal to physically appear as a certain gender, while many stop with breast implants but don't have other parts converted.

     These are not all the same.

     Since s/he hangs out with Holly, maybe I should suggest the hot red-headed choir member treat her friend to an extreme make-over.

     (Encounter Christ while having a Brazilian wax?

(That'll separate the trannys from the crossys from the transgenders.)

✂ -

Standing at the back doors, I was shaking hands with people as they exit the sanctuary.

"Reverend, good sermon."

(TICS: "Tell me, what was your favorite part?"

✂ -

Standing at the back doors, I was shaking hands with people as they exit the sanctuary.

Parishioner # 58.

Man needs more than a hearing aid!

He'll be looking right at me, and I'll start to talk to him, he still goes "Huh?"

I used to wonder if he's day-dreaming so badly that he doesn't even realize that the person standing in front of him – the person he's looking at through those unwashed glasses of his – has lips that are moving?

Doesn't that clue him in to listen harder?

Nope!

(TICS: "I hate small talk on a good day, and this isn't working for me!")

"How you doing today?"

"Huh?"

I repeat myself.

"Oh, I been better!"

"What's going on?"

"It's my bad knee!"

People lingering outside in the sunlight, holding up the line (as they take forever on the wide porch in front of the doorframe without moving off to the side), forcing me to entertain those still waiting to leave.

"Do you need to sit down until the line moves out there?"

"Huh?"

I repeat myself so he can read my lips.

"No, I can walk!"

I used to think it was just his way, now I think it's because he can't hear a thing, and is probably inwardly a million miles away.

(His daughter told me he's been diagnosed with early stage dementia.)

I try to be compassionate and understanding but some things just irritate like sand in your thong! – "Huh?"

✂- -

Parishioner # 38 isn't much different.

I've learned not to say too much all at once to her.

"So I was talking with Mrs Church – 'Uh-huh' – about this petition she wants to leave out – 'Uh-huh' – so every one can sign it – 'Uh-huh' – within a couple of weeks, but what I'm wondering – 'Uh-huh' – and maybe you can help me, is ..."

Yes.

She "Uh-huhs" that much in the middle of whoever is speaking to her!

It's like she's not even listening to what people are telling her in her rush to that next "Uh-huh"! Maybe she thinks that encourages people to think that she's paying attention, I dunno.

(TICS: "Just an absent-minded habit, I hope?")

Now I'm wondering if maybe all her "Uh-huhs" are a sign of early dementia too.

As she said, "Like my father used to say! 'More paws, less jaws!' Which meant, work more, talk less."

Maybe that explains it.

But what hasn't been explained to me is why she takes such pride in bragging how she's never gone to a doctor.

"What do you do if you get sick?" I'd asked one time.

"We have a vet who lives next door, I see him."

A vet.

A doctor for animals.

"When I had that bad knee, he gave me a shot of what they use on horses, and that fixed me right up!"

Horse drugs.

Great.

(Makes me cringe – Ezek xxiii. 20.)

"Huh?"

"Uh-huh!"

✂ -

Standing at the back doors, I was shaking hands with people as they exit the sanctuary.

Was told Parishioner # 63's sister-in-law's husband died unexpectedly.

"Wake's today, burial tomorrow morning."

"Thanks for telling me."

Usually I'll attend the wake for a parishioner's extended family (to support my parishioner), but a husband's brother-in-law, usually not.

Still

it was at Bergerac

and just so I could get another look at Paget, I'd go.

✂ -

She was at the door, greeting people going in, and I took notice of Paget's figure, standing in the doorframe, hoping she didn't notice my noticing.

A black dress with grey sides and sleeves, black nylons, and boots. I was enjoying the sight of her.

Exactly as I remember her.

Exactly as she is in my dreams.

(TICS: "I can't speak for anyone else, but I don't mind the sek-zay!"

(i.e. she's not just sexy, she is Sek-Zay!)

"What brings you in?"

Checked for her engagement ring – yes, still there.

Damnit!

I really shouldn't indulge – but eff-me sideways! – if she isn't still the sexiest woman in the world to me!

"Parishioner's relative. It's my day off."

"I could tell, the way your shirt's unbuttoned."

Hand to my chest, checking the top button was done, "Is it obscene?"

"Maybe if you were four or five buttons undone, but not like you are."

(TICS: "I'm happy to unbutton and show off my hairy chest if you want.")

"OK, good."

We shared a smile and Paget did that Patches thing again, where she holds a smile while slowly glancing away from me, then back again to lift her eyebrows invitingly.

I asked how her aunt and uncle were, and had they relocated safely?

They had.

Had to prod myself to walk away because it'd be so easy to just stand there all day talking with her. I went up to the main floor and to the table, signed the guest book, took a memorial card and another few of the Bergerac business cards (since her picture is on the back), then moved through the Slumber Room looking for Parishioner # 63, or her husband.

They weren't there.

It wasn't a wasted visit.

Not after the sight of Paget in that outfit!

Lust was stirring an inner warmth
that tingling growing in my rod and tackle
and I was drifting away on the feeling of desire spreading through me.

Longer from hip to shoulder than from hip to ankle, the word "long" described her more than any other. Wide shoulders, long supple neck. Long, slender fingers. Long hair and lashes.

(TICS: "Baby's still got it all!")

Were I there to do the funeral, I'd take my usual place on that corner couch and sit quietly; present and available should anyone need a priest to talk with. But I hadn't been asked to do the service, so I returned to the lower lobby where Paget was at the door.

Rather than indulge myself by staring, ogling, and gawking, I considered discretion and valor, and made my exit rather than lurk around the place.

Didn't want to creep her out by being there beyond what was customary.

I hoped that my having popped in would also send the message that my feelings were not hurt that I wasn't asked to do the funeral

nor that I would hold a grudge about it.

✂ -

Ran into Parishioner # 63 and her husband on their way into Bergerac as I was leaving.

Turned around and went back inside with them to talk for a bit

(got a bonus Paget gawk that way).

✂ -

Whenever the AA group has an open meeting at church, I try to get to it.

Sunday evenings – not always the best time for me.

Not being an alcoholic, I go to hear the stories of how other addicts cope with their addictions (never know when something might be adaptable for me, or my clients). Having a non-alcohol addiction didn't qualify me for speaking (probably wouldn't even if I could) but I was invited to sit in and listen.

The different faces of addiction are many and varied.

But the character of addiction is always the same underneath.

I wonder sometimes, if I would still get the same invite to the meetings if I was in off the street rather than the parish priest.

But so long as I was the priest and I was invited, I get there whenever I can.

Some groups are limited strictly to professionals for an added layer of identity protection, but those are up in the cities, not usually found out in the country.

One thing I've been blessed with is a poker face (an impassive, almost "unreadable" expression to which I joke; "My face, was frozen like this"). I hoped it was firmly in place, given how my inner response was jarred to see the church's Choir Mistress there.

Alcohol and sex addiction often go together.

Bi-polar often gets into the mix of excessive sex and too much drinking.

But like me, she sat quietly and listened supportively.

✂- -

Couldn't delay any longer!

I didn't want to go and tempt fate by fondling a trigger, but I wasn't being given much of a choice!

My response was being demanded, and now it's being demanded by the whole Vestry!

Why aren't I putting out the petition to block the porn shop in town?

The town clerk wasn't as helpful as I'd hoped she'd be.

Needed to get help from somewhere.

So ...

Returning to the city porn shop I used to frequent one or two times a week (following every visit to Patches), it felt weird walking back inside after being away for ... how many years now?

The owner behind the counter and I had had many good talks throughout the years, ranging from favorite performers, to how he was a fan of 70s porn, and loved the modern European stuff because they have better production values.

(Read: sound, lighting, directing, costuming, plotting, chicks.)

He used to give me free rentals all the time.

I was a preferred customer, or as he said it, "Purr-verd-ded" customer.

I wouldn't say we were friends, but when he met Selena Steele (read: my favorite actress) at an Adult Awards Convention, he had her autograph a younger picture of herself for me.

As the owner of two of the six porn shops in the city (and two strip clubs that weren't doing as well), he knew how to reward his "loyal" customers.

"Mr Pervert!" he called out jovially as I entered (I always wished he'd not announce my entrance, but at least he did so with the common mispronunciation) and to show I was remembered.

I returned the greeting using his name, and went to the counter.

Seeing him again was like running into a favorite teacher from school.

Sadly, the velvet furniture he used to have in the porn shop had been relocated to one of his strip clubs for its VIP lounge.

Being there again, leaning against the counter again, I was awash in memories.

Feeling calm.

Feeling bliss.

The ratty curtain was still there, reminding me of the last time I'd been in the shop, and why I'd stopped coming by.

The portly owner and I caught up and I lied about having a fiancée who was why I stopped coming to the store, and that I'd married her. That she still wouldn't let me watch porn. Of course I'd tried showing her couples' videos! Such as – and I rambled off some titles and studios!

Had to let him know he was preaching to the choir.

"Wasn't me showed her the crap. That was her ex. No, I've tried explaining to her about the porn made by women, for women, and some of the big-budget stuff, and parodies."

He extended a fist across the counter for me to bump with my own.

Kindred spirits.

It was a lot like coming home again, and I could tell the chemicals were pumping back through my system, just like old times.

But I was just on a fact-finding trip
      not there to rent videos.

Or, that was how Lust was rationalizing and justifying the visit, hoping for temptation to stir.

It wanted to arise!

To live again!

The chemical boost would need to be watched; make sure it didn't draw me to a relapse, since I was starting to feel those old familiar stirrings.

That told me it was time I got the hell out of there!

As soon as I could work it into a conversation, I mentioned seeing a small town shop with a sign, "Parking in the Rear."

How funny was that?

Response I got was a lot more than I'd expected
      and just what I needed!

"Used to have a guy working for me at my other shop. He got it in his head he wanted to be his own boss. And since he'd been a manager for me, he knew the suppliers and distributors, and how to order inventory. He knew how to get a license to open a store, but his dumb-ass didn't know the first thing about state restrictions. So he got a loan, put a down payment on a store in some bum-fuck, hick town, somewhere an hour away, sunk all his money into buying product, and then he couldn't open! Dumb ass! He tried coming back to work for me, sell me everything he had. Told him to go fuck hisself!"

Thing is, the owner was so eager to reveal his insider know-how, that if I'd been a competitor about to open my own shop, he would've just given me a lot of the info I'd need to open a shop successfully. Like, list your shop as a T-shirt apparel store, not a smut shop. "Just sell one T-shirt, and they can't touch you for adding to your core product."

I knew he'd be the one to talk to, but you can't finagle a spontaneous conversation by phone.

I appreciated talking with him like old times, from across the empty showroom as I browsed, looking at the box jackets for any new actresses who might resemble Paget by face or figure. No such luck! Still, it allowed me the chance to stroll the aisles as if I were a serious shopper before moving to leave.

"Nothing tonight?"

I said, "Sorry."

"What'd you come in for, then? Not to shoot the shit."

(TICS: "Exactly that!")

"Just curious about what's new," I lied. "If there's anything the wifey might like."

Feigning it as an afterthought, he offered me six more free rentals.

Just to keep me coming back.

I lied again (ends justify the means – in this case – maintain my sobriety).

Said I was going out of town on vacation for two weeks.

That's how I got out of the store without a purchase or a rental.

"See? You got the info you needed, so it's OK you were in there," Lust consoled me, colorizing my view of the place to jump start my next trance-phase.

Seeing Patches again
    unexpectedly
        and after all this time
has caused more ripples in my sobriety than I'd initially thought after finding Paget at Bergerac.

✂------------------------------

Wondered during the hour-long drive back if I should

1) either encourage Mrs Church in her pre-emptive strike against the un-opened shop, or 2) spare her from wasting more of her time (by telling her the shop could never, legally, open).

But then
    if I did that

>   she'd want to know
>   how did I know it couldn't?

No way to explain how I'd gained the "unpriestly" knowledge I'd just learned.

People expect their clergy to be ignorant, naive, sheltered, unaware, and unworldly, and not know anything about how the world really is.

Decided by the time I got back; I'd just have to let her go on wasting her time protesting against something that was never going to happen.

To save my own ass, I couldn't say anything.

And since there'd be no point to it anyway, I'd let her put out her petition.

✂ -

II.

If it's in the Bible, I should be able to talk about it.

Right?

Tell that to the church prudes, or even to Mrs Church, whose view will be: "It may well be in the Bible, but that does not mean you have to talk about it, or, make us talk about it! Don't you know how uncomfortable *that* is?!"

("that" read: human sexual activity.)

✂ -

Another Baptism today.

I had the young mother stand by the font, holding her baby, as I poured the Holy Water over the little one's head, "I Baptize you in the name of the Father, Son, and Holy Ghost."

I prefer mothers hold their babies.

Mrs Church would rather see me hold the baby and parade it up and down the center aisle for everyone to gawk at, but that's not my scene. Let the mother and her baby have their moment, and if you want pictures after service, I can certainly stand there next to the beaming parents and crying infant.

(TICS: "Anybody seen my ear plugs?")

Won't see that family again until its time for the baby to get Confirmed or married.

Went off without a hitch

unless you want to count Parishioner # 8, who fainted half-way during the service.

Everyone thought he'd just fallen asleep, but when he didn't wake up at the end of worship we all got concerned.

I shook his shoulder, and he tipped over onto his side.

The paramedics were called, and he was carried away on a stretcher while still unconscious.

Dehydration.

✂ -

Sex addiction is a thing!

Client # 20 and I met before he was a client, and before he knew I was a sex addiction counselor. He'd attended a funeral I officiated at Bergerac for a non-church goer whose family wanted a religious send-off.

Soon as he recognized me at our first session all he could talk about was how attractive the platinum blonde was (she'd been at the funeral and reception but was also the librarian I had been hot for). So I knew exactly who he was talking about.

As he said, the blonde sent him into such a frenzy he had to lock himself in the rest room and rub one out.

Twice.

Before I'd even started the funeral service!

His thing: funeral hook-ups.

It's becoming a thing – people trolling funerals for sex partners. Usually, they will meet at the funeral and go elsewhere for a tryst.

My client and his latest partner got busy in the rest

room at Bergerac's closest competitor (over the county line).

She was 92.

✂ -

Don't just blow that off by thinking he's a pervert taking advantage of an elderly woman.

Or that he's aroused by the elderly (Gerontophilia).

As he described it, it was an opportunistic tryst.

For one thing, studies indicate sexual activity is life-long, from birth to death, for men and women. True, frequency may decline with age, but there are many folks (both genders) who remain sexually active into their 80s and 90s.

(The engine may run slower, but it's stll going!)

So, get over the ageist stereotypes.

For another thing, there is such a thing as "sexual bereavement" which occurs after a long-term relationship loss. The lack of touch which follows the death of a partner (it may not always be sexual) is something that people need, and miss. To supply that deficiency, they may turn to others for physical contact.

In short: the idea of an elderly woman looking for sex with an attractive young person is not unheard of, and it may even have been mutually beneficial for both partners.

Just saying.

"Solace sex" if you're looking for a term.

Probably "Sexual Bereavement" from her point of view (read: she was missing sex, and wanted to get some.)

It's really a shame we don't have more attention given to the study of elder sexuality, because it is a very real thing, and it should not be blown off as some kind of bad joke (had almost chosen that for my PhD dissertation topic).

I have not yet been approached by an elderly person as a potential client who

1) wants to talk about sex after the death of their spouse, or

2) presents as a sex addict.

I am ready and willing to enter into sessions with them in a way that takes them seriously.

✂ -

Client # 20 delighted in sharing with me this bit of advice learned from his experience: "That's why it's always a good idea to have some heavily lubricated condoms before you get to a funeral home!"

I replied, "Good advice, actually, since studies do show STD's are on the rise in the elderly demographic."

(You wanna think I am, but I am not making this up!)

✂ -

From the clinic to the hospital.

While visiting Parishioner # 8 he shared with me how he was brought in for dehydration, but that they were now at him for the same thing that's had him in and out of the hospital multiple times for being in pain.

His doctor was insisting he have an operation.

Had been advising it for a while.

Parishioner # 8 didn't want to have it.

I asked, "Do you think, maybe, the reason you're always in pain is because you won't have that operation? Maybe if you did, then you wouldn't always be in pain?"

He's convinced he'll never live through the surgery.

I prayed with him, promised to be there the next day to drive him back home.

All I can do.

I can lead the sheep to a stream, but I cannot make them drink or bathe.

✂ -

Half my congregation is made up of two, intertwined families.

What you're looking at is how multiple generations from each family have married into the other. Half the congregation is either a Chandler, or a Hammett.

Makes the church feel more like a family chapel than anything.

A severe problem that's left minefields all over the place.

Piss off any one person, and half the congregation might disappear in seconds.

So you can understand why it is, exactly, that I can only admire Holly from afar, and must never, ever, touch her.

Forget that when she took me with her on a shopping errand she'd led me into the store's lingerie section

to ask my opinion of a skimpy little number.

Clearly, Holly was interested.

(You'd call that a "gimme" hint I'm sure.)

But "interested" in what?

A casual fling?

The ego boost of being able to seduce a priest?

(That's actually a "type" – priest groupies – we call them "Cassock Chasers" and "Vicar Chicks" by the way; cross-reference with hierophilia.)

So when I tell you her name is Holly Hammett, you'll know the exact WHY behind my not acting on – and accepting – the signs and hints she's dropped my way.

✂ -

Parishioner # 51 has, on many occasions, fallen asleep during worship.

He's not alone in that.

But he is the only one who snores.

(The stereotype, right?

(Sermons put people to sleep.)

Now, me, I could just lean closer to the microphone and increase my volume to wake him up, but why?

You see, if a person is sitting in church and they feel comfortable, and they're relaxed, and my voice is so soothing that they nod off (and I've been told my voice is very soothing), then let them fall asleep.

From my point of view, they might really need a snooze.

I could take offense, but why bother?

I'm not a bang-on-the-pulpit, scream-at-the-top-of-my-voice, fire-and-brimstone, keep-everybody-awake preacher. My preaching style is more relaxed and calm.

I aim to reflect God's love and acceptance, not wrath.

A love that is not conditional, but universally felt for all living beings.

My Theology is that we have been given God's forgiveness, and that forgiveness will never be taken away. So why berate people with "feel guilty" and "repent you awful sinners" when that is not God's message sent through Christ?

As a Christian priest, my job is to meet people where they are at, and to help them connect with God in whichever way works best for them.

If they're Spiritual, but not religious, I'm good with that.

But getting back to my point, the Bible does talk about God sending people messages through their dreams, so yeah, if someone nods off in church, maybe they needed to so God could tell them something.

I won't ever say that is not possible (although whether or not the person hears God's message is entirely different).

My personal views; I do not speak on behalf of my denomination.

Just letting you know what kind of a priest I am.

✂ -

There're a lot of stereotypes floating around, so let me share my approach to Christianity. Unfortunately, you will not find this view more often.

On Sunday mornings when I'm in the pulpit I use a lot of Jesus Christ language. But the other six and a half days of the week I use more Judeo-Christian language (what Christians call "God the Father"), which isn't to say I dismiss Christ, but I'm just not name-dropping at every opportunity.

For me it's all about the Great Command – "Love your neighbor" (Mt xxii. 37-39; Mk xii. 29-31; Lk x. 26-28; Jn xiii. 34-35), and a big part of love is acceptance.

Acceptance of others for where they are at, and what their chosen beliefs are. Mine is a "both/and" approach to non-Christian faiths, instead of that dreaded "either/or" attitude which is rampant. In their fevered quest to "Make the Whole World Christian" most Christians forget that back in the Biblical era there were many different religious persuasions, and Christ never said "Convert all pagan heathens under threat of death!"

If our approach to the Great Commission (make disciples) is not informed by, nor in line with, the Great Command (love thy neighbor), then we are making disciples in the very worst way imaginable (i.e. the most un-Christ-like way), so now you know my position:

love (by acceptance) rather than proselytize.

✂- -

An abbreviated Theological Quadrilogy:

1) Christ is the poster child for God's love for all humanity (John iii. 16).

2) Propitiation – the ancient practice of sacrificing an animal to God to have your sins forgiven. Christ, as the "Lamb of God," was a perfect sacrifice for the sins of all humanity so that such an ancient sacrificial practice would no longer be necessary.

We have an After-Easter relationship with God, which involves

> Christ died on the cross
> our sins are forgiven
> Christ was resurrected and ascended to God.

This means that our prayers should shift from "Please forgive me" groveling, to a gift-receiving "Thank-you, God" instead. With that joy in our hearts, we should fight against sin not because we are afraid of punishment, but because it is our way of honoring Christ, and recognizing the value of his death on that cross. That is what replaced the need for using scapegoats and other animal sacrifices to gain pardon from God. Christ became the last (the one and only) sacrifice needing to ever be made again for the purpose of sin forgiveness.

The hiccup though is that so many people are happier with a black-and-white/right-and-wrong/good-and-evil way of thinking. That may be developmentally normal for kids, but many adults don't grow out of that way of thinking. Hence the whole "God-punishes-sinners" notion (a very Old Testament way of thinking) remains alive and well.

Another indication of where our stated beliefs are contrary to how we think.

✂ -

God will not take away an already-given-forgiveness no matter what we do.

(read: "Is God's love conditional? Cuz that's what we're saying if we think God forgives, revokes forgiveness, gives it back, withdraws it, etc. etc.)

Given once and forever, that should fill us with joy and assurance.

And our desire to fight sin should arise from our wanting to recognize and honor what God gave to us, rather than from a fear of being spanked for misbehaving!

Now consider, what have we given back to God?

Obedience to what God said, or total compliance with Church policy instead?

✂ -

We should not be clinging to God-still-punishes-and-judges, because if God did, then why the hell did Christ come to earth, live as a human, and die as an atonement for humanity's sin? Are we gonna forget all that his gesture of love means, just to stick to something we were taught as children?

Think it through.

Now, if you're comfortable with the God of vengeance and judgment that you find in the OT, that's your inalienable human right. But if you call yourself a Christian, that means you should believe in Christ as the symbol of God's love and forgiveness, and embrace the NT as first and foremost rather than continue on with OT wrath, judgement and punishment.

✂- -

Getting back from the tangent I was on:

3) Jesus, as a Jew, speaking to Jews, used a Jewish point of reference which the Jews understood. Keep in mind, Judaism doesn't hold a belief in hell. Then, the death of Jesus and resurrection of Christ, (still pre-Christian). A lot of Christians overlook how the Christian perspective isn't reflected in the four Gospels – unless you take the Papal editorializing of original documents as Gospel-truth.

4) desire not to sin, instead of only avoiding sin to stay in God's good graces and avoid hell.

Behavior modification through fear?

Look into your own heart, and be honest with yourself.

God gave you Free Will for a choice.

Own who you are (what you think, what you feel, and acknowledge your you-ness) in your prayers.

Have an honest relationship with God.

Stop thinking you can pull the wool over God's eyes by pretending to be what you truly aren't. As though if you don't say it, God won't hear it.

✂- -

I'd preach that quadrilogy on Sundays if I didn't have to worry about certain aggrieved parishioners getting on the phone to the bishop and insisting I get yanked out of Saint Mary's, or worse, accusing me of Amyraldism (read: a less severe version of Calvinism).

My Theology isn't exactly orthodox, nor is it non-kosher; but it does skirt the edge enough that it'll probably make some at D-house very nervous about what's going on out here in the boonies!

> There's a liberal Theologian in the pulpit!
> Yikes!
> Horrors!

✂ -

Fortunately for me, most attractive, sexy, young women are not found in church any more.

It's been a blessing to me to be surrounded by women I'm not sexually attracted to.

It's a challenge for me though, whenever an attractive, sexy, woman is visiting a parishioner and joins them in the pews on a Sunday morning.

Hot chick.

SPOTLIGHT!!!

I instinctively zero right in on them.

The only full color person in a world that's black, white, and grey.

So, with her there, the rest of the world fades away.

I feel guilty for feeling thankful we don't have many visitors like that.

It's why I asked to be moved out to a country parish.

Get away from the city allure and all its temptations.

Jokes on me!

Good, one, God!

Solve one problem, only to have it replaced by more of the same!

(Triggers!)

Out and about in this small country town, and I'm surrounded by cowgirls in their
- tight-ass jeans
- plaid shirts tied above the naval

- slim and sexy figures.

No matter where you go, a change of location will not free you from your temptations.

Temptations always go with you.

And now, I'm a rural priest; probably for life.

No one asks to be moved here.

I did.

From one frying pan into another frying pan.

The fire's still there.

✂ -

Whenever I see a beautiful woman across a crowded room, my mind starts weaving a tapestry of possibility.

I begin to imagine how

she would be as my wife,

how she behaves sexually.

Trouble is, 99% of the time, my fantasy idea of her is not at all close to who she is as an actual person.

My Lust-enflamed imagination will create a personality and a history for her, as I'd like her to be. The way I'd need her to be (a whore in the bedroom, hostess in the church kitchen).

I've had several relationships with kitchen hostess types, but they bore me sexually.

I've had a few relationships with bedroom whore types, but they couldn't be faithful.

Like Dr Frankenstein, I'm looking to build the perfect woman, who is a loyal wife, willing, able, and free enough with herself to be sexually exciting for my Jekyll/Hyde thingy.

(Someone in touch with her "inner slut.")

You'd think you're not gonna find them in church, but that's just more stereotyping.

(Although: virgins pretending to be harlots; not for me.)

Used to be I was too fussy as you've said; and I still am.

But now, if a woman is drawn to me, what I agonize over is: is it <u>what</u> I am that appeals to her, or <u>who</u> I am?

(Perfect example: can she accept I'm a priest finalizing my PhD dissertation in Sexology, or am I expected to not have anything whatever to do with talking about sex?

(See the difference?)

Clergy dating is a problem.

And not just because of my Theology.

✂ -

III.

Feeling a mood for being nostalgic (but knowing that was just Lust's way of getting me to backslide), I dug out the portrait photos I'd taken of Patches back during our nine months together.

Flipping through the prints reminded me of happier times.

I love the ones of her in the tight spandex dress. You know, the kind with the wide scoop neck, below-the elbow sleeves, and a skirt that ends just below the hips.

Trouble with that photoset is the dress.

It gives a pleasing length to her neck and torso.

But, it also makes her legs look only half as long.

She hates that photoset because of how she thinks it makes her look disproportionate.

I love that photoset because of how damn sexy she looks with her figure in that dress.

And for the fond memories of the way that material felt once I was allowed to get my hands on her.

And then
a couple more frames
and wa-lah!
A before-and-after photoset
with her hair tussled into an after-coitus-in-the-woods do
for my personal viewing pleasure.

✂ -

As both Patches and Paget, the lower lids of her downturned eyes appear as a straight line running across her face, defining smooth cheeks, chin, and nose below, while also accentuating the sunrise curve to her dark eyes above. Thin eyebrows take sharp downward angles at their ends, and with eye shadow and mascara, the soulfulness in her eyes really expands. The under-eye crinkles that appear with her smile – along with that deep dimple below the left side of her mouth (noticeable with her happier smiles, but absent from her forced smiles) illumine her countenance with a sensuality I could never escape while beholding her beauty.

Thin lips (which look fuller when she wears lipstick).

Dimples in-between her smile-lines and the corners of her mouth.

Her beauty, and dark chocolate eyes are magnetic.

The pics of her in a bikini.

She also hated that photoset as Patches
probably still would as Paget!

"Look at my fat legs!" she'd wailed when seeing those prints that first time.

She looks fabulously sexy to me, but looking at her standing knee-deep in a pool, her self-consciousness was somewhat revealed ("We have to burn these, right now!" and we did, but then I just reprinted a private set for myself to not show her.) As Sek-Zay as I find her, her figure appears to be one size smaller above than her proportions are from the waist down. It doesn't detract from her sex appeal, but I knew she didn't like to think of herself as "curvy" and the bikini snaps also displayed her muscular arms (which I'd never noticed back then). I still can't help wondering, when she looks in a mirror does she see some fun house mirror caricature with an exaggeratedly small torso and head, framed by swollen lumberjack arms, and a ballooned-up bottom two sizes bigger?

Not how I see her!

I'm biased, I admit, and there's a lot I didn't notice about her at first back when she kept most of her clothes on whenever we got together, but even if she is a bit larger than I usually go for, the shape of her did redefine for me the proportions I find sexy on a woman (used to be only slim and athletic got my attention). Maybe that's because of my falling in love with her, or maybe because she is my every porn fantasy made flesh and come to life!

I'll repeat myself:

"She looks fabulously Sek-Zay to me!"

✂ -

Had three funerals in two weeks.

That's a lot of Paget!!!

With her intense dark eyes, long lashes, crooked smile, uneven laugh lines, and pink lips, she stood at the door like Cyranose always did, opening it for people as they came in.

Our eyes met as I entered, joined her there at the threshold to greet folks passing through the entryway, and soon as I could, I dropped my gaze to double-check for her diamond engagement ring.

She was engaged so I didn't want to bring up our past which I missed, nor get into the whole "why-did-you-disappear-after-I-asked-you-to-marry-me" thing, as that might jeopardize my on-going status as Bergerac's go-to priest.

My musings were short lived though.

Duty calls.

Gotta keep it all professional.

Not get pervy.

✂ -

Funeral # 1 of 3

The decedent – natural causes.

Paget hit me with the bad news after the service was over. Her understudy was out running around the cars, making sure each one had a roof sign. She was going around getting all the drivers squared away in procession order while I waited in the hearse, with its door open for the breeze.

The elbow tray between the bucket seats had a well filled with empty gum wrappers, local maps, bottle of water, and some CDs. Metal: Halestorm, Leave's Eyes, Evanescence, In This Moment, Megan McCauley, t..a.T.u., Porcelain Black, The Pretty Reckless.

Still listens to what she used to.

I smirked at the idea of her jamming and headbanging while a filled body bag was in back. Who'd object to the volume she cranked the radio up to?

(TICS: "Trying to raise the dead with this music?")

Once the cortege (read: motorcade) was set to pull out, she joined me in the Bergerac Yukon (read: non-traditional hearse), noticed my smirk, and smiled in amusement at my smirk.

She twisted the ignition.

I pulled the door shut.

In gear, and rolling, "Sorry. The Air Conditioner is broken."

Sweltering hot day.

"Still want to ride with me?"

(Did I?)

Her high heel poised over the brake pedal.

"Last chance."

I didn't reach for the door handle.

(Like I'd ever pass up a chance to be near her?)

Got out onto the road, made a right to head through the village then out of town. Cop there to stop any traffic that might happen to pass us as we went through.

She wouldn't roll down the window, and I couldn't roll down the passenger's side window without forcing us to endure that godawful wobbling noise car windows make when a driver's side is up but others are down.

Paget told me, "I hate spiders, and there's one right there! It made a web in-between the mirror and the window frame."

Within the hot vehicle, she shivered.

I smiled.

Hers is a cute shiver.

Cruising at a healthy 40 mph as we crossed the county line, I commented, "If we weren't leading the procession I'd have you pull over so I could get rid of it for you."

She looked at me in pretend shock, "But it's one of God's creatures!"

At Bergerac she'd been too busy to mention it because of being distracted by work (when I could've gotten rid of it while we'd been waiting), but I figured I'd just make a point of getting rid of it once we got to the cemetery.

She drove, I enjoyed the scenery.

I couldn't take my eyes off her knees.

She noticed, and pretended to scratch an itch on her thigh which inched up her skirt.

She didn't tug it back down.

As lovers, we could chat about anything.

As ex-lovers I wasn't sure what we could chat about.

Especially since you know where my mind was.

✂ -

Typical burial service runs 10 – 15 minutes.

Took 45 minutes for the last of the family to leave!

Only then did she gesture for the vault guy to lower the casket into the grave.

Whole time all I could think about was
Paget and I
    alone in the cemetery
        with a vehicle pretending to be a hearse
           able to stretch out in back
                getting busy...

✂ -

Thing with me is
    just because I think thoughts
        doesn't mean I always act on them anymore.
    I have my boundaries, and I keep to them.

(Yes, I'm aware pride goes before a fall. I still have triggers but so long as I keep a self-awareness for nearing any risky potentialities I can function within my boundaries.)

I have an imagination, often incited by Lust, and it leads to all kinds if writing projects. Maybe one of these days I'll actually complete one rather than letting them all go unfinished.

✂ -

Last to leave the cemetery, we went back without other vehicles escorting us, and I had to bite my tongue rather than ask Paget to take us parking somewhere. To shake the Lust-induced fantasy out of my mind, I made conversation by asking about how she was adjusting to Bergerac.

She shared, "We had a funeral yesterday, and the sister of the deceased was a nasty woman. Master of back-handed compliments. I dunno, that must be some defense mechanism or something. But she wasn't happy. If she didn't know my Uncle from church, she'd probably give us a shitty review online."

Left hand on the wheel, her right palm rested over it, thumb and forefinger rubbing the diamond of her engagement ring. By watching her, instead of the road in front of us, I became suddenly aware of something I hadn't ever consciously noticed before!

Other than her coat with the elbow patches, she always wears black!

She's just much more stylish about it than I am.

"Black's an expected work thing," she shrugged.

"I'd think you'd want to get away from that dour, gaunt, unsmiling, ghoul image."

"Think about it like this: suppose I wore red, and didn't know that the person who'd died was killed in a car crash? Meeting the family for the first time; my wearing red would just remind them of all the blood. Not good."

"No, that wouldn't be."

"It's not just red, you know. Any color might bring up a bad association. With my luck, I could be wearing blue, and a family would come in to talk about a decedent who drowned. I don't need to upset them double, you know? At least all black is expected and it makes shopping a whole lot easier."

Don't I know it!

✂ -

As I recall, all her undies are black, too.

✂ -

Funeral # 2 of 3

The decedent – heart attack.

Was always known for saying at every dinner, "Save your fork, the best is yet to come!"

Laid out in the casket, her head on the pillow, fork in hand.

In both hands.

In pocket of her blouse.

Tucked behind an ear.

Each person who came into the wake placed a fork somewhere in the casket with her. Made doing the 20 minute service easier – just tied "The best is yet to come" into my message. Left a dessert/afterlife tie-in hanging in the air as hinted at.

The family was happy.

I was slipped an extra hundred in gratuities as people left.

After the last person exited and she shut the glass doors behind them, Paget rounded on me, smiling with that extra dimple below the left side of her mouth, "Half of that goes to the house."

✂ -

Flirting is the way people signal their receptivity to each other.

Dare I hope for a reunion with Patches, now that she's Paget?

What about that damn engagement ring?

In the Biblical era once a woman was engaged, she was as good as already married. Only married women could be guilty of adultery, and I did not want to be the reason for Paget's being condemned for sin.

(See what I mean about the whole irrational faith rising up when rational thought and common sense should disprove it?)

✂ -

Paget opened the Bergerac doors with a wide glowing smile, "We have to stop meeting like this."

"Every time is like the first time."

"I think I know what you mean," she answered, eyebrows lifted suggestively.

Tease!

Funeral # 3 of 3.

The decedent – natural causes.

Paget pulled me aside
    into the sales room
    closed the door
    got my hopes up
but it was before a service, and she'd never jeopardize her job, any more than I would mine.

"The family flew in this morning, and is flying back out tonight after dinner. If that doesn't say how inconvenient death is for people, I don't know what does. All they want is the service here, and that's it. No burial. No reception afterwards, so don't announce any. They're only doing something for just family. It's the quick in and out."

Static made her black cotton dress cling to her body, revealing the indentation lines where the elastic of her undergarments pressed into her supple ...

I was distracted, I admit.

Gotta stop myself!

And even with her being engaged, Lust was still aroused by her!

That's a risk to my boundaries!

✂ -

When introduced I noticed her high heels made the widow as tall as I was, but then once I was at the podium I didn't notice that she'd changed from her heels into black fuzzy slippers with white trim and poms.

It wasn't until I was at the door by Paget afterwards that we both noticed the widow walking out in those slippers, carrying her shoes by the heels.

Whatever comforts people in their grief, that's what I say.

✂ -

Afterwards I helped Paget go through the room and fold up the chairs, turn out the lights, and lock up. She was removing her key from the outer door when I made an attempt at letting her know I could accept that things could not go back to how they'd been for us.

It was heavy-handed, and awkward, "Do you have a church planned for the wedding?"

"Uh, er."

"Your engagement ring. I'm thinking it was passed down from your fiancée's grandmother. Family heirloom kind of thing."

(TICS: "And it explains why you disappeared on me.")

Wondered, how would I feel officiating her wedding to someone who wasn't me, after all fifty times she and I had ...

"There's no fiancée." She twisted the ring around her finger, "I only wear it because it keeps the wolves at bay."

"Ah!"

(TICS: "Was that the antique you were shopping for the time we met?")

"You know, guys find out what I do and then they're interested in me for that, and not for who I am."

(TICS: "Don't fault them for wanting her, just how they'd use her only to satisfy their own morbid curiosity about having cold hands on their genitals. Scumbags!"

(TICS: "So why did you disappear on me? What happened?")

You know how there's always that one moment which turns the key and opens the door? I like to think that because we had that in common – jobs that make people think of us as what we do, and not for who we are – that we both took notice of each other and contemplated resuming what we used to get up to together.

To me, she was Patches-Paget.

To others, she might just be "the Funeral Directoress."

I liked to think I was not just "The Collar" to her.

Yeah, I could relate to what she was saying since there have been women who wanted to date me not for who I am as a person, but because I'm a priest. There'd always be the expectation that I'm a priest 24/7, and never, ever, allowed to let my hair down.

That unspoken expectation – that I can only embody the stereotype

nor never, ever, get up to all the hi-jinx Patches and I used to get up to.

✂ -

Would she and I have resumed things on the Bergerac doorstep right then and there if her intern hadn't picked that exact moment to drive into the parking lot because he'd left something behind in the office?

Cursing Paget's understudy (by the way, "Undertaker" is not a recognized job title in this state), I walked to my car, Lust inflaming my imagination with scenarios of Paget and I doing what Patches and I used to do.

To get that back, I'd need to be around more often!

One of the things which can lead to people hooking up is if they see a lot of each other. Priests are associated with death and funerals, and I am Bergerac's go-to priest.

Unfortunately – for me – the established pattern seemed to be multiple funerals for a few weeks, then no funerals at all for a few months.

I spent the night tossing and turning.

✂ -

Is it monstrously evil for me to wish for more funerals?

✂ -

IV.

I have a wingback chair set in the rectory's bay window.

My housekeeper calls it my "Time Out" space.

She's not far wrong.

I spend thirty minutes a day in private prayer while seated in that chair.

When it's a slow morning I may follow that half hour with an hour of reading (I keep track of time by using a kitchen timer as an alarm).

It's my daily refuge.

Years ago I bought one of those hippie egg-shaped wicker chairs with the puffy cushions to be my prayer chair (got it from a thrift store). The shape, the sense of being enclosed while sitting in that seat had been my imitation prayer niche like those found in medieval cathedral walls (monks used to sit in those when praying, but these days they often contain statuary).

My spirituality is what is known as "contemplative" in that I am renewed while in solitary prayer rather than by being in communal worship. That might sound odd for a priest to say, but when you think about it, when I am at the altar and pulpit leading worship, I am leading worship for others, not myself. To be crass, my focus is on the performance, rather than my being in prayer. A lot of clergy fall into the trap of thinking that when they're leading worship that counts as their being in worship; but I don't see how they can claim that, not when practical concerns for lighting, sound, and awareness of your audience, all distract you away from focusing on remembering your lines, and good showmanship.

Yes, there's a degree of theatricality to Sunday morning worship.

Though there's no real call for theatricality while doing funerals.

✂ -

As far as everyone in church knew, I'd only recently met the new funeral directress in town.

Yes, I wanted to swim in my memories.

Relive each and every time we'd been together.

Make new memories together.

My inner addict wanted to be let out
> and once out, it would do something stupid
>> and that stupidity would get me busted.

> Another priest screwing a parishioner.

Except – I wasn't.

When we first met
> I didn't know who she was.
> She didn't know who I was.

I had not abused my authority as a priest – she didn't attend Saint Mary's.

I wasn't her counselor.

She wasn't my client.

Should I suggest she needed counseling?

Is she already in a 12-step group?

Seeing a counselor?

Why haven't we gone back to our old routine?

All I did know for sure was that I was in love all over again.

> Paget!

> My drug-of-choice.

As she said early on in our acquaintance, "Guys can't keep sex in perspective. Either they get jealous, or possessive. That's why so many people are hung up on marriage. It's the idea of owning your spouse as your personal sexual property."

(Which, according to a recent survey, 40% of people think marriage is an antiquated idea now-a-days, and I knew from that chat what Patches' opinion had been. Of course, in my love and sex addiction, I'd conveniently forgotten she'd said that, and asked her to marry me anyway because, as she surmised, I'd wanted her all to myself.)

Almost four years since I last saw her, and I'm still impatient for Paget to take a permanent place within my life.

("That's not a sign of enduring love, but of the depth of your addiction," according to Rhys.

(TICS: "That'll kill the greeting card business, saying 'true love' is only an addiction, and it never lasts and that the longer the memories linger, the stronger the addiction is."

(But if you really wanna talk terms, here are just a few to turn romantic greeting-card love strictly clinical:

(Osculation – kissing

(Estrous – sexual receptivity

(Tumescence – male swelling to erection/ detumescence – male deflating

(Intromission – when a penis enters a vagina)

Called out of my musings and to the counter I stepped up, paid for my tea (with two Cassis flavor shots), and waited until it was passed across to me.

I thanked the barista and left the coffee house to stroll along the village square to think up a sermon.

Instead I mused about the coffee shop owner, a former member of Saint Mary's. The last time he'd attended worship was my first Sunday in the pulpit. Curiosity satisfied about the new guy, he hasn't been back since. Cassis may not be too widely know in our area because back around 1900, some Blackcurrant was imported with an undetected fungus. That infection, "White pine Blister Rust" almost decimated the Whitebark, Limber, Sugar, and Western White Pine industries. So, to save the pine trees, Blackcurrants were banned, and today, over 100 years later, no one really knows about Cassis anymore. But since the owner likes to "stick-it" to those in power he gets his jollys having Blackcurrant products available.

(Ex-parishioner # 1: a rebel with a fruity cause).

On the far side of the square, I noticed Paget jogging past, her long dark hair done up in a ponytail. Those skin-tight black yoga pants with pink accents and ball cap.

My heart rate increased, and I stood transfixed until she'd gone the length of the square and vanished behind the far building. I headed that way, lamenting how, by the time I crossed the square, she'd be so far up that road that I wouldn't get a good gawk of her perfect bouncing butt in those sport pants.

✂ -

All I could do was mourn the loss of such a vision!

✂ -

I was asked to drive Parishioner # 8 to

his follow-up appointment with his doctor, and then to

the hospital for his surgery.

He gave me an envelope once we were parked in the hospital lot and the car was turned off.

"Open it later," he'd said. Then told me where I could find the spare key to his house. "I didn't save all that money so she could tan that wrinkly ass of hers!"

I remained silent.

He'd said his sister couldn't be bothered to drive him to the hospital (to be honest, I doubted that he'd even called her to ask for a ride).

"You promise me? You promise me, and I'll believe you, cuz you're a priest."

"I promise."

Getting out of the car, I heard him grumble, "Good. Now I can die in peace."

✂ -

Got him checked in, and stayed with Parishioner # 8 in the prep room until the orderlies and nurses came in to roll him away.

"Remember what you promised me! Remember?"

"Yes."

"Promise?"

I tried to hide my exasperated sigh; looked him in the eye, and answered, "Yes. I remember my promise. But I don't want to have to do that. So you. Get well!"

"It's outta my hands, Father."

✂ -

Parishioner # 8 came through surgery and was in recovery, sitting up and smiling.

Sat with him for a while afterwards.

Said a prayer with him.

✂ -

5

Pentecost (iv)

I.

9 am

Standing at the back doors, I was shaking hands with people as they exit the sanctuary.

Parishioner # 92:

"Father, I got this letter from Fr Whozzat, at Saint Simons. You should read it!"

(TICS: "And then you want me to write something for you to brag about?")

I laid it on thick

    with a sincere smile

    taking the page

      "I look forward to reading it."

Then, instead of leaving, she circled around to talk with someone she'd missed, meaning I'd likely have to talk with her some more as she came back through the exit line.

(Probably also expect me to have read her letter before she comes back up to the door. She's impatient like that. The whole world revolves around her notions of how everything should be rather than her accepting things for how they are.)

✂ -

Standing at the back doors, I was shaking hands with people as they exit the sanctuary.

Parishioner # 46 is a dreamer.

She's a great one for ideas, and to be put on a "visionary planning" committee, but she's a disaster if placed in charge of things.

Both her attention span, and interest, dwindle quick if she's not flooded with non-stop praise for her efforts.

Her interest (in whatever she's doing) fizzles as soon as she thinks no one is noticing.

She wanted to teach the children's lesson during worship, and had come up with "the kindly old Grandmother" as a character to do it in. Without a single compliment (from anyone other than me), once service was over, she quit, having only done one lesson.

So, I came up with a high visibility/low responsibility option to keep her active and involved.

I pulled her aside once and had asked her to update the narthex bulletin board every month.

Got two months on that.

Then she got bored, gave up, whatever.

That's when I had to start coming up with excuses not to accept her offers to help on various projects.

Wouldn't be fair to ask six people to be on Parishioner # 46's "Cheerleading Committee" so that there'd be half a dozen folks always ready to praise and extol a certain individual.

Sounded good in theory, but in practice it wouldn't be long before

the "Cheerleading Committee" needed its own "Morale Booster Committee"

who in turn would then need their spirits lifted by a sub-committee.

Where would it end?

✂ -

Complication is, Parishioner # 46 is a blogger.

So she sits at home on her computer, writing online trash talk about whatever, just to get a "hit" of approval. Each time someone online "likes" or "thumbs up" whatever bile she's spewing, it's a fresh dose, and to feed the approval addiction, she gets nastier and meaner with every posted blog as she goes.

I wonder if I should try encouraging her to seek counseling for that.

Though, not with me.

(Makes my stomach turn with dread whenever the notion – of my name coming up in one of her blogs – pops up.)

✂ -

Standing at the back doors, I was shaking hands with people as they exit the sanctuary.

Parishioner # 88 eats every meal as if it were going to be her last.

Her mother had died unexpectedly one afternoon while cooking a favorite meal without ever having the chance to eat that meal.

Which had left the impression on a young # 88 to make every meal satisfying so that when she died it would be after having had an enjoyable last meal.

I wonder if she's had Gout, or if she'll get it someday (even though women usually don't).

✂ -

Standing at the back doors, I was shaking hands with people as they exit the sanctuary.

Parishioner # 30 is a hugger.

Whenever she comes up to me with open arms I'm reminded of how that seminar lacked a method for handling the situation of "when clergy don't want to hug, but parishioners do" (because the insurance idiots were more intent on sending their message of: "Priests, don't ever have sex with your parishioners".

(TICS: "Is it OK to have sex with ex-lovers? How about with a certain brunette funeral directress with glasses?")

Because # 30 is a parishioner, I hug back.

Gotta be polite.
Show the love of Christ to all.

✂ -

Standing at the back doors, I was shaking hands with people as they exit the sanctuary.
"Reverend, good sermon."
(TICS: "Tell me, which part really spoke to you?"

✂ -

Parishioners # 84 and # 92 are a "tag-team" of criticism.
I've dubbed them the "Cathedral Sisters".
There are two types of parishioners to watch out for:
The first, those who cozy up to you the day you start (cuz they're pushing an agenda they want you to adopt).
The second, and more toxic, are those who talk about how they believe in "Full Disclosure" (read: they'll be watching closely for any mistakes, and as soon as you make one, they'll be sure to tell everyone they've ever met about how badly you effed up).

✂ -

Some parishioners – I hate to say – would be happier somewhere else.
Of course, I doubt parishioner # 92 (Cathedral Sister # 1) would ever be happy anywhere. I doubt she'll ever find any priest who measures up to her unrealistic standards.
Such as
1) that whatever she feels strongly about, I need to feel just as passionately about.
2) I need to spearhead every single social justice issue on the board, even those the Saint Mary's congregation never heard of (yet she remains mute on the issue of protesting the genital mutilation of young girls by certain second and third world religious cultures).

3) take everything hyper seriously, like she does.

4) have no sense of humor, never make a joke, and don't let people laugh during a worship service.

(TICS: "Most people who don't enjoy humor are also likely to have endured a shame-based upbringing, making them the protectors of family secrets.")

5) there better be no spelling mistakes or type-o's in the weekly bulletin (I imagine she'd have had a coronary if she'd been in worship that Sunday when the bulletin prayer which was supposed to read "recovery of sight to the blind" read "recovery of sight to the blonde" instead.)

I have to ask – when will it all end?

She's a prime example of today's "Episcopalian militant" SJW.

(And we thought Mrs Grundy was bad!!!??!!!)

✂ -

Sometime in the night, Parishioner # 8 had died.

I hurried in soon as I got the call from Paget after service.

("I knew you'd be busy, so I waited before calling. I hope that was alright.")

Said we'd meet up there, but I got there first.

Parishioner # 8 was still stretched out on his white hospital deathbed.

Tubes still up his nose.

Machines still wired to him.

An IV drip of something not dripping.

I prayed. Anointed his forehead with oil.

Heard the scuff of rubber shoes, knew a nurse had just entered the room.

To her credit, she waited until I was finished.

"Father, thank-you."

She gestured to the chairs, and we sat on the side of the room away from the bed and windows as two nurses came in to unhook him and remove all the tubing.

HIPAA privacy laws; she couldn't tell me what had happened.

"The last time he spoke, he asked me to remind you of your promise?"

"The last time I spoke with him, he was very complimentary of you. For the way you've been looking after him."

She brightened to hear that.

I was lying my ass off.

He'd never mentioned her.

Patches once commented (I forget the conversation, but remember what she said), "People in the caring professions don't often hear anyone say 'thank you'."

I thought this nurse could do with hearing how her efforts did comfort someone in need.

If not Parishioner # 8, then somebody, I'm sure.

✂ -

He'd been so convinced he'd die going into surgery that I suspect Parishioner # 8 gave up on life, even though he'd come through, and I'd sighed in relief to see him in recovery.

It's always awkward, to hear about a parishioner's death from the funeral home instead of hearing about it from other parishioners first.

Happens that way most of the time, actually.

You'd think I'd be used to it by now.

(TICS: "Shouldn't I know a parishioner died
before
the funeral home calls me?")

Paget arrived in her all-black and heels, with a severe expression, and collapsible gurney to take the body away.

Figuring she'd been having a bad day, I wanted to go to her and hug her, cheer her up, make her laugh. Then Lust dared to hope that maybe, she'd come into the hospital room, saw me talking with the nurse, and got jealous.

Excused myself from the nurse and left with Paget and my parishioner's body in the black bag.

Looked at her.

She didn't say a thing to me.

I was afraid of saying the wrong thing to her.

Neither of us spoke.

Until

we passed through the back door of the hospital and found ourselves on the loading dock.

"Where's my SUV?"

You ever have one of those times when you're feeling really horny, but then it turns into a laugh, and the sex is forgotten as you enjoy a non-sexual experience with your lover? I had to spell it out: "You lost your hearse?"

"Shut up. Where's my SUV?"

"Are you sure this is where you parked it?"

"They don't have two loading docks here, do they?"

I began looking through the lot for the Bergerac monster truck (a black GMC Yukon XL).

Didn't see it.

"You lost your hearse."

"Why would someone steal it?"

(TICS: "Halloween's in a couple months, maybe they're planning ahead?")

Which is when security came through the same door we had and noted, "Sir, you can't park there."

Turning to him, I saw him notice my dog collar, realize his error, and immediately turn to Paget.

She was getting frantic, not having a vehicle for the body on the stretcher beside her.

Not having the vehicle which contained her collection of Metal CDs.

"Where's my SUV?!"

"We moved it. You can't park there, ma'am."

"Fine! Soon as I have him loaded up, we'll be out of here. Where's my hearse?!"

"Didn't look like one. I'll let you off with a warning this time."

(In seminary I'd worked part-time as a security guard – only job I could find that would pay me to sit and read – and that required an annual seminar, the gist of which was: "You are not a cop, don't act like one!" I don't think this guy had taken that NYS required seminar yet.)

Needless to say I waited with Parishioner # 8 while she followed the self-important doughnut muncher to her vehicle, then drove back to the loading dock.

The stretcher's legs fold up as it's pushed into the vehicle, some fancy contraption thing which cost ten thousand or more. I helped her load Parishioner # 8 into the "hearse".

Slamming the back door, "Day from hell," was all she said in parting.

I felt bad for her, having a bad day.

Only in my world does a sexy funeral directress lose her hearse.

Parishioner # 8's words, from our drive to the hospital returned to me: "If I die, I want you to go into my house, take my coin collection and all the cash under the mattress in my guest room. Don't let my sister get the money. She'd only hock the rare coins, and use the cash to take a frivolous trip to the Bahamas."

The "hearse" tore out of the lot as I started for my car.

Bergerac served as the town morgue, so even though Paget collected the body, there was no guarantee that Bergerac would be holding # 8's funeral service.

I drove back, my thoughts all over the place.

Parishioner # 8 had lived two houses down from the rectory.

My window of opportunity to get into the house before his sister swooped down like a vulture was closing. For all I knew, his sister had already been notified of his death and was looting his place.

Or, she was en route, flying across the state on her broom.

Driving past Bergerac, I saw Paget unloading him from the truck while still turning it all over in my mind.

He'd been more interested in his sister not having the money than he was in how I spent it, or even if I cashed in the rare coins.

Was his sister as bad as he said?

Would she opt for direct cremation, then flush his ashes, and never spend a penny on a memorial for him (as he'd prophesized)?

Back on my street, I slowed to look at Parishioner # 8's house as I passed it.

No cars on the street or in the drive-way.

No lights on inside.

Should I keep my promise?

✂ -

Parked in the rectory garage, I looked at the envelope he'd given me the day of his operation.

I'd forgotten it in the car.

It contained a hand-written note of thanks, and mentioned the gift of cash he'd slipped inside.

Fifty bucks.

His way of saying thanks for my being there for him.

The thought occurred

no one needed to know he'd given me <u>ONLY</u> fifty.

Could've been more than fifty inside, with how the note was worded.

Had he counted on that?

Probably.

Tricky old coot (said affectionately).

Tucking the empty envelope into my coat's inner pocket, I decided I'd fulfill the spirit of what he wanted, and walked along the street to his house like I had every right to do so.

Found the spare key where he said it'd be.

Let myself into the empty home.

✂ -

His rare coin collection was worthless.

From what I could see the oldest coin was stamped 1902.

They'd all been cleaned and polished.

(Years ago, a parishioner at my city church who collected

rare coins had shared with me that once a coin is cleaned its value to a collector is decreased. Cleaning = erosion.)

I left them behind.

Not only would his sister not get much for the coins, but I'm sure he would've been delighted to think of her spending more money (in time and gas) trying to sell a worthless collection than what she'd actually make from the sale.

Besides, taking that large, album-sized container out of the house would be too obvious.

(Figured a pocketful of cash was more easily hidden.)

✄ -

My heart sank!

I'm rounding down; but he'd squirreled away over three thousand under that mattress!

✄ -

Stuffed all my pockets (and a paper shopping bag taken from the kitchen) with the cash.

Remade the guest bed.

Locked the door.

Replaced the key.

Left the house loaded down, and went straight to the church office.

I put as many of the highest denomination bills as I could into the envelope he'd addressed to me.

With his handwritten note inside, and his handwriting on the outside, I dropped the fattened envelope into the collection plate on the altar.

Returning to the rectory with the rest of the cash in that paper bag, I spent a sleepless night wondering what I was going to do with that extra two thou.

I wouldn't be able to use his money to buy him a tombstone without a lot of questions being asked.

✄ -

The Memorial for Parishioner # 8 had been scheduled with Paget.

I then did what no priest should ever have to do on a Sunday morning immediately after a worship service:

I lied my ass off to my parishioners!

✂ -

Before anyone had arrived in church, I'd snatched that first envelope out of the collection plate where I'd put it.

Getting to my office, I taped it to a second, larger, and fully stuffed, manila envelope.

I then placed both on the table where my tellers would find them when they counted the "plate take" after service.

From there I took my place at the double doors to greet people on their way in for Sunday morning worship.

✂ -

Parishioner # 43 – always on her way into church, has to ask with a smile, "We starting on time this morning, Father?"

It's not a dig at me, exactly.

She's trying to make a joke about that family which always comes in late.

Any dig at me has to do with my stalling for that family.

"You know Father, your starting late for them only encourages them to be even later. They plan on being late so everyone knows they're here."

(TICS: "That's Christian love for you – right there!")

✂ -

One minute before the bell rang, little over half the pews were empty, and the precentor (read: hymn leader), with twinkling eyes, and mischievous smile at the back of the sanctuary, about to process in, commented, "We're filled to capacity, better lock the doors!"

I like having someone around who prefers theatrical terms rather than always using a strictly religious frame of reference. And I think he liked having a priest who wasn't always correcting him to say things with a lofty pomp instead.

✂ -

For a nondescript Sunday, the service went good.
    You just wouldn't know it
            not if you only saw the frowns worn by the entire Sourpuss family.

✂ -

Standing at the double doors, I was shaking hands with people as they exit the sanctuary.

Parishioner # 3 kept her white hair cut short.

A former school teacher who used to love reading, knitting, and going for walks in the woods.

She's nearly blind (macular degeneration), and practically deaf (cheap hearing aids).

Looking at me all she sees is a big white blur with unkempt hair (I'd asked).

Her pet cat was taken away by a daughter who was worried she would trip over the animal curling around her cankles.

I met her staring gaze.

My heart breaks.

To love to read, and not able to see.

To love music, and not able to hear.

To want furry companionship, but be kept alone.

✂ -

Standing at the double doors, I was shaking hands with people as they exit the sanctuary.

You'd say Parishioner # 52 is a creepy-looking old lady with pale white skin, whiter hair, and uneven lipstick that leaves streaks and splotches on her withered lips.

Although not attracted to her specifically, she did sport that alluring look which has always got my motor running! So I can't help dubbing her with the name "Ohgeegee".

Story is, when her husband died seventeen years ago, she trashed a rainbow colored wardrobe and began to wear nothing but black, including a wide brimmed hat.

Parishioner # 52 hadn't yet met someone new, and has voluntarily stayed in mourning.

Some people don't let themselves move on.

(Ohgeegee – O-G-G – "Original Gothic Girl")

She slipped me a reminder note while requesting, "Father, could you stop by this week?"

"Certainly. Is there something you want to talk about?"

"I have a new cat, and I'd like you to bless him."

"Of course, I'd be delighted."

✂ -

Standing at the double doors, I was shaking hands with people as they exit the sanctuary.

Not one for prayers by phone, Parishioner # 73 asks me to visit and pray with him in person.

I don't mind that since I also feel prayer misses something when done by phone.

What I do mind – and strongly object to – is the way that, after I've extended a hand for him to shake, he pauses long enough to pick his nose before taking my hand in his.

✂ -

It's as I pray: "People are strange – God love'em!"

✂ -

I call our church tellers the "Count" and "Countess" and yes, they are a married couple – and no, they should not be counting weekly offerings and tithes <u>together</u>!

(But what do you do with a volunteer organization, when no one else wants the job?

(And you, as the priest, should never handle $$$$$.)

I stepped into my office to hear their questions, asked with raised voices. They often talk at such a volume (I usually expect to find them arguing when I enter the room, but they aren't; they're just both hard of hearing).

I explained, "The morning I took him to surgery, he gave me these envelopes and asked me to hold onto them. Just in case something happened to him, and he was sure it would."

The Count had a chin beard (no moustache), which he strokes when in deep thought.

"His letter doesn't say he wants it to be a restricted donation."

"No. He mentioned that to me in conversation the last time I spoke with him at the hospital. That we should spend it on getting a new sound system."

"He didn't write that down, neither."

"We've all heard him complain about it," the Countess interjected.

"I have," agreed the Count with a nod.

"Others have too," he added, and wrote it into the ledger as a restricted memorial.

Church donations: three types

1) "**Restricted**" which by state law has to be spent on whatever the donor specifies the money is to be used for (i.e. things like new hymnals, a sound system, new altar clothes, paving a parking lot, buying new light fixtures, whatever). Typically involves lawyers and wills.

2) "**Designated**" which is defined by the parish vestry on what they want to use it for. The vestry could later change their mind about what the money is spent on - if some other need ever comes up, but it would require a formal vote, and need to be entered into the parish minutes.

3) "**Undesignated**" is typically presumed to go into the general fund, and be used for operating expenses like staff salaries, utilities, maintenance, etc.

After counting out the three thousand plus "Restricted" donation, the Countess questioned, "What do we do about filing the form, since he doesn't write any of this down specifically?"

"If you just summarize our chat, write it out, then we'll all sign it, and file that away with the empty envelopes in case we're ever questioned."

"Sounds like a plan," the Count said in his deep, grumbly, gruff and loud, voice.

✂ -

I didn't celebrate like I'd gotten away with something.

Rather, I did something that made me feel even worse

I walked back over to Parishioner # 8's house.

✂ -

I'd never met his sister before and had only his perception of what she's like.

He wasn't wrong.

His house was stripped and emptied within four hours of my keeping my promise to him.

The movers and cleaners had been working all Sunday morning and his sister was there in the midst of it.

Horrible woman!

Told the movers to just trash everything in the portable dumpster set up in the drive-way!

✂ -

"We'll be having a memorial service –"

"I can't make it."

"If you tell me when you could, we can reschedule accordingly."

"I don't have time!" and she briskly moved away from me.

That is when I glanced down and noticed the heap of an emptied coin album in an almost-full trash can. Cover torn to shreds, pages ripped apart, emptied and discarded like nothing. The VHS of his favorite movie also in the bin.

Parishioner # 8 may not have known the first thing about collecting coins, but it had been a hobby he cared about (evidenced by the album he'd kept).

I felt badly I hadn't taken that album away with me when I'd had the chance.

I plucked up the VHS tape just to be defiant.

Walking away from a life being strip-mined for all valuables (the rest being obliterated), my conscience was clear about the money (and VHS tape under my jacket), but a guilty conscience followed me as I pondered, had he only had the surgery because I'd encouraged him to do so?

If I had not suggested he have it, would he still be alive?

In continual pain, but alive?

✂ -

During his funeral (at Bergerac, not in the church, thanks to his horrible sister) I spoke about how he'd been a good-natured retiree with a hearty belly laugh.

I spoke about how everyone called him "Andy" because his surname was Anderson, and how that nickname originated during his time in the Navy.

I mentioned how he was a widower, without kids, so Andy hadn't had anyone to drive him to doctor appointments, or to the hospital. That led to his asking me to take him since he'd surrendered his license earlier in the year (TICS: "Unlike some elderly who keep their licenses and still drive while being a hazardous risk to themselves and others!").

I didn't go into the details, but Andy was fascinated with the mob. Even though he'd only been one quarter

Italian, he had assumed that ethnic identity with the furor of a pure blood.

The Godfather was his favorite movie.

(I'd slipped his VHS copy into the – rented – casket with him.)

Other things I'd noted while writing his eulogy – but discarded when I gave it – had been how he wasn't one of Mrs Church's favorite people, and how he and his sister were deeply estranged.

(Could've said that last, since his sister couldn't be bothered to attend his funeral.

(Or even how she didn't want a military honor guard salute for him.

(After ransacking his bank accounts, I heard she was on the next plane going to Hawaii.)

She'd refused a public obituary in any newspaper, and there weren't even ten people at the service for her brother.

Horrible woman.

✂ -

Direct cremation is when a body is picked up where the person died and taken straight to a crematorium.

A direct funeral is to go straight into the casket and then onto the floor for visitation (although in all honesty, you don't want to go the direct funeral route, no matter how much you think you'll save).

✂ -

Paget joined me at the casket after everyone else had left.
Standing
with one hand set over the other in front of her
ankles together
her usual work pose.
(TICS: "Are those stockings pure silk?")
After a moment she inquired, "Were you two close?"
"No," I answered, looking at him in the casket. "No, not really. But I liked him."

Cutting corners, the horrible sister saved a buck by not having him embalmed, which left Andy looking sickly and emaciated rather than returning him to some semblance of health.

"I could hear that in the way you spoke about him."

"He reminded me of my Grandfather."

It was from Paget that I'd learned about
the honor guard being declined
a Hawaiian flight needing to be caught
and no, the funeral home didn't need to reschedule since she'd miss it no matter when it was scheduled for (and Andy's sister was alright with that.

(Knowing the sister wouldn't be there, Paget had arranged for the Honor Guard salute anyway – something that had me fall more in love with her than I already was!)

"She didn't seem too broken up about it," I added.

When dealing with family issues of every stripe, I find it helpful to remind myself that

a) you never know what goes on behind closed doors, and

b) that there's a side we show to the world, and the private side of ourselves we keep hidden (I wondered what secrets Patches-Paget – in her black dress, heels, and matching silk – still kept from me).

Paget stayed beside me a moment at the casket, offered a smile while telling me, "I don't think they've spoken to each other since their mother died ten years ago."

I was in my thoughts.

Didn't say anything.

A moment passed and my yearning to again do what we used to do, sparked within me.

Sputtered.

Faded.

Paget said, "You know, I used to always tear up whenever they play TAPS.

"Way I stopped that was, I bit my tongue. Literally, I have to bite down on it. And you know, that works for a lot of other things, too!"

With downcast eyes, and after another moment of silence, she added, "Take your time. I'll be in the office."

After a few moments I left Andy and went to leave.

Paused at her office door to let her know I was going.

"I wanted to say I'm sorry about the other day at the hospital." she said, moving out from behind the over-sized dark oak desk.

And so there'd be no mistaking her intent
she raised her eyebrows suggestively
while slowly lifting her skirt.
She turned.
Bent over,
elbows on her desktop.

✂- -

"Make sure you don't fall in love this time," she said firmly while refitting her black G-string.

Was that an apology
with a renewal of our old habits?

✂- -

Leaving Bergerac and walking back to church

I wondered: how many other mourners had she comforted in the way she'd just comforted me?

I realized there was no chance in hell I could ever not be in love with her, and not have my cooled ardor resurrected to life with the heat to rival a volcano.

Just had to remember
KEEP MY MOUTH SHUT!!!!
SAY NO MORE WORDS OF LOVE
TO HER!!!!

It'd be the only way to make sure she didn't run away on me again.

I was on a high
spring in my step

every Patches memory enfolding me
my Mistress has returned!
Things were back to the way they
should've always stayed!

✂ -

Patches-Paget.
The only woman in full color within my black and white world.

✂ -

With her back in my life, I could focus on her, and ignore everyone else.
Yes, that's an indication of what my addiction is like.
No rubber-necking.
No gawking.
No skirt-chasing.
No bar sex pick-ups.
No phone sex apps.
Total focus upon one person.
She, My Object of Desire,
Paget!

✂ -

II.

Never thought it would happen to me!
I often get so busy I forget to make the time to cook something, which means I'll be working, and suddenly realize I'm hungry and need to eat. But, hungry right then – can't wait!
So I started to stock up on assorted meal drinks (usually the ones for dieters or weight-lifters), and keep them on hand so I'm getting my nutrients each day. Down side of that is, I'll have a banana and hard-boiled egg

for breakfast, a too-large dinner around 8 or 9 p, and a protein/diet shake during the day.

That's why the church ladies keep telling me "You need someone to look after you."

Yet I tell them flat out, and even remind them til I'm blue in the face, that my doctor wants me to cut down on sugar so I don't become diabetic, and then, at the very next potluck, what happens?

"Father, have that last cookie. It's lonely!"

"Father, here's a piece of cake for you."

"Father, I made you this pie."

"Father, I got you this cannoli."

"Father, have you gained weight?"

So much for "being taken care of."

✂ -

Regarding my on-the-job-frustration; I think of it like this

19 out of 20 parish conflicts stem from

1) a detail-oriented control-freak church leadership

2) a congregation that is too easy-going

3) a priest who's more a "Spirit-of-the-Law" than a "Letter-of-the-Law" type.

Now, the congregation will never say anything against the leadership.

And the matriarchal (A-type) leadership all have broomsticks up the bum-bum, and get their panties in a twist over any error or oversight, which makes me wonder: if mistakes throw them out of whack that easily, then clearly their concern is not on worship, but on human shortcomings instead.

(TICS: "Do you only come to church to count my mistakes?")

✂ -

I'm thinking: perfectionism.

I'm thinking: shame-based upbringings.

I'm thinking, instead of taking offense and insult, maybe I should have more compassion for them and their – probably – unacknowledged childhood traumas.

✂ -

Parish Anniversary coming up!

This Sunday kicks off our month-long celebration of the building

all that went into it

and a memorial service for the original congregation.

Piece by piece, bit by bit, a reflection of all that went into making Saint Mary's Episcopal what it is.

The most distinctive feature of Saint Mary's is how the chancel area imitates a medieval cathedral.

I love this!

A pulpitum separates the chancel from the pews. That's the wall-to-wall fencing (with gate) you sometimes see cutting the altar area off from the congregation in the nave. Here it's made of ornately carved wood, and has six support beams, three on either side. It doesn't extend all the way up to the vaulted ceiling, so a wooden arch spans the part above the center opening, joining the two separate sides. That arch is capped by a carved wooden cross.

All along the top, are raised wooden accents.

The reason Saint Mary's has a very understated Communion railing is because it is fitted in-between those six pulpitum support beams.

Looking at the altar space from the pews, you can see the raised pulpit to the left side (thankfully missing the clergy snuffer overhead i.e. abat-voix, canopy, sounding board – basically, the thing that looks like a droppable lid), and the podium to the right (a carved eagle supporting the over-sized Bible on its out-stretched wings).

There are three short pews behind the podium, and the organist sits at the keyboard behind the pulpit, leaving her invisible to the congregation in the nave. Priest and

verger on one side, precentor, choir, and deacon (when/
if one visits) on the other. One acolyte on either side.
Everybody in robes, facing center (except the organist),
dying for a fan in the summer months, yet comfortable
all winter while the congregation shivers.

A total of five tiers lead up to the altar from the floor
of the nave.

The ancient architectural style has been imitated
perfectly, not that you'd expect such craftsmanship
and historical detail
in a small town church.

A testimony to how individual parishioners do make
a difference!

(Also hinted at how "High Church" the parish used
to be, but thankfully, isn't so any longer.)

If this church hadn't counted such gifted and skilled
wood workers in its congregation (like Mr Church, and his
father, and Grandfather), it may not look the way it does now.

✂ -

The two congregations may share a building, but by and
large, they don't intermix.

Best I can manage is an annual parish pot-luck
following a single 10 am worship service.

Didn't have to sell a joint luncheon as vigorously
as usual (thanks to it being held on the last Sunday of
the month, at the end of our month-long anniversary
celebration).

✂ -

For weekly mid-day prayers, I'd gotten the small group to
start using the Episcopal rosary as a prayer discipline. At
first there had been protests, but now that they've tried it,
and like it, the group expressed an interest in making it
a regular part of the service. I wondered if that was what
Parishioner # 21 wanted to talk about Monday when she
asked for a moment.

No, not about the rosary.

I pulled up a folding chair outside the altar railing for her to sit.

She was clearly nervous, running the wooden rosary through her stubby fingers, as she struggled with what she needed to say.

Seated inside the altar railing on that beautiful (and very uncomfortable) ornately carved wood chair (with very thin velvet cushion), I waited silently.

She was in great emotional distress.

Her personal preference had her move from the chair to the altar railing, where she knelt.

Protestants don't do "Confession" in closets behind a mesh screen; it's voluntary; not required, so we sit face to face, on either side of the railing to speak with an awareness that God is present between the priest and penitent. Protestant clergy do not offer absolution, rather, we remind people that God has already forgiven them.

The Church is not part of that equation, and if it is, it shouldn't be!

"It's tearing me up, inside!" she began.

Deep breath.

Baby steps.

One admission at a time.

"This isn't the sort of thing a priest should have to hear!"

Sobs.

Tissue dabbing her nose.

I waited.

She finally blurted out how she'd been having erotic dreams about another parishioner.

(TICS: "Is that all? I'm supposed to be shocked and appalled by that?")

✂ -

I leaned forward.

Offered her my hands.

I led the prayer, "Dear Lord, this is Diana, and I pray

your healing mercies be upon her this evening as she goes to sleep. May her hours of rest refresh her, and renew her sense of connection to you. I pray your Spirit watch over her, and guide her dreams to reveal your glorious presence in her life, rather than letting her dreams be about something else.

"Lord, help her to find you in all places during both her waking and sleeping, her dreaming, and her conscious thoughts. Please strengthen her as she struggles to stay within your light. Help her to continue to step out of the darkness, and deliver her from those powers, and presences, which seek to tear her away from you."

I closed the prayer, she thanked me profusely, dried her eyes, and left, leaving me to lock up, and check my cell phone for missed calls.

No calls.

I wondered how long it would take before someone needed a funeral.

✂ -

It's a sad truth – there is a clergy double standard.

People can be rude to us, but we can't be rude in return.

Another occupational hazard.

Parishioner # 10, what an effing – hold on (thanks for reminding me), Jesus died on the cross for them the same as he did for me.

(TICS: "Jesus loves you, the rest of us just think you're a total asshole."

(Sums it up perfectly.)

✂ -

Most people seem to think that as a Priest, I eat, sleep, shit, and breathe religion.

They'll give me gifts of religious art work, and books of faith that they've read.

But I don't decorate with pictures of a bloody Christ hanging on a cross in anguish (the more pained and tormented you see the Christ, the older the iconography is. With the softening of sensibilities over time, the expression of agony on the Christ figure attached to the cross has lessened). I thank parishioners for their generosity and thinking of me, but really

I don't have time to read their books

in addition to all the books the bishop wants his clergy to read

nor even those I actually want to be reading

✂ -

Another example of where my personal interest caused a conflict with my professional image

never criticize

any artwork

decorating your church

because you never know whose family donated it!

✂ -

Flashback:

Do you remember back to when I had to come here for an interview?

(First step in the "Call System" process: you post your resume at the diocesan office and website, second is that a delegation from an interested parish "Search Committee" will visit you at the church you're serving, get a sense of your style for leading worship, how you preach and present. Get some gossip on your track record there. That delegation then returns to their own church, gives a report, and if that Vestry concurs, you get asked to come to their parish for a formal interview.

(Now, the bishop could appoint a priest somewhere, but usually, they're ineffective leaders, hired to keep the office chair warm, and they only live to pass the buck. In cases like this I'm sure they let the various parish Search Committees do their thing just so the bishop doesn't have to worry about anything other than his golf game.)

After my interview with the Saint Mary's Vestry, I was asked to step out of the room for them to vote on me.

After a (nearly) unanimous vote, I was accepted as their new parish priest.

(I wasn't told who had issue with my credentials as a Pastoral Counselor, but I've since gotten a good guess on who's threatened I might deduce their sex addiction secrets ...

and it's not who you'd expect!

(That's the quirk. A lot of people who want to keep their sex addiction a secret will posture as though sex addiction is not a real thing.)

I accepted their job offer and after saying the interview's closing prayer, was given the grand tour by the church warden, Mrs Felicity Church (not her real name). The tour began in the sanctuary where she stopped suddenly. From the middle of the center aisle we paused to take a look at the stained glass triptych windows high above the pulpit, the center one showing a figure in white standing before a kneeling figure. The two windows on either side had one figure each and extended the landscape.

"That's Simon Peter, with James and John in the side windows, and Jesus at the Transfiguration in Matthew 17, Mark 9, and Luke 9. Gorgeous, isn't it? They don't make windows like that any more."

"No, they don't. And restorers aren't easy to find, either."

Mrs Church turned around to draw my attention to the back of the sanctuary and the over-sized portrait of Saint Mary hanging there.

Story goes (and I didn't know any of this at the time): back after the church building had first been erected, one of its leading parishioners (Mr Church's Great-Grandfather) came across this oil painting while overseas, and brought it back for the church (at great personal expense, including shipping) just so the new building would have a portrait of its namesake. Mrs Church had delighted in telling me, with a wide smile, "This is Mary as an old woman. Here, you can see the Communion bread she's taking out to those early believers. I think this would've been about the time that Paul was ..."

That was the exact moment when I fell from her good graces

she stopped smiling

and had become my "nemesis" as you like calling her.

(Four minutes after she had voted in favor of my calling to be her new parish priest!)

It wasn't because I corrected her.

It was because I spoiled her delight in that cherished, and beloved, heirloom painting by noticing the details of
- the solitary figure's tanned complexion
- her long ankle-length white hair
- the red cloak she's wearing
- the desertscape in the background.

Open mouth, insert ...

✂ -

I should've known better, yet still made the mistake:

"Actually, I think this is Saint Mary of Egypt. I say that because she's commonly shown in religious paintings as wearing red and having three loaves of bread, which she took with her into the desert for her solitary retreat."

Her story goes:

Saint Mary of Egypt was a wild woman who traded sex for personal favors. Her *vita* says she refused monetary payment for sex and was simply a promiscuous beggar.

Blur the tradition over time and you get: Saint Mary the Egyptian prostitute.

Not Saint Mary the mother of Jesus.

An honest mistake.

Mr Church's Great-Grandfather had probably never ever heard of Saint Mary of Egypt.

So, it won't surprise you to hear that Mrs Church has been trying to have that painting removed ever since I started at this parish.

To date, she hasn't told anyone why she wants to have that over-sized portrait taken down. And as a kind of unspoken concession/olive-branch, I haven't mentioned the mistaken identity of the portrait's subject to anyone else.

Maybe she thought I would open my big mouth again. I didn't.

Blunder in once – my bad.

Blunder twice – careless.

Blunder thrice – unpardonable!

I learned from souring Mrs Church's delight in the family heirloom.

And given how many relatives she has in the parish, I'm surprised no action has ever been taken to remove that painting, which is why I'm always happy to see it hanging there every Sunday morning in worship.

A secret too shameful to share?

Seriously?

It's not that big a deal!

Saint Mary of Egypt is still a "Saint Mary."

✄ -

I watched Mrs Church bite her tongue at the vestry meeting when mention of the portrait as "Mary the mother of Jesus" came up during a recap of our on-going anniversary celebration plans.

I leaned forward in my chair, and suggested a gentle reminder: "We really should remember not to invest too much in that identity, because it can get very close to idolizing that identity. The Church should not become an idol to replace God. Remember in the Old Testament how the Israelites came to worship the bronze serpent and in worshipping that device of salvation, forgot who their salvation came from."

Yes, I B-S-ed my way through, and Mrs Church at least nodded.

Maybe I wasn't such a screw-up in her eyes?
That my discretion could be trusted?
That I wasn't a threat to her family's reputation.
That I cared enough to let her save face for her family?
One can hope.

✄ -

"It would've been so nice if we could've had the bishop come out to join us in our celebration!" Cathedral Sister # 1 lamented to the whole Vestry.

It was no secret she blamed me for the lack of a guest in the big chair, as though I'd forgotten to make a formal invitation.

(TICS: "The hour drive back from Saint Mary's would only make them late for their Sunday Golf game. So it doesn't surprise me no one from D-House wants to come out.")

✄ -

Flashback:

My favorite class in seminary.

Several classmates ended up dropping out of the class, and I'd started to think of it like that Agatha Christie mystery where the ten people are gathered together, then picked off one at a time.

Who in the class of 18 would drop (out) next?

(At the end of four years, only 8 of us graduated.)

We had a liberal professor who offered our class a challenge: "Try reading the Bible in a new way.

"For example, don't open it with the preconceived idea that sex is bad or evil. But start reading the Bible as though sex is a good thing. And see what that gets you."

Most of my classmates wanted to argue with her about the authority of Jesus' statement in Matt v. 27-28 ("Look with Lust in the eye, and you've already done it").

Me? I've always liked the academic exercises, and the open-mindedness of my professors willing to encourage free thinking, rather than quell it the way the Church does.

What I found was that half the time the Bible mentions sex it's in a positive way. Half of the time it mentions sex in a negative way, but of those negatives, sex is not discussed as the sex act itself, but for how sex was used by pagan fertility cults in pagan worship led by temple prostitutes.

✂ -

Given Mrs Church's reaction to the portrait of Saint Mary of Egypt hanging up in the church sanctuary - instead of it being Mary Mum - you can understand

I don't dare go up against a prudish church matriarch by preaching a sex-positive ethic from the pulpit.

I don't believe the church roof would cave in

but I do suspect the bishop would be prodded to fire me for it.

✂ -

Not exactly a heresy, but certainly a brow furrower.

It's palpable!

This notion that you don't talk about sex in church.

It's a presence that casts a long shadow!

No sex talk in church.

It's a tangible – invisible – wall!

Yet sex is repeatedly mentioned in the Bible!

The Church's immovable legacy: sex – don't enjoy it.

SEX – don't talk about it, otherwise you might want to do It!

As though talking about sex is the same as physically having sex.

Effing insane!!

✂ -

So many cling to the falsehood that if they have sex then they can't also have religion.

Either/or.

One or the other.

That's a bullshit ideal.

Way way back the earliest Christians embraced a theology of the body being a weakness which drags the soul down into the muck and mire of condemnation.

Yet there was also a belief that, through the body, one's spirituality could be enhanced through sexual activity.

But the seething masses could not be controlled by the minority unless the masses were convinced they had something to lose (eternal soul), and only the minority (Church) could provide the means to never lose it.

Sadly, the vilification of sex was just about numbers (read: a membership scheme).

✂ -

Sex Addiction is a thing!

Client # 7's rant reminded me of those frumpy, f-ugly women at the Annual Convention who protest porn out of jealousy.

They never want sex.

Yet they demand their husbands not ever have sex without them.

Basically: limit the sexual options a man has.

Such was how my client was feeling.

Lot of anger for his wife.

She clings to the idea that if they have sex then they can't also have religion.

Not both.

Never both!

✂ -

Saint Augustine of Hippo (354-430 AD) prayed it best:
"I had prayed to you for chastity and said, 'Give me chastity and continence, but not yet.' For

> *I was afraid that you would answer my prayer*
> *at once, and cure me too soon of the disease of*
> *lust, which I wanted satisfied, not quelled."*

✂ -

Sounds like sex addiction to me (long before sex addiction was even known to be a thing).

Don't presume that the church's sex-negative perspective is all there is, and that you've already heard everything.

You haven't.

There is a sex-positive perspective in the Bible which is just as valid, yet not widely known anymore.

There're reasons why the Church has been struggling with sexuality for centuries.

I think that struggle is still around because it is based on a misperception that gets all the attention.

A gross misunderstanding!

A despicable membership campaign.

Which has become so internalized (over time, and through every generation since it started), that it's mutated into far more than it was, and has become more insidious than ever before.

✂ -

Too much of anything good becomes bad.

There will always be those who abuse anything good.

So:

> moderation is key.

✂ -

Sex addiction is a thing!

Client # 25, about to leave again for college, wrapping a dish scrubbing pad around himself while self-pleasuring because he thought the abrasive texture would scratch and be so unpleasant that he'd be able to stop masturbating.

No such luck.

Too moist to be wholly unpleasant.

That he kept using the pad indicated how badly he wanted to quit his behavior.

That he was thinking of moving on to using sandpaper ... !?!

(TICS: "That would be a lot drier and more abrasive.")

(He was thinking out loud, that since the abrasive pad was not working, he needed to try something dry. If I seriously thought he'd do it, I'd have to involve authorities about the potential for self-harm.

(Just remember self-flagellation – the medieval practice of monks and nuns to harm their flesh so they'd keep their souls pure. A deep, deep shame that they did not understand how the body works of its own accord and not because of demonic influences way back when.)

Well, the Church's enduring legacy on sex ...

How do you argue with that?

✂ -

I always enjoy the country nights for how quiet, and peaceful they are.

Cold nights with clear skies, there are more stars than you'd ever imagine.

The rectory and church buildings are so old they retain the summer heat well into the Fall, and they hold onto the winter cold well into Spring.

Up the road from the village square, in any direction, you'll find a dozen floral shops, plant nurseries, vegetable and fruit stands, cows grazing in horse fields.

Every so often a cow will get out of its pasture and linger at a road-side ditch.

A little more often you'll see horses being ridden down the streets in the village square as the riders like to get them out of the stables to go someplace a little different.

And then there's the poultry running loose, and crossing roads.

✂ -

III.

One of the larger portions of a priest's job is research.
    So you have to love doing it
        being in a library
           going through old books
               looking up facts
                  double-checking things
                     basically, you should enjoy always
being on the hunt for more and more knowledge.

(And have a yen for sexy librarians before your former Mistress turns back up.)

When I suffer the sin of greed, it's this – I'm greedy for knowledge.

And in a vocation which prizes workaholism; when it comes time for me to do research on something interesting, I do tend to overwork when I know I shouldn't.

✂ -

Regarding sermons, they don't come out pre-written, unless you want to cheat by going online to any of the websites which offer someone else's sermon for download.

But here's my "professional pride" showing through – I don't like doing "reruns."

Because I enjoy research and writing, I've made that a personal policy.

I stick to the three-year lectionary cycle as much as possible, that way, if I'm ever stuck, and I have no other choice, I can whip out one of my sermons from years ago, and preach it again.

My homiletics professor at seminary claimed that sermons are like a meal.

You don't remember what you had for dinner, but you remember you ate.

People won't remember a sermon, but they'll remember sitting through something.

Having that archive of oldies-but-goodies eliminates a lot of the stress of worrying (in case of a week that's so

busy I don't have time to write one up fresh) that I won't
have a message to preach every Sunday.

It may be a "rerun"

but I can honestly claim that every sermon I
preach is still "all mine!"

✂ -

My Myers-Briggs type is INTP-A (the "Logician" –
Assertive).

My Enneagram type is a 5 (the "Investigator").

I come up as belonging to a minority of the
population (3%).

(My "Lovetype" match is the INFJ – labeled "the
Mystic Writer" and as an Enneagram type 4, belongs to
that type which is just 2% of the population.)

(And you won't find many of my type/category in
ministry either.)

I favor Narrative Theology and Narrative Therapy.

I have a journalist's cynicism.

An artist's appreciation for beauty.

(And I've been told that if the church thing doesn't work
out, I could always get a job as Seth Rogan's stunt double.)

So, for a guy like me

with my Free Will intact

- I'm curious.
- Inquisitive.
- Question authority.
- Never happy with the institutional
  status quo.
- Nor with accepting things in blind
  obedience without question.
- I wonder about the "What If" possibilities.

Don't you?

✂ -

I'm a bachelor

working within a culture that broadcasts the message

I'm not allowed to have sex
unless I get married and want to make babies
(why condemn those who are single – with no desire to
procreate – to a prison of sexlessness?).

The great irony is, Paul extolled the
virtues of being single yet the church (which should
encourage and support celibacy), looks at unmarried
priests like we're all kiddie fiddlers or homosexuals.

No, I'm not looking to excuse my non-marital sexual
hijinks through eisegesis
(making it seem like the Bible says what I want
it to say)
but that through good exegesis
(what the Bible actually does say)
I'm calling the status quo into question!

Outside of the Bible, our modern views of sex have their
roots in the attitudes of Paul (a sex addict), Saint Augustine
(another sex addict), Thomas Aquinas (yet another sex
addict), and Saint Jerome (a homosexual). Not to mention
all the popes, cardinals, bishops, priests and televangelists
who have been preaching a sex-negative perspective based
on the faulty premise of others since the near beginning!

Again, if it's in the Bible, then shouldn't we be talking
about it?

✂ -

Mary Magdalene's Day.
July 22nd.
The Church's Feast Day for the most celebrated
working girl in history.

Who says religion can't be titillating?

✂ -

In Sunday's sermon I talked about how
it wasn't until 574 AD, that Pope Gregory the Great
preached a sermon in which he declared Mary Mag had
been a prostitute (what other explanation is there for a

single woman with money? Lk viii. 3 – a widow with an inheritance wouldn't stay single for long).

It is widely accepted that she came from the town of Magdala, which had a reputation for being a wild, happening, and sinful place.

✂ -

Yes! YES YES YESY YES!!!
I do feel trapped a lot of the time!
Imprisoned!
Stifled!
That's what happens when you disagree with the status quo in a system you're part of. So don't envy me. I'm just happy that I have someone I can be honest with, and tell my thoughts to.

Thanks again for letting me!

Still, let me state flat out that I'm not trying to plant seeds of doubt, I'm merely raising questions that I hope will get you

thinking things through

to get a sense of how you feel about what you believe.

These are the kind of steps I took on my seminary journey to grow closer to God.

Maybe, by looking for your answers, you'll be helped to do the same.

✂ -

My job requires me to be friendly with everyone
(and yes, there are lonely people who take advantage of that).

Just bear in mind, that while I'm being "friendly" I would not say that also means I count everyone as being my "friend".

Many parishioners probably feel closer to me than I feel towards them.

In my seven years at Saint Mary's there have been two couples who wanted to think of themselves as my best friends.

The constant invites to their homes

the continual Bible studies

the seats saved at tables during Coffee Hour.

Conversations that aren't about anything other than religion.

No conception of how I don't always want to talk shop.

You see, it isn't me they want around

it is The Collar, pure and simple.

Sure, they said I could stop by and visit unannounced, and that I could tell them whatever secrets I wanted to talk about. But the reality is

any crack in the shell

or scratch in the veneer

and they get uncomfortable.

Soon as I'm not The Collar, religious addicts aren't interested in anything I have to say.

And you know that's the case because they rush to interrupt with platitudes and lame Bible references as though that's the magic cure-all to make everything alright.

They don't want intelligent conversation.

Once they realized I wouldn't be making weekly visits (look at my schedule, it is just not possible to let any one family monopolize my time) both couples stopped coming to Saint Mary's.

It's not about me, for who I am.

It's all about me, wearing The Collar.

And about their needing to be seen as my inner circle, as though I'm JC and they're my most trusted apostles or something!

Fuck that, and the horse it rode in on!

Now, those people I do consider my "friends" will have no expectations of my thoughts and behaviors. I can "let my hair down" around them; and they can listen to me rant and vent about my job, even read these letters, and never respond with

"You shouldn't be feeling that way!"
"How can you say that?"
"You don't really think that way, do you?"

People with those reactions to my innermost thoughts and ideas will hold the expectation that I embody the stereotype, rather than my being allowed to be myself.

For them, I'm my job (read: "The Collar"), and not a human being.

So thank-you
for letting me be me.

✂ -

11 am

Standing at the double doors, I was shaking hands with people as they exit the sanctuary.

Parishioner # 12 cried out the loudest when the podium was moved.

As the number of choir members grew, the furniture needed to be rearranged.

Call it "Growing Pains" if you like.

Some prefer to have a large choir.

Some didn't care where the podium was.

Yet Parishioner # 12, along with a few others of the grey-haired guild, had major issues when they needed to start turning to the far right (rather than looking to the mid-right) to see the lector.

✂ -

You hear it in churches all the time.

The seven deadliest words.

The first objection to any change
"We've never done it that way before!"

Bear in mind, the objection was not so much the physical placement of the podium, but that moving it meant change

207

and change means something is now different from how it used to be.

✂ -

Standing at the back doors, I was shaking hands with people as they exit the sanctuary.

Parishioner # 41 quilted for a hobby.

She'd made a blanket large enough to overhang a king-sized bed.

Donated it to the church raffle for a fund raising prize.

Parishioner # 41 was devastated when it didn't go for more than two hundred.

After all her careful work, she'd expected it would fetch at least three times as much.

(The picture of her holding it spread open, which ran on the local newspaper's front page, didn't draw the raffle crowd we'd hoped for.)

✂ -

Standing at the double doors, I was shaking hands with people as they exit the sanctuary.

I took the opportunity to pray it's not too soon to be asking our resident "Roadkill Lady" if she would mind making something for the parish Pot Luck next week, as she'd only just started coming back to Sunday morning worship services.

"I'd be happy to, if you're sure you want me to."

"I'd love it if you did!"

Her smiled brightened, and I could sense her heart lifted.

I smiled.

She left.

I knew I'd have to make a show of being seen to eat whatever it was she brought in.

I'd have to go first.

Overlook the uncomfortable glances.

Ignore the clearing throats.

Shush all the, "Father are you sure you want to be eating *that*?" sort of comments.

(TICS: "Woodchuck and Skunk Soufflé. Yum!!" – not really.)

I had a woman willing to come back to church, and as The Collar, I needed to set the example of welcoming her back fully.

Free and clear from the rumors and gossip which surrounded her.

Isolated her.

For me, this is ministry: extending to others the love of God by showing my human acceptance of them as people.

✂ -

6

Pentecost (v)

I.

It doesn't take a pervert to see how so many positions, phrases, and actions, are used/done in church which are sexually suggestive.

Religious kink and fetishes (Pecattiphilia, Homilophilia, and Theophilia to name a few).

Take kneeling (for example):

> Kneel in prayer.
> Kneel to give oral.
> Kneel at the altar railing as a humble penitent.
> Kneel as a BDSM submissive before their dominant.
> Kneel for Confession.
> Kneel to align the "naughty bits" for doggie style.

(TICS: "As I say, 'Crying out "Oh God!" in bed does, indeed, count as prayer!'")

✂ -

YES!!! It's a prayer of celebration for the joys of our physical bodies as a part of God's creation.

God created us with an enjoyment of sexual activity, so don't tell me **only a sex addict would say that**!!

You need to divorce Church morals from Divine truth.

(Which can be confusing, given our twenty-first century sex-negative view of sex beside Church celebrations like July 22nd and October 8th as Saint Mary the Harlot's Day.)

✂ -

Every so often there's a client and the best way to help them is to offer education.

(Psychoeducation through bibliotherapy whenever possible.

(Provided the client reads and would read the books I loan. Too often though, I'll loan out a book then never get it back.)

Educated thinking will – hopefully – counteract any "distorted" thinking.

Distorted thinking is when irregular behavior is normalized in a client's mind (read: mistaken for being socially acceptable and/or common).

For a sex addict, distorted thinking is when they convince themselves that their waitress isn't being nice to them because it's her job. They're thinking the waitress is being nice to them because the waitress wants their body, and so they respond to that distortion of perception with inappropriate behavior (stalking) and/ or verbal comments (harassment) because they cannot concieve that the waitress is just scrambling for tips, not sex partners.

Yes, there are lonely people who mistake the friendliness of a waitress as flirtatious interest, but the difference is not in making that mistake (or in leaving their phone number written on a napkin). The difference is that distorted thinking will lead the customer to camp out in the parking lot to wait for the waitress when their shift ends. The addict will not see anything wrong with that because – in their mind – the waitress signaled an interest and desire in seeing them again.

The addict doesn't perceive a distinction in-between customer service and personal interest, plus, after perceiving (what they imagine is) the slightest interest, their responses carry them overboard in their attempts to seduce their object of desire.

This can make them very scary.

Although most of them are very harmless, there are those addicts who don't hear "No" whenever/however clearly the word is spoken.

Like client # 13: "She doesn't mean it!"

"She told you she wasn't interested," I pointed out.

"By phone!"

"You said by e-mail."

"And by text, all of them, but she doesn't mean any of that!"

"Why not?"

"Because there's someone behind her, with a gun to her head, making her say that!"

I asked, "A gun to her head?"

(TICS: "Don't you hear how crazy you sound?")

"Not literally, hopefully! But making her do it, that's what's important!"

See what I mean?

Not **gullable**.

Deluded.

Distorted thinking does not let him see reality, nor how deperately he's grasping for straws beyond his reach. In his mind, that "gun-to-the-head" theory was completely possible, even if unlikely, it was still possible.

Like, one-in-a-bazillion possible.

But that barely-even-possible is exaggerated in his thinking to be an absolute.

Sex addiction is a thing!

✂ -

A large part of what I love about parish ministry is that the days are seldom the same.

Some days start much earlier than others, and some a little later.

Some are non-stop activity, some are laid back and spent reading.

Spring to summer is typically slower paced, and that's why I haven't had much to do lately, and certainly not as much to tell you as usual. Usually it'll be back-to-school time when things pick back up. Labor Day, as the last summer hurrah, right?

(Last year my summer was filled with funerals and Cyranose.)

Funny how the circadian rhythms work, isn't it?

As a person, I'm a night owl and hate mornings.

DSPS (Delayed Sleep Phase Disorder).

But as a priest people presume I'm a morning person.

"This is the country, everyone's a farmer," Mrs Church had argued my second year. "People want to see you out and about in the morning!"

By which, she meant, one parishioner in particular, wanted to bump into me at the post office every morning because that is how she interacted with my predecessor (heaven forbid the new priest change things and not start his day before the crack of dawn!).

Turns out, that parishioner got over it.

And this business about farmers?

Kelly's family are the only farmers in the congregation.

Pray with me, "People are strange – God love'em!"

✂ -

Anyway, boundaries. That's where I was going.

My office hours start later than for most folks only because I don't punch a clock, leave the office, and have alone time after 5pm. More often than not I'm at church in meetings or study groups until 8:30-9pm.

Just because I am on salary does not mean I work 24/7.

Gone are the days when a priest could plan on working in the morning, and at night, but have the afternoon off in-between. Now it's non-stop with all sorts of crap that has little to do with parish ministry out in the sticks.

The institutional Church with it's one-size-fits-all approach.

Everything is arranged and planned with the large urban churches in mind.

(TICS: "'Benign Neglect' as my seminary mentor called it.)

Stop me if I said this already, but I'm not a workaholic.

Not because it irritates the Churches and Cathederal Sisters, but because I know when I need to stop.

When I need time for myself.

When I need to rest.

But I'm a minority in the clergy since most are workaholics.

(TICS: "More power to them.")

When they collapse from exhaustion or get hospitalized, I'll still be going.

Slow and steady.

Pacing myself.

Gotta have your priorities in line.

Ironic since, as a bachelor, I don't have a family suffering my absence, and yet how many clergy have family problems (infidelity, abandonment, separation, divorce) because of clergy workaholism and poor boundaries?

Sorry (not really), but I refuse to run myself ragged for anyone.

And if any of the Godfather's staff question me, I'll remind them of their constant lecturing about "self care." I'm actually doing what they recommend I do, yet they dare fault me for it because I had to let something slide, so their latest report didn't get filed in time?

As I've said, pastoral ministry first.

Ecclesiastical shenanningans (i.e. their endless, pointless, reports) last.

The motto I try to live by:

"People before paperwork."

✂ -

"Inkie" the black cat from hell, hissed.

Took repeated swipes at me as we went through the

agenda for Convention since this year will be her first as Saint Mary's lay delegate.

Her devil cat bit a chunk from my hand when Parishioner # 52 wasn't looking.

I thought black cats were supposed to be laid-back, and easy-going.

Don't they have a reputation for being "lap fungus"?

I've heard they settle in on a person and don't move.

Maybe on my parishioner's always-black lap, but I couldn't help wondering as I left "Are you sure this rescue doesn't need an exorcism instead of a blessing?"

✂ -

Funerals don't depress me near as much as nursing home visits.

At the one out here, there's this alcove

it's like a coat room inside the fire escape exit to the courtyard.

Lined with chairs instead of coat racks.

Old recliners that no longer recline.

Threadbare.

Soiled.

Musty smelling.

Urine soaked.

Every time I've been by to visit someone, the same elderly folks are sitting in the same ratty chairs.

("Ratty-ratty-rat-rat" as Patches said that time – we were against the outside of my car, in a movie theater parking lot when a rat scurried over our feet.)

I imagine these old folks are parked there in those chairs every day.

Arguing with raised voices if someone takes their seat.

Passing down the hallway, it saddens me, seeing them there.

Every time.

Every damn time!

The same faces.

In the same chairs.
Wasting away.
Waiting for death.
I question their quality of life.
But then
    budget cuts
        staff shortages
            state politicians regulating everything.
I imagine the underpaid and overworked staff probably find their lives are made easier by setting someone someplace where they won't make a fuss.

Where they'll sit quietly all day long.

And not run away.

    Life as a fixture.

✂ -

Elderly woman walking down the hall in her slacks.

Ploppings of excrement pressed and dropping out of her pant leg with every step
    leaving a trail of plump, squished, plump, squished, etc. on down the hallway.

Just another day at the nursing home.

✂ -

Parishioner # 5 is a crusty, opinionated, old guy who is difficult to talk to.

He doesn't see anything in any way other than his own.

Surprising for WWII veteran, who'd served in multiple foreign countries, he's unable to put himself in another's shoes to imagine their perspective.

(I hear from other parishioners how his personality had really changed since he had his heart attack ten years ago.)

He complains about the changes he's seen happen to the church over the years.

Good thing he doesn't have a cane.

I'd be worried he'd be taking a swing at me; he gets that worked up.

Story is: he had some Huguenot ancestors who had been persecuted and murdered by Papists for religious differences. His hatred of all things remotely Roman Catholic made sense.

Thing is though, that since Saint Mary's has a few features his home parish hadn't had back when he was growing up, Saint Mary's can't possibly be a truly Episcopalian Church in his mind, despite the red double doors fronting the village square. As though his ("High Church") home parish alone defined all things Episcopalian, and that no other Episcopal Church ever could be as authentically Episcopalian.

(Episcopal church doors are painted red to symbolize Christ's blood [through the blood we enter salvation]; or the blood of the martyrs; or to brag that the mortgage was paid off; or as a sign to show off we're different; or even because it references Exodus xii. 23. Why ever it started, it's now church tradition [which yes, some churches break by painting their doors some other color].)

Maybe he had a point with the décor, the genuflections, the rituals, the rites, the incense, and the pew calisthenics.

(TICS: "You wanna spout 'Denominational Pride' then you tell me, what exactly does the label 'Episcopalian' even mean?")

✂- -

He'd been watching a Western on his small TV when I'd arrived, and from that we started talking about movies. From westerns (his favorite), to noir (my favorite) to silent movies (mutual appreciation, though not a first choice).

Took him up and off about how "Birth of a Nation" (1915) has "way too many parallels with today's culture.

"More than any of us want to admit!

"If you can't break away from racial politics, you'll be offended. But if you watch it as a good-vs-evil story, then it works just fine! The good guys are white, the bad guys are black. Like the cowboys in the old Westerns. White hats, and black hats. It's one hundredth anniversary wasn't too long ago.

"They won't let me watch it down in the rec room!"

Waving his copy of the DVD at me, "Can I watch it at the church?!"

(TICS: "How? It's a shame you voted against the proposal for a wide screen. What'd you call it? Oh, right! 'Jumbotron.' You said Jesus didn't need one on the mount, so the church didn't need one now.")

I was familiar with the movie.

✂ -

Flashback:

My Film Studies class in college had been taught by a professor who refused to watch any movie which manipulated him into rooting for the KKK. Of course, that only encouraged me to go out, rent it, watch it, and form my own opinion.

DW Griffith, the film's director, also made a movie called "The White Rose" (1923). In which a priest gets a young woman pregnant and abandons her.

Wrote my final paper on "White Rose" because I'd heard that The Scarlet Letter was another one of those pieces of fiction the professor avoided.

✂ -

Parishioner # 5 does still get to church every so often, but only when his family decides to get up early and take him.

He's in the nursing home because his kids just don't think he should be living alone. Which he wouldn't have been, since he and Parishioner # 7 had spoken to me about doing their wedding back during my first year at St Mary's.

But then, with his getting remarried, his kids would've been out of their inheritance when # 5 dies.

Heaven forbid!

✂ -

Kids, to keep themselves happy (and protect every penny of their inheritances), need him to stay single.

✂ -

Mrs Church raged over the phone: "Father! I've just heard some disturbing news!"

"Which is?"

"You're not letting someone use the church! Shouldn't it be available to anyone who wants to use it? Don't you think a member of over seventy-five years should be allowed?! That's what I think!"

Calmly, I asked, "Do you know what movie he wants to show?"

She screeched, "I don't see how that matters! Silent movies! Buster Keaton. Charlie Chaplain. That sort! He's a veteran! He's a member of the church! He should be allowed to use the fellowship hall!"

That was her stand, and I was amused by the irony.

I'd expected to be the one advocating in favor of a movie screening while she'd be the opposition. Rather, I tried anticipating her reaction, had responded accordingly, and still brought her wrath down upon me!

(TICS: "There's no way I can win with you, is there?")

"If he wants to watch a patriotic movie about history, we should let him! That's what I think. I'm about to make up some flyers to post around town."

✂ -

Sometimes, God pulls a fast one.

✂ -

Once she came up for air, I said, "If we're going to do this, then we'll need to do it as a 'double-feature,' and call it 'silent movie night' that way, what we're showing gets down-played."

"Father! I don't think too many people will turn out for it anyway."

(The temptation to instigate and provoke was too great for me to bear!)

She'd never seen the movie.

Probably never heard about it.

"Father. I think we should let him show his movie. I already told him he could."

(TICS: "Of course you did!"

(One of her guiding lights is that we should never do anything that will upset those parishioners who are in their "golden years" which is really just her defending her preference to not let anything change, since the older folks will protest each and every change anyway.)

As if brainstorming, and thinking out loud, I went with, "As a double feature, let's start with *the Tramp*, and then we'll show *Birth of a Nation*. That way, hopefully, no one will really stick around long enough to get to the part when the KKK rides into town. That sound alright?"

I heard a pin drop.

She stammered after a momentary inability to form any words at all: "The – Kay. Kay. Kay?"

It's like I could hear her stomach sinking with her falling jaw.

"They – they're in the movie?"

"Not the first half."

I was enjoying myself too much, I know.

I reigned it it.

You'd be proud.

"I only saw the movie once. Back in college. It's three hours long. But I do remember that the second half of the movie is about how they formed to rebel against political corruption. They're the heroes by the end."

She burst, "WE CAN'T SHOW A MOVIE LIKE THAT!"

(TICS: "A movie like *'that'* – priceless!)

"The nursing home won't let him show it there, and it really is a classic. Cinema history. For a silent movie, it was way ahead of its time as far as how movies were made back then. The Civil War fight scenes were the *Saving Private Ryan* of their time."

(I shouldn't need to remind you I'm not a Klan supporter, but do you think she could tell I was enjoying myself?)

Mrs Church protested, "WE CAN'T LET HIM INVITE THE WHOLE TOWN TO WATCH THAT IN OUR CHURCH!"

(TICS: "But he's a long-time member. Shouldn't he be allowed? Seventy-five years, and you did already give him permission and you are making up some flyers.")

She decreed, in her wisdom, "*You* need to tell him he can't!"

(TICS: "I already told him he couldn't. But then you went ahead and told him he could.")

✂ -

I know, I know.

I'm a horrible example.

I shouldn't think such things.

I shouldn't say stuff like that.

I shouldn't be human.

Yada yada yada. Blah blah blah.

But damn, if her discomfort didn't make up for all the years of Church business I've already endured!

✂ -

Personally, I had no objection to his watching that movie
in church
on our bitty 20 inch TV
in the fellowship hall.

But the thing is, he wanted to invite everyone in the community to a movie night so he wouldn't have to sit through all three hours alone.

I was just trying to avoid the picketing and protesting.

✂ -

A letter came today, with the diocesan seal on it.

My stomach sank in dread, like always.

(You remember that panic you had as a kid, every time an adult yelled out your name?

(Or whenever we got called to the principal's office?

(Like that.)

The Bishop's signature at the bottom.

Not an excusal from attending Convention.

Damn!

(They never grant two excusals two years in a row.)

Not a complaint from any parishioners

thankfully.

Not a disciplinary letter

fortunately.

It was much worse.

Read it through.

Twice.

He's personally asking me to take a seat on the Diocesan Discernment Team.

My eyes rolled.

(TICS: "More meetings? Are you effing serious??!!!")

My acceptance to be announced at Annual Convention.

Just what I need!

Right?

Why me?

Takes me at least an hour to drive one way to/from D-House up in the city!

Can't ever say "No" to my boss.

Could you say "No" to yours?

✂ -

To escape from that bummer letter I stretched out on my office couch before mid-day prayers, and just allowed myself to retreat into fond thoughts about Paget.

✂ -

Parishioner # 25

is a twice divorced man who'd retired from working as an accountant.

He's planted himself in the pew his family always sat in, because that's how he feels connected to them since all but his mother have died, and she'd just been transferred from the hospital to a nursing home. I promised to get up to see her.

He often stays late on Mondays to ask me questions about the sermon from the day before.

"About your sermon, yesterday."

"Yes?"

"You've now repeated that message three times. First when you talked about the evil of a tea addiction. Then your addiction to buying books. And now, you're talking about it again. You should focus on telling us what we're doing right."

Interesting what people hear.

The sermon hadn't said anything about anyone doing anything wrong, and my reference to myself was a matter of convenience, in that I debate with myself:

Am I putting my needs before what God is asking me to do?

And isn't that such a foundational dilemma, and basic question?

(So much so that it bears repeating every so often?)

Parishioner # 25 worries that if one person takes offense and leaves the church because of a sermon message, then others would follow, and the small church's already low attendance will be decimated.

(TICS: "No one else remembers my sermons from week to week. Why do you? You're not one of those who take notes. Guilty conscience maybe?

(TICS: "So, all I should be preaching are fluffy, feel-good, puff-pieces?")

I also think that he tends to underestimate the community. While yes, they are mostly farmers, and retired factory workers who haven't gone on to college or higher education (like he and I had), that did not automatically make them uneducated simpletons.

And yet, he was born and raised in the area, so I wondered if maybe his lifetime of experience with the townsfolk should outweigh my seven years.

✂ -

My weekly visitation list is written up on Sunday mornings from the prayer requests that come in during worship. Finding out who's sick, or going to a doctor's appointment, is a good way to know who I need to get out and see, or at least call on the phone.

Nursing home visits.

Hospital visits.

Home visits.

Lunches.

Cup of tea at the coffee shop.

Running into people in the square.

Being a priest is to be with people at the best of times, and the worst.

Weddings, baptisms, and Confirmations – the best.

Death, funerals, and will readings – the worst.

Fellowship and community – the best.

Bitter words and petty arguments – the worst.

Illness - the worst.

Recovery – the best.

The joke's evolved. How's it go?

The three times people need the church is when they're

bred, wed, and dead.

Carried, married, and buried.

Hatched, matched, and dispatched.

Otherwise, church attendance is pretty much down across the board. Doesn't matter which denom we talk about
folks will always return when one of these three milestones in life occur (birth, wedding, death).

✂ -

II.

I'd arranged for three of us to present a funeral preplanning workshop.
Mostly to keep myself in check, because if it were just me and Paget
I might be a little too flirtatious in front of my assembled parishioners and folks from town. I talked about
- hymn selection
- scripture readings
- prayers
- eulogy writing tips, and advised people to write down their eulogies and memories to share, because when standing before a crowd, folks sometimes break down and can't finish. With it being written down someone else (read: me) can step in and finish reading it for them.

Paget then talked them through, step by step, from
- initial meeting (insurance forms and paperwork to bring in)
- planning services (calling hours, embalming, cremation, scheduling)

- viewings (if any, and if so, what clothes to bring, jewelry, what can be put in casket with the decedent, what is taken out before burial/cremation, if anything)
- committal (funeral home co-ordinates with vault company who sets up chairs and tents; then co-ordinates with cemetery, to confirm plots and that the grave is in the right spot [there've been two local misburials that I know of!]).

She is a capable public speaker and while I enjoyed the soft lilt in Paget's voice, my eyes were too busy enjoying the sight and shape of her to catch all the details of what she was saying.

✂ -

"Thank-you, Father, this was a great idea!" Paget said lifting her eyebrows suggestively as we moved to the double doors in back of the sanctuary.

Wasn't there a moment before the first person came up to exit with a complimentary review of our joint lecture/seminar.

"I'm glad you two thought to do this," said Parishioner #73 (he's on the board which oversees the local cemetery.

(His portion of the presentation had started off by telling about the cemetery relocation back in the 1800s; and that the village green out in the square used to be the cemetery (close by the church as you'd expect). Having arrested everyone's attention with that anecdote the nose picker then gave the cemetery/burial portion of our three-part program, and went through talking about

- vaults
- plots
- state laws and
- how people cannot be buried with the cremated remains of their beloved pet dogs (but that if he didn't see it, he didn't know it, and he wasn't

always watching to see what went into the ground).

✂ -

Paget waited while I shut off the lights and locked up Saint Mary's.

We walked across the village square side by side.

A priest, a funeral director, a vet, and a librarian, walk into a bar...

and they're a barbershop quartet who solve crimes
starting with the case of poisoned wine.
(*locals too afraid to take Communion.*)

✂ -

I pulled away from my inner joy and musings when a drunk at the bar called out, "You're both dressed all in black! You been to a funeral or something?"

Sunday evening
forgot
I'd pulled out the tab in my collar.

We had the attention of the whole bar.

"Yes, we were. Thanks!"

✂ -

I was smirking all the way to the table we were taken to in a side room.

The music started again, and wasn't as overloud as it would've been had we stayed in the front room.

"Sorry, I couldn't help myself back there," Paget said as I pulled out a chair for her.

"It was a good comeback."

Paget was decked out in her finest tight blouse and matching skirt.

She shared how she doesn't often wear a pencil skirt because she needs a wider range of movement. "I figure a presentation won't need me to be bending over and lifting a body, so why not be a little fancier than usual?"

(TICS: "You're elegant, fancy, feminine and drop-dead Sek-Zay on an average day – even though your arms are more muscular then mine.")

We talked about work (the funerals we'd done together), about her uncle's ill sense of humor ("horse-killer"), and how we both liked Copthorne.

"I was missing it, that's why I came back. My uncle wanted my cousin and brother to take over the business, but they didn't want to. And since they don't, there's no need for me to be feeling homesick while working at a funeral home far away."

(TICS: "You sure you didn't get fired for having funeral hookups on the job?"

(TICS: "Not that I'm complaining.")

"Your uncle told me you'd been in medical school?"

"I switched to mortuary science. Not as much pressure. It's easier to make mistakes."

"Mistakes made with the dead won't kill anybody."

"Exactly!" she smiled. "Something I haven't missed, though, is fertilizer season."

"The scent in the air?"

"Try dealing with that while you're in a cemetery doing a burial."

"Been there. Done that."

"So, other than funerals for us, and preplanning lectures, what does a priest do when it's not Sunday morning?"

"Solve crimes. Do exorcisms. Have affairs."

She couldn't tell how to receive that answer.

I held the pause, though.

I typically do.

When asked a question I don't know the answer to, I make one up. Then I'll pause, let it sink in, and if the fake answer is bought, I'll confess I made it up (for those who know me, they know to ask immediately:

"Are you making that up?"

(Of course, I'd never lie to her when asked a direct question).

"Yeah. Haven't you ever noticed how the only time priests are the main characters in a story, they're either solving crimes, doing exorcisms, or having affairs as a crisis of faith? Most of the time we're just in the background, shown doing baptisms, weddings, funerals, sometimes preaching, but the focus is usually on the other characters. We're typically seen, but rarely heard."

"You know, now that you mention it, that's a lot like with funeral directors, too!"

(TICS: "Horror movies. Ghouls haunting mausoleums. Lurking in cemeteries.")

✂ -

Why she wanted to be a funeral director.

The story goes:

"First funeral I ever went to.

"Neighbor, down the street. An Irish guy. It was in his house, not a funeral home.

"My father took me with him to the wake, and we got there and went up to the coffin, and looked inside. There was no body. We were puzzled, turned around, saw a group in the far corner, drinking beer and laughing. We went over so my father could ask where the decedent was.

"They'd taken him out, propped him up in the corner, put a beer in his hand, the brother said how they were all having a last drink with him.

"That's when I first thought about being a funeral director, because they looked like they were having fun! I didn't know it was the alcohol, but a couple years later, I found out what wakes were like in funeral homes, and state laws that you can't eat or drink in the buildings, and I went from that to going to medical school, but then back to it, and here I am!"

(TICS: "And I'm so glad you are!")

We'd never really shared before, but she confided how she'd been interning for her license and needed some

229

hours. Her uncle needed help one day, so she came out to Copthorne, got her hours, and stopped into the coffee house for a brew before the long drive back.

She could do with other relaxations as well, and figured a priest was good for an attachment-free quickie. Rather than go to her car, she lingered in the antique store doorway to see if I'd follow her into the shop. If I did, she'd know she could have me.

And have me she had.

(TICS: "Complete with my being completely attached to you!")

✂ -

Forgive the belabored detail, but this was a huge event for me!

(Plus, rewriting it lets me think about Paget some more, which gets me some fresh hits, so I probably should not be writing this out in such prolonged detail, but I'm gonna, and I'll also enjoy each fix as I go.)

Being out with her

away from work distractions!

Our conversation drifted on and I shared how I find that people act differently around me once they see The Collar. They put on their "best church behavior" and I asked if she found people act differently around her.

"People are surprised when they find out what I do. They say things like 'you don't look like a funeral director' or if I'm picking someone up, they're asking if I 'have someone to help me'. Usually I go by myself and don't need help."

Elbows on the table, wine glass held in both hands, she replied, "Sometimes, people will have it in mind that only a man can do my job, and they'll be a bit condescending. Like that security goof at the hospital with my hearse. Sometimes I'll fake it during a pick-up. You know. 'Helpless little me can't lift the body, would a big strong fella like you help?'

"But when making the arrangements, I think most people are comforted to have a woman doing that. Usually though, I think sometimes, that people have no idea what it means to be a funeral director. Act differently though? I dunno. I've seen, pretend sadness, maybe? Like they weren't feeling it, but thought it was expected."

"There's a bad joke I hear too often. That priests only work one day a week. If people only knew the rest of it."

"That you solve crimes. Do exorcisms, have affairs," she echoed my earlier answer.

"Exactly!"

We talked about professional commonalities, like our unpredictable schedules, and there not being any such thing as a "typical" week. Mine may start in an office, and hers may start with a 5 am home pick-up, but neither is an everyday pattern.

"I can have a few weeks of inactivity, and then a week of non-stop, morning-to-late-at-night days filled with doing bulletins, sermons, eulogies, prayer services, visits, wakes, funerals, annual convention, and so on."

It was nice to have someone listen.

Somebody who related.

Someone genuinely interested.

Somebody who sympathized with the professional lifestyle.

Someone aware of the pressures of being self-employed, and the ever-constant temptation to blow off work sometimes.

(Call it a "sanity day".)

✂ -

Which is what we joked our waitress was doing, since the service was so slow, given how NOT busy the place was and how flirty she was being with the guys at the bar.

Once she finally did get back to us in the side room, I ordered another of my usual – Cardinal (three-quarters red wine, one-quarter Crème de Cassis.

(Which the bar only stocked because the coffee house had started to first.)

She'd ordered another Grasshopper (milk with Crème de Mint and Crème de Cocoa).

Paget and I shared in telling the story her uncle had told me about my predecessor:

"He was running late, and once he got to the cemetery, everyone was relieved to see him hobbling along. Your uncle looked away from him, glanced to the family at the grave, and when he turned back around, the priest was gone!"

She inserted, "Vanished!"

"Then, this frail, withered hand and arm ..."

"Came reaching up from the earth like the dead rising back to life."

"The elderly priest had tripped and fallen into an open grave!"

(Fortunately, he hadn't been hurt by his tumble because of the soft mud.)

She roared with laughter, even though we'd both taken turns telling the story. I was heart-warmed because this was the first time we'd finished each other's thoughts. Were we moving back towards how it was between us near the end of our first 9 months together?

(Cold fear inside – would she run off on me again?)

(TICS: "Wish I could trust I'd see more of you tomorrow. All I'm imagining is that you'll wake-up with a hang-over-like response. Immediately groan and regret it, as soon as you recall how you opened up to me. And then, your distancer-pursuer pattern will start over again."

(It's a fear of the vulnerability within intimacy that she's dealing with.)

You know how you tell yourself "The one thing I won't ask them about is ... _____"? But then, as soon as you run out of things to say, the first thing you do is voice whatever it was you didn't want to say?

(TICS: "Why did you run away after my proposal?")

I didn't voice it, but it was there on my tongue.

Paget rescued me by adding, "My uncle's full of stories!"

(TICS: "And prone to beating a dead horse joke to death.")

"He says that's a way he can connect with everybody. Everyone's always got a story. All it takes is to get them started. Do you find that works for you, too?"

"Telling stories? Not to sound contrary, but no."

She was puzzled.

"In my line of work, except when preaching or teaching, it would not be good for me to do more talking than anyone else."

"So how do you get people to open up, and share, then?"

Looking into her eyes, I paused.

Waited.

And waited.

She shifted in her seat.

From her brown eyes I could see she was debating that bread basket on the table between us. Reaching for it, she asked, "I mean, really? You know what I'm asking, right?"

I smiled. "People hate silence. When they don't know what to say, I wait. Usually, the silence gets them talking again."

With a laugh, she threw half her roll at me.

I flicked it back at her, my dignity maintained since we were the only two in the side room; and no one visible through the open doorway (or glass wall beside our table) was looking our way.

"Seriously though. With clients I'll use trivia to break the ice. Same kind of idea as telling stories, I guess."

"Are you a trivia buff?"

"Don't know if I'd say it like that. I collect trivia, sure. I try to pick up something from everyone."

Easing back in her seat, she paused a moment, then smiled widely. "Here's some trivia for you. How social views of death have changed. Back in the 1800s, once a couple got married, they'd start saving up for their markers. That's why the older monuments are more ornate than our modern ones. Used to be, they reflected the life a person lived.

"Like a forever testimony in stone."

I smiled. "Headstone trivia. Wow. But did you know that the Bara of Madagascar, and the Cubeo of South America include sexual activities as part of their funeral and grief processes?

"Their way of turning the grief and anger at a death into joy."

"Sex trivia, wow," she teased by mimicry.

We shared a warm smile, then she told me the story of her break-up from her fiancée (cheating) being a good portion of why she'd moved to Copthorne to get away from him when our second round arrived.

"Your dinners will be out in a moment."

(TICS: "And probably be cold by the time you get them to us!")

"And probably be cold by the time she brings it out to us," Paget whispered when the barmaid/waitress left the room.

She and I might only be together for the sex, but we do have a lot in common.

Yet I don't dare point that out to her!

She is pretty, and fun, so even if we end up back on that roller coaster of hooking up, breaking up, getting back together, her running away from me, then coming back – ad nauseum – I'd continually return to her.

✂ -

The irony of my saying what I'm about to say is not lost on me:

> *the male orgasm should not be considered*
> *the "Holy Grail" of a sexual encounter.*

I say that because I enjoy it when a woman and I take our time – sure, variety is nice (so the occasional fast & frantic can be a treat), but by and large, I'm drawn towards those women who are not in a hurry for sex to be over.

See, for me, I just like being touched, so cuddling during – and after – sends me.

(Touch Deprivation issues.)

But those women who think the only point of sex is to get the guy off, well, they're the ones who get frustrated with me.

And the magic of Patches is that she never gave up mid-coitus to run off like so many others had. Rather, she always stayed until the end, usually finding her satisfaction a few times before my finish. That's not bragging – it's celebrating!

Back then, and now!

✂ -

"Don't fall in love."

I was starting to dread hearing her say those words every time.

✂ -

I was back in love with her all over again.

Only this time it was sweeter than before, as I was in love with Paget!

Not "Patches".

✂ -

Don't tell me **Even when it's bad, sex is good** cuz to a sex addict, one orgasm is too much, and one thousand orgasms are never enough.

✂ -

Yeah, I'm flawed.

Think of me as a noir "anti-hero" if you want.

The picaro in a Picaresque.

I'm not PC.

I won't apologize for that.

Way too many TICS these days!

Yet, to keep my job (and maintain self-preservation), I also have to keep quiet and not share what I really think and feel.

Otherwise I'll be defrocked faster than the current bishop can lift his robes and bend over his secretary.

✂ -

I find small talk to be a ridiculous waste of time.

I don't have the "gift of gab," and don't want it.

I've no love for keeping up appearances.

The insincerity of
        artifice
        affectation
        posing
        posturing
            bore me
            grate on my nerves.

Wear thin, and tax, my patience.

I'm happiest when left to myself.

Just let me go about my business at odd hours, I am not hurting anyone, nor vandalizing anything.

I hate crowds, which is why I enjoy small congregations.

And yes, more often than I like, I'm forced to ponder
        am I in the right line of work?

Not for spiritual or theological reasons
    but strictly for religious appearance reasons.

✂ -

III.

Sex addiction is a thing!

Had a walk-in at the clinic.

Tall, thin woman, long cascading black curls. Blue eyes. Pointy nose. Thin lips.

Long neck, deeply lined.

Compact, tight body.

"What can I do for you?"

"Er ... Father, is it?"

"Father. Pastor. Padre. Your Eminence. Use whatever you're comfortable with."

"How about I just call you Reverend?"

"If you like," I forced a smile.

(TICS: "Reverend is actually an adjective, and the proper form is 'The Reverend' followed by my name. But everyone uses it as a title anyway, so go ahead.")

"I think my daughter is a sex addict. I don't know what to do with her."

With continual prompting and a hell of a lot of patience

and uninterrupted silence

I eventually got the story from her.

Teen aged-daughter, car broke down on way back from a school function. She started to hitch hike, got picked up by a friend, and traded sex for a ride home.

(TICS: "Bad decisions don't make for an addiction.")

"We'll schedule an appointment."

"But you need to see her as soon as possible!"

"Of course. How about Friday then, say this time?"

(TICS: "If I can't get an open room here, we'll meet at my church office.")

"Oh, no. I have my Bowling league that day."

(TICS: "<u>Not</u> an emergency then!")

I typically work one or two days a week at the clinic, depending

and offered my next available appointment.

She wasn't happy I wouldn't drop everything for her crisis.

But you know

realistically

if she can't skip Bowling

then it's not really a crisis.

I explained how I worked

that there was a window in the door

and she was welcome to look through the window at anytime (her daughter is a minor), as my chair is in full view of the window,

but in order to establish a rapport, her daughter could not be inhibited in what she said by having her mother in the same room.

"But you'll tell me everything, right?"

"I'll tell you everything I say to her, but I will not repeat what she says to me. She'll need to be able to trust that I'm not just another adult who will tell her parents everything she says. If she doesn't trust me, then she'll never open up, which means we'll never get to the root of her behavior."

She didn't like that.

Probably won't like anything I do.

There was paperwork to be filled out first, but I wanted her daughter to see the signing, as a kind of proof that I wouldn't be telling her mother about our sessions (that my office was a safe place where she could share, and her parents would not be informed).

From what I was told, it didn't sound like addiction to me. Might be a behavior pattern that could potentially lead to addiction, but I'd start from an insecure attachment approach and work backwards. Stats suggest that promiscuity is more evident in women with avoidant attachment styles. Women with sex addiction typically have a history of childhood and/or sexual abuse (though not always) while women with fearful-avoidant attachment styles tend to have the strongest sexual aversion (the approach/avoidance cycle is pretty common).

She hated what I said next:

"Let's make two appointments. One for her, and one for you. That way, you and I aren't rushed when we sit down and go over what I've told her" (it was bullshit, but it served its purpose. Getting the mother into a session for a full hour, instead of just for ten minutes after cutting her daughter's session short.

(Family settings do contribute to addiction.)

✂ -

PARISH REFLECTIONS:

You'd be surprised how often a parishioner goes to the hospital and I don't hear about it until after they got home, and additional recovery time has passed.

And then, they bitch that I never went to see them in hospital.

I WASN'T TOLD!

I can't visit if I'm not told!

Of course, on a practical note, unless it's life and death, no one thinks to call in the priest.

Or they think someone else has told me
    and while everybody is thinking that someone else has told me
        nobody has actually told me a thing!

I'd rather get the same news
    a dozen different times
        from a dozen different people
            than never hear the news once!

Sorry.

I'm just tired of being bitched at
    for not doing something
        when I was not told there was something I needed to do.

I'm not a mind-reader!

✂ -

You guessed it!

Of course it was Cathedral Sister # 1/parishioner # 92!

I am just not her idea of what a priest is supposed to be.

Screw that.

I'm me!

✂ -

Cathedral Sister # 1 has a passion for Convention and diocesan holitics!

(It's not politics in church, but holy – holi – holitics.)

She lives for that bullshit!

She should be the Parish delegate for life. She'd get a free ride to it every year with Saint Mary's paying all expenses.

But ... na-ho!

In her idealism, everyone else at Saint Mary's should care as much about Convention as she does. Especially me! And there should be a different lay delegate every year!

Thing is, as I said – no one else lives for that crap!

I don't!

No one else wants to go.

The parishioners who work aren't going to take vacation time to attend Annual Convention, nor should they be expected to if they don't want to!

The parishioners who are elderly don't want to go, they can't sit still that long, and they shouldn't have to!

(How Parishioner # 52 ever got suckered into going is beyond me!)

But see, it's antics like this which make me wonder if Cathedral Sister # 1 is only as passionate as she is because it feeds a religious addiction.

She can't get a "hit" unless there is someone else to put down so she can think of herself as religiously superior. And since no one wants to go to Convention, she's filled to the gills with people to put down for their lacking a proper attitude and not prioritizing the Church the way they should. As she's repeatedly told me, it's part of my job to make parishioners prioritize it!

Errr ...

Umm ...

Thing is: how do I sell people on something I don't like doing?

✂ -

If you liked everything about your job then it wouldn't be work.

Yeah yeah yeah.

✂ -

It's a truth in parish ministry that the longer you stay at a church, the less revered you are by the congregation.

"Longevity breeds discourtesy," that'd be the saying!

People get used to you, and you become family rather than God's proxy on Earth, as was the old concept when priests were placed up on pedestals.

We've been knocked off those high pedestals.

Something that has both good, and bad, points.

✂ -

You wouldn't think it, but yes – there is a kind of parishioner who gets off on hounding and harassing and criticizing their priest.

The agenda of such "rabid sheep" is simple. To harry the priest until the priest resigns from that parish. Usually, they do it for no reason other than how causing a priest to move puts another feather in their cap.

And the most insidious part of it is
       the priest is a sitting duck!
Because we're called to "love our neighbor"
       we are not allowed to strike back.
Because of "turn the other cheek"
       we're expected to not return fire.
This is how priests are victimized by some parishioners.

The ones that gossip, lie, and spread their opinions as though what they're saying is holy writ. Sadly, there is also a kind of parishioner who goes along with the first, and echos every gripe.

One good thing, most of my parishioners don't have a high opinion of Cathedral Sister # 1 to begin with. She'll start in on me, and the joke now is other parishioners coming up to me with jovial smirks, and teasing me after her latest, "Father, you just can't do anything right."

You see, the Cathedral Sisters want to turn Saint Mary's into a mini Saint Thomas.

(The larger parish they transferred from.)

241

The bad news for them is that the Saint Mary's congregation is maybe one eighth the size of the Saint Thomas congregation, and it doesn't want to become Junior St Tommy!

(TICS: "Why did you really leave Saint Thomas to come here?")

✄ -

I had to laugh when you asked why I don't just pack it in, let the Churches and Cathederals win, and move to another parish.

I've asked myself that a lot, actually.

But the reality is, every church has someone just like them.

Was Mrs Grundy before the Churches. Then the Cathederals.

No matter where I go, there'll always be someone who doesn't like how I do things
thinks I should do everything their way, not mine
and is hyper-critical and overly-demanding.

In the end, why go through the hassle of moving,
getting re-established
losing all the wonderful connections I've made here in Copthorne
just to escape a quartet of nasty people who are convinced their mission from God is to make my life hell?

It's not like there won't be someone else to take their place no matter where I go.

Like the Chinese proverb, "The devil you know is better than the devil you don't know."

✄ -

9 am

Standing at the double doors, I was shaking hands with people as they exit the sanctuary.

Cathedral Sister # 1: "Father, do you know Father Dullard?"

I don't.

"He reads two thousand pages a month."

(TICS: "Good for him.")

"How much do you read in a month?"

I've never counted.

You see, what's going on with her is I'm not giving her anything to brag about to her ECW friends from the other parishes when they get together.

(You'd think it a cardinal sin the way she carries on!)

Which isn't to say I'm inefficient or ineffective.

It just says I know my boundaries.

Like I said before, I may be on-call 24/7 but that does not mean I'm working 24/7.

So while other priests may run themselves ragged, and be working every hour of every day, I refuse to.

I know my limits.

Check the stats:

Only 10% of those who start in ministry, retire from ministry.

The vast majority drop out of ministry before their fifth anniversary.

So don't tell me that after fifteen plus years in the collar that she has nothing to brag about. She does. She just doesn't want to brag about what she can actually, and legitimately, brag about:

- I'm not an alcoholic
- I'm no longer an addict who still acts out (Paget excluded)
- I haven't had a nervous breakdown
- I'm good at what I do – like counseling sex addicts, preaching, leading worship, teaching, and visiting.
- I just submitted my PhD dissertation.

She hears her friends talk about their priests and then measures me up as impotent.

My sin – I'm not a workaholic.

But that's the double-standard, right?

It's the priest in the office she wants to brag about, not the person wearing the dog collar.

My values need to be her values, because if I don't value what she values, then she is wrong for having the values she has. And here's the kicker, since she can't be right unless I agree with her, she exerts pressure for me to conform to her notions.

With her there's no room for anything contrary from her parish priest.

You encounter this attitude – as a priest, you are not a person.

You are expected to be the embodiment of unreasonable expectations, rather than be a human being with limitations. So, as a beast of burden, I just need to be whipped harder and put to shame more often

with sharper, and harsher, criticisms.

(TICS: "Forget all the lip-service the diocese gives to clergy self-care at Convention and in their newsletters, because they don't really mean any of it, right? – although honestly – given some of the expectations which come down from on high (work, work, work), they leave us no time to take care of ourselves [unless we're willing to let some things go unfinished by their deadlines].

(TICS: "Just cuz I'm a bachelor doesn't mean I'm not allowed any family time."

(TICS: "Just because I'd spend 'family time' in solitude shouldn't mean I have to spend that time on the clock instead!"

(TICS: "Cathedral Sister # 1, ladies and gentlemen! First to criticize and complain; last to volunteer!")

✂ -

Standing at the double doors, I was shaking hands with people as they exit the sanctuary.

"Father."

"Yes?"

"About these 'riskier' sermons you mentioned today?"

(TICS: "Good! Someone wasn't sleeping!"

(I'd publicly suggested my theme: "If it's in the Bible, we should talk about it. So lets talk about things the Church doesn't talk about. What's on your mind?")

"I have to say, Father, if you're going to talk about homosexuals, then let me know when you're going to."

Glad Parishioner # 33 doesn't want to miss it, I encouraged, "I'm hoping to get topics from the congregation, and then work up a schedule, so you'll know the topics in advance."

"Good! That way I know when I should skip a day."

"Oh?"

"Nothing against you, Father, but my mind's already made up, and I don't want to hear about it anymore."

"Or about the LGBTQ thing!" piped in Parishioner # 62 in line behind him.

"BLT?" I simplified for a laugh; hoping they'll feel me relating to them. "G-Q?"

Nope.

(Every so often I amuse myself, but no one else.)

Alas ...

sigh ...

Oh, well ...

still, I needed their help if I was going to help them.

I started to ask, "Is it the - ?"

Got cut off: "It's all well and good for the Presiding Bishop, and other parishes. But not here at Saint Mary's! I come here to get away from all that, and nothing about sex, neither!"

"No sermons about nudity?"

"No!"

"Adultery?"

"No!"

"Capital punishment?"

"That's OK."

"Slavery?"

"Fine."

"Racism?"

"Alright, I guess."

"Abortion?"

"Nothing to do with sex!"

"I will make sure you know in advance, if I tackle any of those topics in a risky sermon. But how do you feel if I mention them at a Bible Study, or in a lecture series?"

"So long as it's not in church on a Sunday morning!"

(TICS: "Because Sunday mornings are the only time you're ever in church except for fund raisers? Gotcha."

(TICS: "What a shame! It's not surprising, really. I'd expected that kind of reaction from the Sourpuss family, but not others. Yet that's exactly the kind of attitude and mindset I'm trying to reach, and this guy's already slamming the door shut.")

So I pray like always: "People are strange – God love'em!"

✂ -

11 am

Sunday morning worship, and some prayer request cards were slipped to me as people entered Saint Mary's.

Kelly's family asked for celebration prayers that "Elder" would be moving back home. Kelly is looking better, though the almost faded surgery bruising can't be covered by foundation, no matter how much she cakes on.

(TICS: "I hope someone else mentions that to her, so I don't have to.")

✂ -

The mug I keep in the pulpit is white ceramic.

I like to have some hot water with me during services.

(Just don't want people thinking I'm filling it with Vodka like one of my seminary professors did. Especially since Absolut no longer makes the Kurant flavor they used to).

Look inside, you'd see the water is clear
　　but tainted

because of the area's hard water coming out of the tap.

(The well it's drawn from.)

So, although unrelated to its transparency, the impure water tastes like coffee because the countertop appliance used to heat it is also used every Sunday to brew the guest of honor for coffee hour in-between services.

(And coffee drinkers wouldn't notice this taint.)

"Father, I put your hot water up in the pulpit for you."

What can I say to Dottie, who has been getting the water boiling, and setting a steaming mug in the pulpit for me before every service ever since I visited her Grandson in the hospital?

"Thank-you," is what I say.

(TICS: "Is it gonna taste like shitty coffee?")

You know, I type that, and yes. I wonder – am I ungrateful?

Or, just spoiled?

(The single cup coffee maker I have in the rectory kitchen has never been near coffee grounds, and I only ever put bottled water into it, and the boiled water I brew doesn't taste like anything other than plain hot water.

(I don't even put tea bags where the coffee should go.

(I wait 'til the water's in a mug before adding the tea bags.)

People going thirsty in the world, and I'm bitching about flavored water, right?

I don't hate myself for that, it's just my compassion fatigue has me feeling so burnt out on the plight of others that I've grown numb to suffering. That's what I resent!

To want to care, but lack the spark of an emotion to bring myself to it.

You said that time how it's my **empathic** nature being over-loaded, and leading me to feeling emotionally drained. I figured it was just my introverted nature.

We'll have to revisit that sometime.

✂ -

Dottie's amazing.

At 80 years-old, she's still Bowling.

She's the one who pinched my ass that time!

The one who sat on my lap and complained her seat was lumpy!

(It had been at a church dinner; she'd gotten up to get a dessert, so I took her seat to ask someone at that table a quick question. When she returned to the table too quickly, Dottie had simply slid right onto my lap without pause!)

Why can't elderly people all be as happy and cheerful?

Someone should tell Mrs Church that you can't be angry with someone as carefree and effervescent as Dottie is.

(She's described Mrs Church as "the woman who never smiles," and confided to me that Mrs Church's disapproving frown makes her laugh.)

✂ -

Flashback:

Dottie had been one of my first home visits.

I arrived while she was peeling apples for a pie.

When she went to answer her phone, she left me with a knife, pile of apples, and an unspoken request that I continue quartering them the way she'd just started.

It's my thing: when visiting a parishioner, I try to take part in whatever they're doing rather than expect them to stop.

I was cutting the apples and feeling pretty good about not dropping any when one slipped out of my fingers.

I tossed it in the trash and kept on going.

When Dottie returned from her call, I mentioned the lone casualty of my clumsiness, and you could see the expression drop on her face.

I had wasted something!

(How terrible to throw a dirtied apple slice in the trash!)

Excusing myself to the wash room, I was coming back into the kitchen in time to notice her rummaging in the waste bin. She didn't know I saw her pluck the slice from the trash, rinse it off in the sink and add it back into the bowl of sliced apple wedges fated to be baked into her pie.

(She grew up during the Great Depression and doesn't throw anything away.)

Yet I should add how Dottie is one of those in the Grey-Haired Guild who will not eat any of the roadkill casseroles cooked by Parishioner # 31 in her backyard barbeque pit (remember, that's just a rumor), but you get my point –

a person will excuse whatever they do, but condemn someone else when that other does the very same thing – or something quite similar.

It's how folks vent their self-loathing and ease their confusion about second-guessing what they do.

✂ -

Standing at the back doors, I was shaking hands with people as they exit the sanctuary.

Every week, "Reverend, good sermon."

(TICS: "Tell me, what really got your attention?"

✂ -

Standing at the back doors, I was shaking hands with people as they exit the sanctuary.

There's a kind of specialness that happens when a man sees a woman in her undies.

Parishioner # 70 is a divorcee and single mother with two daughters, who recently posted some boudoir photos of herself online at Myface.

The story is: my parishioner's sister gave her a studio certificate to help my parishioner build an enticing online dating profile with alluring pix.

True, she's a little bigger than slender, but also true is that while she is larger than I generally like, her figure is proportional

which always looks good in pictures.

And then we have to acknowledge how amazing many women look dressed up in retro-1920s underwear and stockings when they're photographed on a crushed velvet couch.

Butt ... who am I kidding?

Yes, I did let her keep her modesty by pretending that I hadn't seen her online pictures.

(TICS: "No. No! I didn't see the photos where you're showing a lace thong riding down the valley of your bared intergluteal cleft!")

She asked if I thought her modeling for such pix was sinful.

My reply: "Nope."

✂ -

7

Pentecost (vi)

I.

Making my rounds.

First: Paget.

An ex-parishioner had died in hospice, I went to Bergerac to get the details (why do it over the phone?).

I get there:

First, the details on the service – the funeral was planned for the Monday after Carnival weekend.

Then, "I've got something to show you."

(TICS: "AND I WANNA SEE IT!!!")

She led me by hand into the "Slumber/Reposing Room" and waited to see if I'd notice.

"The couch is new."

"Try it out."

I sat on the new velvet, eased back.

"I hope you won't miss the old one."

I nodded at its comfort.

(TICS: "Didn't think the old one needed to be replaced.")

One hand on the arm rest, other on the cushion beside me, I pushed myself up and down to make a show of testing its bounce.

Stepping over, she nudged my knees open with hers, a suggestive lift to her eyebrows.

Watched her
kneeling.

✂ -

Again, "Don't fall in love."

✂ -

All I could focus on was whether or not she'd bought this new couch as a way of making an apology for disappearing after my proposal.

Had she bought this new couch because she knew it's where I always sat during visitation for those funerals I officiated?

Did that make this velvet couch a gift just for me?

Almost commented about our having "broken it in" but didn't.

Figured the best response to give – with her fearful-avoidant attachment style – was a non-committal one, so I bit my tongue rather than mention anything remotely commitment related. Such folks may give gifts to people they care for, but they'd never verbalize their caring. Instead, they blow off the significance of their feelings, and shy away from whoever, rather than risk getting attached (i.e. bound, obligated, responsible for another's hapPENIS).

(Emotionally, like a skittish cat who slowly approaches you but is always alert and ready to run away if you lift your arm too high, or move too quickly.)

My strategy could only be to simply live for the moment

enjoy whatever Paget and I did together

and never, ever, talk in terms of anything bonding us to each other.

Nor any serious mention of any perceived future togetherness in-between us.

Instead – wait for her to voice it first.

In her time, and if/when she's ever ready.

In the meanwhile, I wrestled with not presuming my interpretation was accurate (that this velvet couch was her gift to me).

I wanted the new couch to hold some significant meaning to her so that I could then turn it around for myself that I also

had a significant meaning to her

since she knew I'd benefit from its unnecessary purchase.

✂ -

Me, over-analyzing
over-thinking
over-intellectualizing again.
It usually helps me avoid slipping back into love-and-sex addictive patterns.
But you know I already have since
I was clearly making too much of a trifle.
That's the heartbeat of my addiction.
Always looking for significant meaning to bond me to my "object of desire" even though she can only ever just be "Paget" to me
part-time lover
occasional mistress
femme fatale
but never monogamous mate.

✂ -

Making my rounds.
Second: Hospital.
"What's going on?" I asked, entering a white room.
"Oh! Today's not a good day."
(TICS: "It's never a good day for you.")
I asked, "Why's that?"
"Oh! I couldn't sleep last night."
(TICS: "Because you nap all day, maybe?")
Parishioner # 14 is in hospital rehab for two broken legs.
She'd driven up to the drive-thru window at a bank, forgot to put her truck in park, and as she climbed down from the high cab to make a deposit, the truck started

rolling away from her. She slipped, fell trying to climb back in.

The bank's drive-thru was closed for two days until after everything was untangled, and the girl from the window got the screams out of her ears.

"What's going on at night? You in a lot of pain?"

"No. Oh! They keep me good on that."

(TICS: "You just like the attention, and acting depressed gets you that attention, right?")

Grump grump grump.

You know, I have to believe people just don't realize what they do!

I make a hospital visit, right?

I'm standing at the patient's bedside.

Not taking her hands in mine, as the insurance company prefers.

I'm saying a prayer for her.

And she reaches over and starts adjusting the bed, like I can't hear the motor whirling as I'm praying for her healing!

Asking God to heal her.

And she's adjusting the effing bed, like it couldn't wait a moment!

That's what I get for keeping the Church's insurance idiots happy!

✂ -

Sex addiction is a thing.

But so are the fake-outs.

Time wasters.

Whether they think they're being cute, or just want a story to tell their friends about going to a sex addiction pastoral counselor, every so often one slips through the screening process.

It's annoying
        aggravating
        irritating
        juvenile

petty

and an effing waste of my time, even though I was paid in advance!

I don't question first session hesitation from a woman, but I do from male clients. "Remind me. I know we talked about it on the phone. But what makes you think you have a problem with sexual addiction?"

The snickers are often a clue, but sometimes, maybe, someone is really, really, shy and just can't bring themselves to open up.

(That's my hidden optimism, wanting to give every potential client the benefit of the doubt rather than presume they're all liars until proven otherwise.)

"Well ... I have to have it."

"Yes but, is that a biological need, or a compulsive need?"

"I don't ... what's the difference?"

"Have you tried to stop having sex?"

"Why would I do that?"

"If you don't want to stop having sex, what makes you think you have a problem?"

"Well, I ..."

"Do you go to a church?"

He gave me that nonverbal response where no, he doesn't

but then

he doesn't dare say that to a priest.

So rather than leave him in awkward silence I continued:

"Do you think sex is a sin?"

"Isn't it?"

"How often do you masturbate?"

"er ... what?"

"When's the last time you had an orgasm?"

"What's that got to do with it?"

"How often do you use porn?"

"Don't you mean 'watch' porn?"

"If you masturbate while watching, that is using. How often do you use porn?"

"I ... I ..."

I paused. My interview style is not as rapid-fire as this reads. There were a lot of lengthy pauses and him sitting there, twiddling his thumbs, struggling for answers.

Generally, I like to get a feel for a person's sincerity before I have them do the intake assessment. Fifteen minute chat, half hour test, then, "See you next time and we'll go over your results."

Something about him just screamed insincerity.

Thought I'd give him a second chance before kicking him out on his imposter ass. Began, "I'm a sex addiction counselor."

"You're dressed like a priest."

"I'm also a priest. Why do you think you are a sex addict?"

"I can't stop."

"Can't stop what?"

"Having sex."

"Why not?

"Have you ever tried to stop?"

"Alright." Took off my glasses, rubbed my eyes, put them back on, and looked straight at him. "How are you having sex?"

"You don't know how to have sex?"

"Do you think being here is a joke?"

"I just gave you a hundred bucks."

"And you think that makes me buy that you're serious?"

"Dude ..." and he was shaking his head. "This ... er ... you're supposed to help me!"

(TICS: "You might want to turn off that tape recorder in your pocket, first.")

✂ -

Gave him a referral to Benson, down the hall. She's more into mindfulness therapy, and that would likely be more helpful – if he was sincere in wanting help.

He was trying to convince me he had a compulsive sex disorder but he wasn't describing compulsive sex habits.

In fact, he was being very secretive for someone who wants to begin counseling.

Being horny all the time didn't make him a sex addict.

Just made him a college student with a – possibly elevated – sex drive.

(Or a journalist with an impotent cover story.)

But not a sex addiction.

Not from the little he was telling me, and therapy only works when the client tells the counselor about their problem without trying to dupe them for some clandestine reason.

✂ -

Got back to church from the clinic, and parked at the curb in the village square.

Pass the carriage step
across the flagstone sidewalk
up to the wide porch
through the double doors
ascend the three steps in the dark bell tower
down the sanctuary's center aisle.

Took my usual seat in the pew beneath a ceiling fan.

The carpeting leads a path to the ornate wooden altar with its marble top (an unnecessary extravagance since the marble is covered by paraments and only ever seen naked once a year (on Good Friday).

My predecessor insisted the church altar had to have a marble top!

"High Church" ponce (not said affectionately).

Meaning, he wanted the Episcopal church (which is Protestant – think "protest") to return to Anglican traditions since Henry VIII hadn't intended a total break with Catholicism.

Before you go thinking it's all fancy with dark hardwood wainscoting and stone walls, let me share

- There are holes in the carpet where the acolyte almost tripped while carrying the cross in front of the procession last Christmas.

- The ceiling is water stained, and there's rotting wood overhead.
- Two of the stained glass windows are starting to bow at the bottom (common with the weight of the glass and lead framing).
- The hardwood seats of the pews have encouraged many parishioners to bring in pillows to sit on, which they leave in their places during the week (one of which I borrow whenever I sit in that pew to meditate and pray).
- The ceiling fans have chains which rattle and sound like old electric typewriters clattering away.
- Inside the bell tower a thick rope hangs through a hole in the trap door so that the bell pull can be used to toll the start of every service.

When not used it's tucked behind a wall hook so it's not left dangling in the middle.

This is a church with a dwindling congregation.

(A few years back they'd needed to do some roof repairs and Mrs Church, as Warden of Saint Mary's, and Parishioner # 24, had gone to D-House and the Standing Committee for a loan, worried all the while that Saint Mary's would be denied the loan and then be closed down, even though it is the oldest original church building.

(The current Cathedral had been rebuilt after the original structure burnt down in 1812; which then passed the title of "Oldest Episcopal Church Building in the Diocese" to Saint Mary's.

(This should be a prestige post, rather, it's whispered about as though the only priests who serve here are those the diocese wants to forget about.)

Thoughts of career advancement/stalemate/suicide occupied me as I sat in the pew after mid-day prayers. I heard the double doors open behind me, and turned in my seat while moving to stand.

My heart dropped when I saw who it was.

It's a miracle my smile didn't drop with my heart.

Christ instructed: "Love your neighbor; give to all who ask of you."

And yet ...
Well, what can I say?
Church Scammers!
Scum!
(Church Scummers?)
I shouldn't judge, I know.
Who am I to talk, right?
But - they steal from the church!
They lie to my face!

✂ -

Convincing tears.
　　Choked up sobs.
　　　　Gasping for breath.
　　　　　Shoulders shaking.
　　　　　　Hands trembling.
She made it to the last pew, and dropped into place.
Waited there for me to join her.
I did.
But I've seen this performance before.
Bought it the first two times.
　　　　　　　　　Not buying it a third.
Seemed to be turning into a day for fake-outs.
　　In a raspy, smoker's voice that she softened as best
she could, "My mother's in hospice, and we don't have
the money to get down there and see her before the end."
　　Slumped on the last pew, she could win an Oscar.
　　Still, she's just a "One Hit Wonder" with that act.
　　Plus, she doesn't keep track of who she's pulled this
scam on already.
　　Previously, it had been her sister who was ill.
　　First time, her daughter was in the hospital.
　　According to other area clergy, her mother has already
died.
　　(TICS: "She was resurrected, but she's now back in
hospice? That sucks.")
　　People like this go from church

> to church
> to church
> to church.

Professional Beggars.

And, to their credit, they get good at performing.

(Saw this all the time at my church in the city.)

But, they also get greedy.

Then stupid.

They visit the same well too many times, and don't keep track.

Cry "Wolf!" too often.

And don't know that area clergy get together for an ecumenical lunch each month, when we swap stories about idiots like her and her whole family!

We don't forget
> we just pretend to.

(To distract from his baldness, her husband has a ring of tattoos from ear to ear around the back of his head.)

✂ -

"I'm sorry to hear that, but we don't have any money to give out."

"But you -"

(TICS: "Gave you money before, the first two times you came by?"

(TICS: "I'm being polite, acting like I don't remember you.")

"Couldn't you ... call some of your parishioners, and ask them to help me?"

"I'm not going to call my parishioners to take up a collection for you."

"Then you must have money in your personal account you could give me."

(Can you believe the nerve?!

("Give to the poor," indeed!

(Throwing the Gospel in my face! "Sell all you have, give it to the poor, follow me."

(Give you all I have and leave myself with nothing?

(I don't think so!)

My ("un-Christian") reaction boiled over, and I could not help myself!

I blurted out, "You've already stopped here twice. First when you daughter was ill, and then when your sister was. Now it's your mother in hospice, out of state, and you have no way to get there."

"All of that happened!"

"Maybe it did. But I take it that neither the church down the road, nor the one up the hill, were able to help you out this time?"

She got hostile: "The Church is supposed to help people in need!"

"Those churches have the money to help you. I've already helped you twice!"

"But they -"

"We don't have the money to help you anymore!"

"How can you be so –"

Sex is not my **dark side** like you say.

Rather, moments like this are!

Regaining my calm, "Hang on, wait here a moment and I'll get you the number for a social assistance program."

With huff and glare, she stormed out.

Guess she wasn't really in need after all.

And surprisingly, after she left, I did not feel

> worse
> guilt
> regret.

Some (like the Cathedral sisters) might say I am not a good Christian for feeling the emotional equivalent of "Good riddance to bad rubbish!"

But I felt ok with it.

✂ -

As a seminary advisor told me, "Be ready for it. You will help those who aren't really in need. And you'll turn away some who really are in need. You never know. But it's not

261

about them, and if they're scamming you. It's all about you, and if you have it in your heart to help."

(TICS: "I'll help you to better yourself by paying for you to take a class to learn how to manage money, and prioritize buying food first, before getting that snazzy wrap-around tattoo, or that Burmese albino python. But no, I won't give you anymore help just so you can treat it like a cash bonus.")

I know.

I'm very un-Christian.

I'm so heartless and cruel.

  And sarcastic.

✂ -

Still...

  opportunity!

I should walk over to Bergerac, give Paget a heads–up in case a certain church scummer ever goes sniffing around for a free funeral after performing an excellent sob story.

✂ -

No guilt.

  No regrets.

  No ethical/moral second-guessing.

  I'm not her priest, she's not my parishioner.

  She's not my client, I'm not her counselor.

  She's almost 30, and I'm just over 50.

  Both consenting adults.

  We're not married, but the Bible doesn't say we have to be.

  Just ...

    her need to stay unattached, and

    my need to be with her, no matter what.

     Funeral Directress and Priest

  A relationship based on sex

    Friends-with-benefits

"Booty call"
            whatever you want to call it.
It may not be everything for me, but it is enough.
Told her about the scammer's mother in hospice.

(As I think it over, I wouldn't have gone out of my way
to warn Cyranose

   (I would've waited until he called me in to do a
service before mentioning it.

      (Like I said, there's a selfishness in addiction.

         (Always motivated by gaining that sweet
reward!)

✂ -

"Don't fall in love."

✂ -

II.

The first costume turned up in church today.

Parishioner # 87, the town Pharmacy's owner, in tri-
cornered hat, long coat, breeches, buckle shoes, and socks
to his knees.

He likes to start wearing his "fancy naval dress"
a week before the carnival so that the cut of his jib no
longer feels awkward once the town starts dressing
up. He likes to tell himself that he sets the mood for
everybody else, and is in fancy dress early to generate
enthusiasm.

As the carnival gets closer, more and more folks will
start following his example and dressing up to get in the
spirit of it before the big weekend arrives.

They've done it that way ever since the latex factory
began sponsoring the carnival as a period event (that
hemorrhoid, who wouldn't sell? His father had been a
Revolutionary War re-enactor who participated mostly
in area events since Copthorne is situated in-between at
least three of them).

I haven't told anyone yet, but I've managed to assemble my own period costume.

That of a "Circuit-Riding Priest".

The week-end of the carnival I'll be in the pulpit decked out in tri-corn hat, wig, black riding coat over a billowy white, puffy shirt, form-fitting black vest, close-fitting trousers, and tan-topped riding boots. My neck scarf has those twin tails. The traditional "Geneva Bands" as they're called, which represent the two sacraments of Baptism and Communion.

This year I won't be accused of not getting into the "spirit of things" like I've been for the past few years.

This year, I'll be in costume like most of the congregation!

✂ -

I know what you're going to say:

"Latex Festival?

"Latex wasn't around in the 1700s.

"What's the revolution got to do with it?"

You'd be right on those points, but consider these facts too:

During the French and Indian War this was a military outpost first, then a medical camp, and then the families came to aid their wounded husbands, sons, and brothers. They settled in, planted roots, and became a community, then a village.

It's industry for cheese evolved after that, and it grew into a town the following century.

More to the point though, are these bits of condom trivia:

- King Charles II's doctor, one Colonel Condom prescribed their use so the king wouldn't keep fathering more and more illegitimate babies (mid-1600s).
- The first written mention of the "Condum" was in a poem from 1706.

- Rubber was first discussed in a French scientific paper published in 1751 (which also revealed the pencil eraser as one practical use for rubber, even though rubber (from plant sap) had been something used by the Mayan, Aztex, and Colmec cultures way back in 1600 BC).
- The Latin word "Condus" (meaning receptacle or vessel) is probably how the name evolved so that by 1785, it was entered into one of the earliest English Language dictionaries.
- "English Raincoats" as the French called them – remember, the Mackintosh was a rubber-lined raincoat (or "French Letters" as the British called them) – were made from linen, or animal intestines, or animal bladders; after being treated with sulfur or lye.
- Casanova was the first guy to inflate each one before using them to make sure there were no holes (the first recorded case of condom inspection – in the 1700s). He also encouraged lemons be cut in half, squeezed out, so that the emptied lemon skin could be used to cover the cervix (a fruity diaphragm).
- Several prominent figures in the 1700s did protest the use of condoms because – get this – they argued using a condom to prevent syphilis encouraged men to have sex with unsafe women. That'd be the Great-Great-Granddaddy of every asinine "STIs and STDs are God's punishment for having sex" argument.

✂ -

The village lawn in late summer was sporting bright flower beds and a change had been made to the banner for Copthorne's 79th Annual Summer Carnival.

Not to put too fine a point on it, but Condoms (not "rubbers") have a good connection to the 1700s, but we don't want to tell that to the guy who refused to sell the abandoned factory.

(Though we probably should compliment the vandals for their historical accuracy since they spray painted "Condom Carnival" across the banner.)

✂ -

Yeah, I researched this
- Condoms were illegal in this country until 1918.
- Condom use can be seen in pre-historic cave paintings in France.
- Condom usage appears in ancient Egyptian artwork.

(Not the "Rubber" we all know, love, and say we use [but really don't], these condom examples are of more primitive forms of sheath contraception.)

I'm not kidding, condom use has a long and illustrious history!

✂ -

You're right; the Church has long opposed sex.
   Just don't get me started on that whole "Natural Law" –
      (people can only have sex when they are married
         (only while trying to make a baby
            (only in the missionary position
               (and to then, never, ever, enjoy the activity)
                  – exclusivist bullshit mentality.

✂ -

I don't believe that a marriage license is the only way to have God-approved sex.
   The Church's practice of instilling guilt and regret has to be removed!
   Asceticism, my ass!
   Seriously!

How many lives have been effed up because we've been force-fed the moronic notion that physical pleasures are meant to be avoided?

Seriously!

God creates us with the capacity to have pleasure.

God creates us with the desire to experience pleasure (it's hard-wired into us).

But then, God suddenly decides that oops – mistake – Adam and Eve! From birth to death "Sex is now the only thing in all creation that is not good for you!"

Seriously?

Do we believe in a god who is that cruel and sadistic?

Did God issue the Commandment "Thou shalt fill yourselves with self-loathing if thee enjoy sex!"

Pretty sure not

    so I'm calling "Bullshit" on that!

And I'm not calling God out for that one.

I'll call out the

    human-founded

       human-created

          human-managed

            Church

               for that disjoint in common sense!

✂ -

Every year I look forward to the "Condom Carnival" to boost my spirits and put me in in a good mood.

The carnival helps keep me centered and connected with the groove and swing of country life.

The high point of the rural year!

From my place on the church porch (in some parishes, the outdoor porch could be labeled a "narthex" but not here at Saint Mary's) I could see the carnival banner hanging from the wires holding up the street light.

I'd love to know how the graffiti artist gets up there without anyone seeing him.

✂ -

The Carnival started seventy-nine years ago, when the factory was in its glory.

And the kids in town have learned to take a great many insults from kids in the neighboring school districts who mock them by using team names like "Cock Thorn Condoms" and "Rubber Rebels" (depending on which side of the county line the games are on).

✂ -

What starts with Parishioner # 87 catches on, and people get caught up in the spirit of the carnival as it draws closer. The shopkeepers and workers around the square usually start dressing up too.

I do my best not to laugh at the girls while I feel sorry for them.

Hooped petticoats bumping into the merchandise on the pharmacy display tables and lower shelves. Not being used to how far out the hoops go, the girls breeze through the store (at the same speed they move at while wearing skin-tight jeans), and a wake of knocked over stuff is left behind their bell-like skirts sweeping the floor.

The girls in the coffee house fare even worse! All those layers of fabric, stockings, shift, stays, petticoat, gown, on top of the heat from the ovens in back, baking the pastries, pies, and desserts.

(Even as I feel bad for the girls in their authentic garb, I can appreciate the community spirit of not going in for the lighter/less layers you get with modern-day cheaply-made [Halloween] costumes for the period.

I appreciate it mostly because I took pains to be as authentic as possible.

✂ -

To give you an idea of what I'm talking about:

A shirt worn by men in the 1700s would hang to the knees and be tucked into breeches (or "spatter dashes" – breeches that extend down to mid-calf, instead of ending at the knee; usually seen worn by background pirates in the movies). Coats were long, and neckwear was commonplace, whether a silk cravat, or a stock.

✂ -

Women's clothing was much more complex:

A shift was worn under everything else, and her stockings were tied by a ribbon above the knees (no garter belts yet, so imagine those ribbons like tourniquet). A woman's stays were kinda like a vest, but they included whalebone and the point was much like a corset, to squeeze a woman's body into an appetizing shape. A gown could come either parted in front (to show off a silk petticoat or embroidered apron), or not be parted at all. There'd be a lace neck kerchief. Sometimes a stomacher was hooked, or pinned, to the bodice of her gown, and would end just above the waistline where the hooped petticoat would be added.

When a woman wore a hat, they had wide brims with shallow crowns, and the only function was to keep their faces out of the sun.

When I first started learning about Georgian fashions, all I could imagine was myself, kneeling down to go in underneath the hem, but then getting lost under the skirt, inside all those layers of fabric from her petticoat, to shift, to ... you get the idea.

✂ -

Sex addiction is a thing!

Women addicted to porn; also a thing!

Client # 14.

According to Pornhub.com (which – take with a gain of salt, they seem to skew the stats by filtering which categories of porn they report, and those they don't mention), the stats for 2019:

30% of porn viewers are women (70% are men).

37% of women viewers watch male gay porn.

During 2019 womens' viewing time increased by 23 seconds (men's by 15).

The average porn viewing time in NYS lasts 10 min, 12 secs.

The US national average lasts 10 min, 36 secs.

Midnight is the peak viewing time.

78% of pornhub visitors are under age 44.

4% of pornhub visitors are over age 65.

There are 115 million visitors each day.

Most website visits are done by cell phone.

If you watched each and every video that was uploaded to that site in 2019, it would take you 169 years to watch it all (presumably without any breaks, and no repeats).

While the online stats are interesting for the picture they show about modern porn consumption and usage, they do not reflect the cultural stigma and negative attitudes voiced about porn when people are in social situations rather than watching privately.

Implicit bias is that "porn is bad".

Explicit bias is, as my client said, "The men in gay porn look better than the men in straight porn."

She's not troubled by her interest in watching porn.

What does trouble her though, is her roommate's reaction to the porn.

"I'm perfectly straight! But she's thinking that because I watch gay porn, and lesbian porn, that I'm going to try having my way with her! And her boyfriend, he just makes it worse with all his jokes about three-ways and foursomes.

"I lost it yesterday, told him my boyfriend's bi, so we could do a four-way! That my guy likes starting down in front and finishing up in back, so he'd love to have a new moon on the full moon tonight!"

✂ -

Yes, sometimes a client can make me laugh.

But I can't ever let it show.

✂ -

Butt ...
                    ethics.

Had to break it down and recap:

"So you're OK with your porn choices.

"You're OK with using.

"You're comfortable with having some time to yourself and your video.

"Yet your roommate is worried your porn choices reveal your inner desires.

"They don't.

"She probably won't understand that.

"So, how can I help you?"

"That's just it, right? How do I get her to understand that just because I watch it, doesn't mean I'm into trying it."

"You've told her that? Just the way you said it to me?"

She nodded.

I jotted down the web address for the pornhub.com statistics.

"It might help if she sees the stats which say it's more common than she thinks. And if she refuses to look, make sure she knows there are no pix or vid clips on that site. It's all graphs, and charts."

She might not look, and that would likely be due to how people are scared that others will notice how interested they really are in porn, and that's the deep, shameful secret which must be protected, right? I said, "You can always bring her to a session if you want. We won't get into anything else, but we can have a talk about porn viewing, the novelty of watching something just because it's new. That finding someone attractive doesn't always mean you're attracted to them. An educational session."

Runs a triangulation risk, and potentially exposes my client's porn addiction issues to her roommate, but

271

it was an offer made in sincerity from my willingness to help, even though it was very unlikely her roommate would ever join us.

Religious prudery from all I've heard about her.

✂ -

III.

Small town carnival parades are often a hodgepodge of unrelated participants showing no unifying theme.

The Latex Festival theme is the eighteenth century, but rather than attempting to parade from that time period, it's a free-for-all! Instead of horse drawn carriages, there are tractors, and fire trucks, mopeds, clowns, dancing schools, boy scout troops, marching school bands, dog walking clubs, company vans for landscaping services, and a pick-up truck towing a cattle cart. Tick me off that Paget and her understudy were driving the Bergerac vehicle (read: that almost-lost hearse), and I wasn't able to ride with her (and then let her ride me).

There were some horses, but that was the horse-riding stable showing off rather than riding in period dress. True, there were a handful of locals walking in the parade and showing off their eighteenth century fashions (as a form of community spirit), but they were grossly outnumbered. The Wellington family had been leading the parade in costume ever since the very first village festival (before it evolved into a town carnival).

Pictures of the eldest Wellingtons walking down the street with the parade trailing behind them are an annual front page image for the Carnival weekend edition of our local paper.

I dunno, maybe I expect too much from people sometimes.

Being in the church float kinda spoiled it for me.

There I was, decked out in my circuit rider finery, tricorn hat, wig, and tan-top boots, looking the part, and stuck in a 1953 lemon yellow pick-up truck, throwing candy at the crowd along the curb while we inched along.

Had a good laugh though. A parishioner's cousin and spouse were in town with their daughters, and the little girl was waving a handwritten sign: "Throw Candy!!!!" while her older sister stood close by with a sign that had an arrow pointing her sister's way with the words "No candy!"

The parade terminates at the farm yard where the carnival attractions are all set up.

It would be another weekend of trampling grass and local EMTs hoping no one trips on the black cables and rubber extension cords stretched this way and that.

✂ -

Wandering around the carnival, there's a disjoint in-between the amusement park rides, game vendors, junk food sellers, and the men dressed in wigs, cravats, weskits, breeches, aprons, ankle socks; and women in their elaborate lace and frilly gowns, hooped petticoats, with towering hairstyles.

From stories I've heard, a lot of the fancy dress was either left over from
- costume parties
- the high school theater department's wardrobe (they did <u>Sweeney Todd</u> 12 years ago, and <u>1776</u> 43 years ago),
- or, just period garb snatched up as soon as the antique stores put it out for sale.

It was almost as though there was a knowing wink, nod, and smile that passed every time one person in period dress walked past another.

I returned more than a few nods, smiles, and winks with the "in-crowd" (read: costumed).

Throughout my wanderings over the damp, matted-down grass, my priest outfit passed those of

Ben Franklin   Daniel Boone

Mozart	JS Bach
Isaac Newton	Voltaire
red coats	Last of the Mohicans
Blackbeard	Scarlet Pimpernel
Captain Hook	Gulliver
Giacomo Casanova	Marquis de Sade.

(Why'd you assume **only *I*** would recognize the last two!)

✂ -

There were several in period dress from the Americas of the 1800s, but still – give them credit for trying.

At least there weren't any cowboys, just cowgirls in country dresses and Western boots (all the line dancing club members wore Davey Crockett coonskin caps).

✂ -

There's a really neat thing they do at this carnival.

It's a *"Name That Chapter and Verse"* competition, in which all the area churches compete for a much prized trophy Cup (which has been collecting dust in Saint Mary's church narthex for the past nine years).

A small, bronze affair on a three tier base (its really just a Ciborium that's missing its lid. I suspect it was a donation made when whichever church donated it came up with the funds to buy itself a replacement Ciborium with a lid).

Originally, the competition was a ticket-selling fund raiser, with the take being divided by the area churches. Once the Baptists accused the Lutherans of not dividing the portions evenly, it was agreed by all that a trophy prize would go to the winner instead.

So, no more cash prize.

✂ -

Flashback:

My first year here, my participation in the contest was a point of contention:

"Every minister in town is on their church's team!"

"But from what I hear, you've won the past two years now without having a priest on your team to boost your score. I'm a cheerleader, not a ringer."

"It doesn't look good for Saint Mary's that we don't have our new priest on our team!"

"You know, you win without your priest, when there are ministers on all the other teams, well, that's a matter of pride for me!"

"'Pride goeth before a fall,'" recited the team's captain. "Proverbs, xvi. 18."

"That's the Spirit! Now get out there, and win one for the Gipper!"

✂ -

I generally avoid sports references, but that was all that came to mind since I'd been on the verge of blurting out, "Give'em hell!"

It's doubtful Mrs Church would've appreciated my cheering.

✂ -

This year's *"Name That Chapter and Verse"* competition:

Spectators drifted in and out of the tent surrounding the contestants' tables, watching for a little while, getting bored, then wandering off for something more thrilling, like a Tilt-a-Whirl, or Magic Mirror Fun House.

The Carnival debate had come up again this past Sunday.

Mrs Church. Every year, as expected: "Our priest needs to be on our team!"

I keep weaseling out of it.

I also speculate that my not joining the team that first year was my third strike where she was concerned (since my first was correcting her about the church portrait, and my second was not letting her take that "slutty painting" down.)

Adjusting my powdered wig I contemplated how Mrs Church can't argue with this year's results:

"The winner, for the tenth year in a row, Saint Mary's Episcopal!"

Say what I do about her, she does bring back the Cup every year.

(TICS: "Did that Baptist just whisper to that Pentecostal that we'd cheated again?")

✂ -

I started to flirt up *Madame de Pompadour*, and might have been getting somewhere until I opened my mouth about her outfit.

WRONG!!

No! Not the king's favorite mistress.

Rather, "I'm Lady Godiva, before she takes that famous horse ride through town."

"Ah, yes. But not in black, I see."

"She wore nothing but her own, long hair," Paget beamed, running her hands through a Rapunzel wig.

Yep.

> Dress for the occasion
>> suggest nudity
>>> entice illicitness
>>>> she had me at her wink from across

the fried dough trailer.

(And she looked great in the electric blue color of her costume!)

I played along, "Yes, I know. But did you know, that the term 'Peeping Tom' comes from how a man named Thomas watched her ride through Coventry. She'd asked no one to look while she took her ride; but he did, and then went blind because of it?"

(TICS: "You might want to tell people you're just dressed as *Marie Antoinette*.")

Her eyes on my lips, hand touching my arm, eyebrows lifting in that way she lifts them,

"She was the first to protest taxes, you know."

"Yes, I know," and I leaned closer to whisper in her ear, "But did you know, she died about 1076?"

"Congratulations!"

(That's a thing she does. Whenever she gets caught in an error, she pretends she was just testing the person who caught her. But with me, she goes a step beyond that by feigning how I'd won the jackpot grand prize.)

"You passed the test." She leaned close to whisper, "Like anyone else is really going to know that."

We both knew she'd gotten the history wrong, and we both pretended she didn't, and we were probably about to sneak off somewhere when one of the church's teens walked by, thinks I'm hitting on someone to get a date, then cheers: "Way to go, Father!"

Ah yes, that's usually a cold shower!

But ... Paget's not deterred.

✂ -

Against the Bergerac SUV, parked against the line of a neighboring cornfield.

(Agoraphilia)

Herdy-gerdy music in the distance.

"Don't fall in love."

✂ -

Ran into Kelly and her sisters all huddled together over a funnel cake held by Kelly's fiancée, who clearly was feeling the deep fried burn from their tasty treat. Given his farm-calloused hands, I'm surprised the temperature was bothering him through the paper plate and his thickened hide.

It was nice to see Kelly without the nose bandages.

Without the discolored bruising.

I don't think her new nose was worth it.

The one she was born with looked better!

None of the girls were in period costume.

Instead they were dressed up in long velvet jackets, suede gloves, tight white pants, knee-hi boots, and helmets.

They'd be riding in the horse show later in the afternoon, and dressed in his jeans and plaid shirt with Stetson hat, Kelly's fiancee was their mascot.

✂ -

The mid-Georgian era has always been my favorite (one of the few times my grades in Social Studies were "A" 100%) thanks in large part to my having read the *Leatherstocking Tales* and the *Scarlet Pimpernel* series in 4th grade.

I've read up on the eighteenth century off and on during the years since then, and it continually fascinates me. So while I enjoy the costume party feel of the carnival, I can't help wishing that people would care more about dressing up (if they didn't), and getting the details right (if they did), although since Paget got it wrong (and I'd forgive her for anything), then I couldn't really hold the bar up too high for everyone else.

Could I?

After all, this is a farming community, and not a lot of folks went to college.

So probably most of what they knew about the Colonial period came from movies, TV shows, and picture books.

What begins as a part-time job while they're in elementary school (family farm), becomes full-time jobs for them after graduating high school (if they stay in school that long.

(Many were home-schooled due to the rigors of a daily farm schedule.)

Even some of those who went to a vocational school – and learned a trade like nursing, cosmetology, or auto mechanics – still returned to work on their family farms.

I pushed myself to get to the point of just being happy that so many had even tried for a costume.

And no, it didn't help me to feel more generous because I won the "Best" costume award!

✂ -

I think I told you already about the clergyman's stock, and how it's pleated linen with the two Geneva bands added. My neck cloth closes in back with Velcro, and when I'd ordered it online, I did splurge and bought mine in white silk.

I wanted to treat myself to something nice to keep the coarseness of the periwig's cascading curls from irritating my neck.

✂ -

Our Episcopal Church comes from the Church of England, which was born from politics, not Theology.

The reason the Church's views bother me so much is because the historic Church's attitudes about sex aren't Theological!

The Church, to guarantee it would have members to fill its pews after the Protestant Reformation (1500s), instituted marriage as a sacrament and suddenly it's available to the poor (previously only the rich got married).

"You want to be married in the eyes of God, promise to raise your kids in our church!"

"You want to make sure the kid is yours? Only marry a virgin!"

And here's the worst bit: in order to keep people dependent on the Church, it had to make sure people needed it. "Come to Church, be forgiven your sins!"

When the Church decreed that sex was evil, it set itself up as the ultimate authority. People tend to have sex, so; make sex a sin that requires the Church to forgive, and POOF! There's an enslaved populace that will always stay in the good graces of the Church.

Like I said, nothing to do with Theology, and everything to do with human greed within a human institution just to satisfy a human minority's lust for power.

(No different that what you see with the Jewish authorities in the gospels.)

My first reason for becoming a priest was because it's easier to change a system from within than it is to make changes from outside it.

But since you challenged me to give you an overview of Episcopalian Church history in just 12 quick points (or less) here it is for you:

313 AD   It becomes legal to be a Christian (Edict of Milan).

597   Saint Augustine of Canterbury (not Augustine of Hippo) brings Christianity to Britain as part of his mission work (though scholars suspect it was brought to the British Isles earlier than this).

1440   Johannes Guttenberg's press for moveable type invented in Germany. After printing Bibles, most presses shifted to printing erotica, which enticed some to want to learn how to read so they could then read those "dirty" stories (although the majority stayed illiterate).

1517   Martin Luther hangs up his "95 Thesis" on a church door (his German translation of the Bible follows).

1519 "Leipzig Debate" – Roman Catholicism outlaws Lutheranism, but the Protestant denomination continues to grow and flourish since the RC army can't arrest Luther and execute him (yes, the Historic Church was a political and military power – remember the Crusades and Inquisition?). ML was protected by a German nobleman, and the Pope didn't dare declare war on Germany just to execute one man (although if he knew how far-ranging that one man's work would divide the Church, the Pope might've invaded after all).

1536 William Tyndale is executed by the RC military for translating the Bible into the English language (his partners complete the full translation within a few years). The reasoning was: once the peasants could read it for themselves, they'd no longer need the Church to explain the Bible to them. Then the importance of the Church would be diminished, and they couldn't have that! So it was illegal, punishable by death, to translate the Bible into any common tongue (unless you were in Germany where the long arm of the Church's army couldn't reach you).

1537   King Henry VIII, desperate for a divorce from Cathy to bed Ann Boleyn, is frustrated by the Pope who has refused to see his envoy (and likewise refused to make a ruling on Henry's request). The Pope, in giving Henry the divorce he wanted would've only caused friction with the other European monarchs, which the Pope wanted to avoid. But Henry didn't like being ignored, so he decided to break away from the church in Rome. The "Act of Supremacy" goes into effect, making King Henry VIII the head of the newly formed Anglican church (instead of the Pope). Henry didn't intend to become a separate denomination and had, at first, just wanted to be "British Catholics."

Protestant denominations developed in Germany and England, independant of each other, yet both arose from reactions to Papal authority and became kindred spirits.

1546   King Henry VIII dies. Roman Catholic buildings (churches, monasteries, convents) are either torn down, or taken over and re-purposed according to the denominational loyalties of whichever monarch comes to sit on the English throne.

1559   Church of England's independence from Rome established through two acts of Parliament: "Act of Supremacy (II)" (1558) and "Act of Uniformity" (1559). This is Queen Elizabeth and her "Elizabethan Settlement" also known as the "Revolution of 1559" depending on which source you reference.

1611   King James Version of the Bible becomes available, the oldest English language translation still widely available today.

1734   The Wesley brothers have their "Moments of Conversion" and both shift from believing Good Works earn salvation, to Luther's view of "Faith alone" as the means to salvation. Arguably, this is the start of the Methodist Movement within the Anglican Church (the Methodys break away to form their own denomination after John Wesley's death in 1791).

1783   End of the War for Independence. The British clergy who had been expelled from the rebellious colonies, slowly returned to America. Colonial Anglicans – who had moved on to other denominations after the British priests were exiled – returned to their original church after the priests returned. New converts joined, children were born into and raised by the denomination, and the Episcopal Church's roots in America were firmly reset.

Skipping over the War of 1812 since you limited me to a dozen points.

Hope that helps you understand it better.

✂ -

After wearing my full circuit rider outfit on Friday for several hours, I hung it up, and to make sure it would still be dry to wear on Sunday, I couldn't wash it. Rather, I spent Saturday using some cologne body spray to douse it and make sure my shirt didn't reek like sour onions. I don't do well in hot weather. I always feel like I'm burning up, and it's unlikely I'm alone in that since perfume and cologne were invented to hide the stink of body odor. Many people wear so much of their designer scents that they are aromatically overpowering (I remember my Uncle always smelled overwhelming), also I figured I can follow Cyranose's example and carry a strong smell for a day.

I stank of overeager maleness in church; although one benefit to being the guy up in the pulpit is that most of my morning is spent so far away from others that they won't be gagging on my animal musk.

No one seemed to notice my scent on their way in to church.

✂ -

11 am.

Standing at the back doors, I was shaking hands with people as they exit the sanctuary.

"Father, glad to see you finally decided to join us in the spirit of the carnival!"

Since the comment didn't mention how I smelled
                                    I was grateful.

✂ -

Standing at the back doors, I was shaking hands with people as they exit the sanctuary.

"Reverend, good sermon."

(TICS: "Are you just saying that?")

✂ -

The Count and Countess had bought themselves George and Martha Washington costumes some years ago for a costume party.

You can tell the costumes were a few years old, because they'd both expanded with age, and the seams and lines of their costumes no longer accommodated their figures.

Still, walking into my office to see a man in powdered wig, and woman with towering white hair (with their full, elborate outfits), seated at the conference table amidst the modern furnishings and purring adding machine, was a pleasant sight.

He was in the middle of talking with the editor of our church newsletter (who did not wear fancy dress for the carnival.

(Some folks get in the spirit, and some – like Diana – don't.)

"... it's so much easier in the Summer. The organist goes around opening all the windows before service. Then I'll go around shutting them afterwards. And when I get to the last one, there's such a reach over the counter, that there's always a few envelopes that fall out of the plate as I'm holding it, and on out into the hedges. I go back later, and get them at my convenience. Trouble is, too many of them turn out to be checks!"

Usually I walk in on some conversation after the contents of the loaded collection plates had been strewn across the conference table.

Going to that table I plucked up an envelope.

That focused their attention on me.

I demonstrated while telling them, "That's why you have to do the 'pinch test.' Only let the fatter ones fall outside. No checks in those, all cash."

"Leave it to Father, to know that!"

"My luck, they'd all be singles!" bemoaned the Count.

(TICS: "From Holly, after a busy Saturday night of pole-dancing?")

I offered, "You have to think like a sinner to help the sinner."

Although we shared a laugh, it's a good thing the Churches and Cathedral sisters weren't there to hear any of what was said.

✂ -

Stopping at the corner bar ("Best Pot Roast Sandwiches"), I took a seat at the counter, removed my wig, and ordered a hamburger, fries, and Guinness.

My reflection in the bar mirror showed a white outline of power across my forehead.

The place was empty.

Most folks were still at the Carnival for its last few Sunday hours. I liked the bar better without the crowd and over-loud jukebox going.

The only other customer was on the last bar stool, hanging on every word spoken by the barber-barmaid in a black tank top, skin tight jeans, and knee-high black suede boots. Her slender figure was leaning on the end of the bar, a tattoo behind her left ear.

All addicts do it: spend hours pretending to listen to things they don't care about all in the patient hope that they'll be the one chosen

> to go somewhere private
> to do a private thing
>> with the women they've been patiently

drooling over.

The barmaid-by-night, and Sunday afternoons (pin-up barber-by-day), is quite probably the closest Copthorne has to a local celebrity, with how every guy in town notices her and every woman ignores her. She can often be seen walking her dog in the village square while running a hula hoop around herself as the dog scurries about. The jealous gossip is that she's a stripper (while a look at her weekly schedule should make any rational mind question: when does she have time to get naked?), and I think of her as "Miss Hollywood" because she's got a year-round tan, perfect white teeth, and never has a hair out of place.

The bar's chairs, tables, and three booths don't match.

The checkerboard tile floor was aged, crumbling, and wherever a square had broken, they'd been replaced by black ones.

Waiting for my food I meandered over to a booth, listening in on their conversation about how she'd like to turn her trailer home into a brothel.

Make all the working girls
and clients
wear masks.

That way, with anonymous identities, no one could get into trouble with the law.

I'm no prude when it comes to prostitution, sex, or porn, so I wasn't scandalized by her dream – just curious to know what planet she was living on
to think masks would stay on
during a police raid.

✄ -

"Everything alright?" the barmaid asked when she came out to the booth to check on me.

The mole on her left cheek rose with her smile, and her shirt was stretched tight across her ample self (to guilt guys into leaving a more generous [pay for the view] gratuity.

(No guilt if you don't look and stare, right?)

Setting my burger back on the plate, I acknowledged, "As always. Thanks. I noticed your sign."

She followed my gesture to the sign taped to the mirror behind the bar, "For Sale" which was the same sign that's been in the front window for all the years I've been here (if not also for some years prior). "SOLD" had been scribbled across it diagonally in black permanent marker.

"Oh, yes! We got a buyer! They'll be closing the place down for a while to renovate. They'd have to, you know? I'm sure they'll be open again soon, though. And I'd imagine they'll keep the Guinness, too. They're going to turn this into an Irish pub."

She knew me only by my drink order.

You use whatever works, right?

(Rev Parishioners-by-number, over here.)

Thoughts of Paget kept me from lusting after the bar-wench.

(But before Paget's return to Copthorne I would've been thinking that if I were to visit the barmaid in her fantasy trailer home of ill repute, I'd only want to see her.

(And, see her without a mask covering up her beauty.)

Focused my thoughts on Paget to distract myself away from the barber-barmaid.

From Paget, to the bar's first claim to (local) fame – the working tap sticking out of the side of a refrigerator at the end of the bar.

A home made oddity which served a practical function.

The second claim was her hot-ass hoopering self.

"When do you close down?"

"Next week, to have the grand re-opening next month."

Her tush in tight blue jeans swished its way back behind the counter.

The guy at the bar jealously watching me.

(TICS: "Like she'd do me any sooner than she'd do you, buddy.")

✂ -

Stepping out of the bar I walked across the village square to Saint Mary's.

Before the raised cement porch and double doors is a flagstone walkway with a carriage step close to the curb.

Imagine a solid concrete block set right in the middle of a patch of lawn, with a step on one side. Used to be, a horse drawn carriage would stop alongside it, and a person would have a high step to get down from their carriage (or to climb back up inside).

Since the need for that had expired with the proliferation of the horseless carriage, the swatch of church lawn has been able to grow up around it, and the ruts of tire paths had been filled in and smoothed over long ago.

And yet, the carriage step remains, used more as a curb-side bench than anything.

Only time it gets used for its original purpose any more is at carnival time, when Kelly's family come to church in a coach and four like they had this morning.

Yet because the sense of tradition must be maintained, the church leaves it there, front and center.

(As I found out, the burnt down church had been an all-wood colonial. The original Episcopal church, it was abandoned once they erected the current structure in wood and stone. The Episcopalians then sold the abandoned church building to the Anabaptists just coming into the area.)

The Baptist church ruins opposite reveal that building's (not original) stone facade had been plastic, which had blackened, lumped up, and had molded around the charred hedges during its "accidental" blaze of glory (one month after the owner had refused to sell the factory property, go figure). After the fire (read: arson), that congregation had then gone over the bridge, up the road, and rented an old snowmobile shop (with floor-to-ceiling windows for a front wall) to be their new worship hall. I'm told that high-trafficked venue was cheaper to rent than removing the debris and rebuilding would be.

I've heard rumors from parishioners that the Baptists weren't selling the charred ruins because once they raise enough cash at their temporary site, they'll rebuild. Something in the deed stipulated that they always had to occupy that location in the square (although they could stay in the new site and continually claim "fund raising goal" indefinitely and repeatedly claim they haven't yet raised enough money to move back.

✂ -

A collective sigh of relief has gone up.

The vendors and park rides, junk food trailers, and gaming stands (which took a week to set up), have vanished.

Gone out of town seemingly over-night.

The carnival is over, the utility station on the farm is back to being unused, and everyone is back to wearing their normal clothes.

The farmer who rents out his property for the event made his annual deposit in the bank today. He doesn't do any farming the rest of the year; just lets his field grow grass and rents it out annually. During the past weekend, he'd made enough money to live on for another two years.

Lucky guy.

After his MBT visit he stops in at Saint Mary's for a chat, and

his annual prayer.

Makes a sizeable donation.

As I go next door to deposit that check, I think –

Lucky church!

✂ -

IV.

Ex-Parishioner # 6 was the sort of @$$ who got off setting one person against another.

All so he could set himself up in the middle and be seen as the "go-to hero" for both sides while pretending to take the side of whoever he was talking to at any given moment.

A very toxic, two-faced, sort of Dumb@$$ dipstick!

✂ -

He'd liked watching movies about Roman Gladiators, and the antebellum south.

He'd liked to see the slaves sexually used and abused.

(Yet I couldn't use slavery and sex to entice him to read the Bible.)

It had been his secret fantasy life.

As he'd said to me once, "Imagine if we still had slaves. Someone – like my son – at college, and the slaves would have to sleep out in the hallway of the dorm. I'd get him a female slave, and so she wouldn't be passed all around the dorm hallways at night, giving it to all the other slaves, he'd have to keep her locked in his room with him.

"And then you, Father, could get yourself a strong man to do all your heavy lifting for you. Wouldn't that be good?"

(TICS: "...?")

Perfect example of how people think of me:

A eunuch.

✂ -

I couldn't mention the slave thing during his eulogy.

I couldn't mention how everything with Ex-Parishioner # 6 involved money.

That he believed everyone valued money the way he did.

How he could not have a single conversation without sharing

- how much he'd made by selling something, and
- how much he'd saved, by buying something for less than its sticker price.

In exact figures, down to the last cent, no less!

(Probably would've gotten a laugh if I'd mentioned it though.

(And also why his funeral was on a weekday, it's cheaper then than on weekends.)

✂ -

There were lustful sparks going off inside me as they always do whenever I'm near her.

I wanted to get some hot oil and massage Paget's whole body.

I wanted to caress her face
    and kiss her deeply.

Paget had shared with me that the family had requested Father Whozzit from the Roman Catholic Church do the funeral.

When Paget had called to tell the family that Father Whozzit was unavailable, Ex-Parishioner # 6's mother had insisted that their priest was on "Administrative Leave." Paget had told her how his name was listed in the newspaper with more than one hundred priests all under investigation, but the stern mother had just repeated – more firmly – "*Administrative Leave.*"

The RC sex abuse scandal again.

Going bankrupt by paying out millions to the victims of sexual abuse done by the priests, who were then quietly pulled from one parish and moved off to another, where they just did the same thing to someone else.

Denial knows no bounds.

And sex addiction is a thing!

✂ -

After the last of the funeral attendees had gone I told Paget, "He joined my church."

I did not add that ex-Parishioner # 6 left within 6 months
        no need for chatter while unzipping her skirt.

✂ -

Refitting our clothes, "Don't fall in love."

✂ -

I'm pretty sure it's not a good thing.
     You know, my hoping for more funerals, just so I get to see more Paget.

✂ -

Seated in a pew after mid-day prayers

sipping my tea

thoughts of Paget broken by the click of Holly's high heels

as she came down the pseudo-stone floor of the side aisle.

She takes that route because it offers her a view of the organist much sooner than she'd have coming down the center aisle.

She slipped out of her overcoat to reveal a tight red dress.

This is what it's like for me.

Knowing that I cannot control Lust's thoughts which pop into my head.

Knowing that all I can control is how long I let those lustful thoughts occupy my attention.

I slid silently to the pew's end, ready to make an exit, yet pausing just a moment in case either of them were going to call out to me for something.

They didn't.

✂- -

Our organist doubles as a "Choir Mistress" (an exacting task-master during rehearsals I've been told. And no, I didn't give her that nick-name. The choir members did; not that they let her know what they call her behind her back!)

I snuck out the back of Saint Mary's nave as Holly began her rehearsal for the solo she'll be singing in Sunday worship (Lauren Daigle's "You Say").

The cliché would be, I ran home for a cold shower.

But I'm long past that method of restraint and distraction.

So, having been there

having done that

this is what makes me a good counselor to my clients.

Just because I think it
    doesn't mean I'm still active in my addiction
(apart from an addiction to Paget).
    I'm able to relate
      understand
        not judge
          but sympathize
with what my clients are going through in their own
addiction/recoveries.

✂ -

Holy Day today, for Saint Mary the Virgin (August 15th).
    Or, as I call it, "Mary Mum's Day".
    The world's most famous unwed mother.

✂ -

Ran into Paget at the coffee house.
    Where we first exchanged words!
    (Arousal by association.
    (Hoped no one noticed the tightening in my pants!)
    Paid for her coffee (two creams, one sugar, espresso shot). Got my tea. Unfortunately I couldn't sit down with her and chat because I had to rush over to church for the mid-day service to celebrate Mary Mum.
    I invited her to come see me at work, but Paget had a family to meet and was on her way back to work herself. "Will you be available if I need you?"
    "Whenever you want.
    "Wherever you want.
    "However you want," I said, enjoying the thrill of sounding like we were having a business chat in front of witnesses, when really, the whole conversation was in personal code.
    "Whatever you want, as soon as you call me."
        Paget has me wrapped around her finger, and I like it!

Since she doesn't take advantage of me through that, I love her all the more!

✂- -

Crossing the village square, hot tea in hand, it occurred to me that casual sex by-passed all the emotional agony of being unloved by my object of desire, and it allowed me to work my way backwards. From physical intimacy to start, moving towards emotional connection as a consummation of the relationship.

That's where I'm at with Paget!

Glorious sex won't be the culmination of our love story.

Rather, you'll know we're in reciprocal love once we're able to spend a platonic night together.

Yes, you could think of it as being backwards.

Inverted is the story of my life.

Still think love and sex addiction is a joke?

✂- -

Standing outside the double doors after mid-day prayers, I was shaking hands with my trio of attendees as they exited and walked towards their cars parked at the curb beyond the carriage step.

Parishioner # 21 had been last.

"Father, can we talk?"

✂- -

We were on opposite sides of the altar rail again.

I sat in silence, waiting for her to start.

Figured it'd be something like unexpected and unanticipated grief, felt for the ex-husband/ex-parishioner who'd just been buried (and whose wake and funeral she'd skipped).

Kneeling at the railing, she began, "Father, I've been thinking about what you said the last time we spoke."

(TICS: "Here it comes.")

"And I probably shouldn't say this, but it wasn't dreams I was having."

(TICS: "You don't want to chat about your grief for ex-parishioner # 6?")

Nope.

> Diana
>> Parishioner # 21
>>> editor of the church newsletter
>>>> had been meeting with Parishioner # 66
>>>>> and they've been growing closer

together.

Imagining Paget's smile and touch, I said, "When we work closely with someone, there's bound to be friendships that develop."

"It's much more than that, Father!"

"Whatever you tell me will remain between the two of us."

She took a moment.

Had to work up the nerve.

"Ever since my divorce ..."

(She spoke with a lot more pauses and extended silences than I'm punctuating.)

Guilty consciences are never easy to talk through.

Confessions like this are not easily made.

" ... I'm worried, Father. If there's a chance he and I ..."

(TICS: "Guessing you're lonely, and if he makes a pass, you'd give in.")

She knew she shouldn't spend time alone with him, but Parishioner # 66 understood her better than her ex-husband ever had. She rarely saw # 66 more than once a week, and that was in church. Knowing she'd be seeing him was something that excited her about coming to church and she knew that was the wrong reason to be attending.

(TICS: "No more wrong than the choir members who skip church if they aren't singing, or the Sunday School teacher who leaves church when there aren't any kids for class.")

Diana was convinced she'd have a much healthier relationship with # 66 than she'd had in her second marriage.

(TICS: "But what about Parishioner # 66's marriage?")

Honestly, she struck me as the type who could fall in love with any man who said "Hello" to her (read: Romance addict).

✂ -

My inner monologue was drifting away.

Dreams and desires? Big whip.

Why couldn't it be Holly, dreaming about having an affair?

Or the bar waitress, confessing to an online porn addiction?

Just not Diana.

Not with sex stuff.

To see her, you wouldn't think sex.

Never think sexy.

She's no where close to being on the menu!

Not even anywhere near the restaurant, know what I mean?

I'm shallow, I know, but that's helped me curtail who I act out with.

A blessing in disguise!

My personal tastes aside though

physical unattractiveness does not disqualify someone from being a sexual being.

I have to continually readjust my thinking.

Stop thinking that only Hollywood sexpot-looking people have sex.

Nope.

God's doing it to me this way, instead.

I prayed with her.

After Diana left, I prayed that she wouldn't start thinking she and I had some kind of twisted connection because I'd listened to her.

One of the saving graces of my addiction is that it is only fueled by a certain type of woman, and if a woman isn't to my taste (read: "my type"), then she does not register as a blip on my radar. I'm a guy, so yes, I enter a room and my eyes look for the most attractive woman first before taking notice of anything else.

It's a guy thing
     not necessarily an addiction thing.

But truthfully, the majority of women are non-entities to me
     sexually speaking.

That is how I can say with confidence
     the women in my congregation are sexually safe from me.

(The great irony being how offended they'd be to hear me say that about them.)

Yet we can't ignore that slim minority, like Holly.

The barber bar-wench "Miss Hollywood".

Or "Legs" at the Easter burial.

The local librarian.

That minority of women who get my motor running.

And with Paget around, those others blur into the background with my focus being wholly on my Funeral Directress friend.

It might sound like being shallow would make it easier to stay sober, but that's misleading. It's not about the number of potential sex partners around (nor even if you're only attracted to a minority). It's all about the addict's desire to have the few they do see, and lust after.

And really, it only ever takes one.

Or even, an old memory of one.

I'd say "They're the ones I can't trust myself to be alone with," but I'd be selling myself short saying something like that. Simply put: I care too much about my job to risk it for a great piece of ass, no matter how sexy she may be.

My cell phone beeped a text:

"Hello Sir! May I reserve you for a service, burial, and lingering next week? I don't have an exact time set with the family yet."

Lingering?

I remembered it:

We'd been at the antique store, refitting our askew clothing, "Do you always take that long? It's like you were lingering *back there."*

Cute.

Lingering. I get it!

Paget's text made me smile and I figured I should also return the humor. I knew she liked medieval fantasy, so I went there to play along –

"Milady, I shall consider the day yours. Just let me know when and how."

Easing back on my office couch (not as nice as the new one at Bergerac), I set aside my phone to fit my headphones in place and start up my mix tape of Symphonic Metal.

Took up my laptop and reviewed my schedule for the next several days.

Be just my luck
> to be out of state, defending my dissertation
> when Paget needs me at Bergerac!

✂ -

This "Year of Letters from a Small Town Priest" continues ...

The Pastoral Noir Trilogy

Series I: Kneeling
Series II: Rug Rash
Series III: Carpet Burnt Knees

AFTERWORD

A picaresque novel is defined as being episodic and satirical, while also posing as a memoir by an outcast.

The preceding has been a dramatization of sex addiction and is intended to be taken as a depiction of this affliction in the hopes that any who suffer from this form of addiction may recognize something in what has been detailed here.

It's a fiction, based on fact.

This novel should, in no way, be confused for a statement against those professions held by these characters, nor should it be taken as a statement against those people who follow these careers.

Rather, it is hoped the message is clear: "Sex addiction can – and does – afflict people from all walks of life; each gender, all ethnicities, and all sexual orientations, from all economic levels."

Denial of (any) addiction is very real, but there is help available for all who wish to accept it. All indications suggest that the best recovery takes place within a combination of individual counseling along with participation in an appropriate 12-Step group.

Don't dismiss your recovery the way these characters do.

They're intended to serve you as a cautionary tale.

(Not to be mistaken for role models.)

Remember, sex addiction is not a fiction!

(For more factual information a good starting place are the books: *Don't Call It Love* [ISBN 978-0-553-35138-5], and *Out of the Shadows* [ISBN 978-1-56838-621-8], both by Patrick Carnes, PhD. Serious students may also want to read the article "Clinical Relevance of the Proposed Sexual Addiction Diagnostic Criteria: Relation to the Sexual Addiction Screening Test – Revised" [American Society of Addiction Medicine, 2014] also by Carnes.)

If you need help, it is available.

For more info, try these websites:

www.sa.org (for marrieds)
www.saa-recovery.org (for singles)
www.slaafws.org (sex and love addicts)
www.sca-recovery.org (sexual compulsives)
www.sexual-recovery.org (sex addiction recovery)
www.COSA-recovery.org (partners of sex addicts)
www.pornaddictsanonymous.org (too many movies)
www.sexhelp.com

ACKNOWLEDGEMENTS

Thanks to the IITAP (International Institute for Trauma and Addiction Professionals) community for all their literature, sobriety kits, materials, and certification programs – without all of your work, guidance, and training, portions of this novel would not have been made possible!

Thanks to the staff, mentors, and teachers who taught me in seminary.

Thanks especially to my clients, parishioners, and co-workers, for providing inspiration and creating a work environment which I hope this novel has celebrated, in the same way my heart celebrates you for being who you are.

Printed in the United States
by Baker & Taylor Publisher Services